I didn't move.
Didn't breathe.
Didn't blink.

"Look."

I couldn't help myself: I looked directly into his eyes.

Which were strangely human. I hadn't expected that. Staring into my eyes, he pressed the tip of his knife into my sternum. I felt the fabric of my shirt rip. Felt the sharp blade of the knife sever the top layers of my skin. The wetness of my blood gathering on the surface.

He leaned back and, pinning me with the knife, reached into a pocket with his free hand.

A domino emerged, and then three more. Four dominoes. Of course: After me, someone would be next. My heart pounded wildly.

Someone in my family.

That was his game.

He wouldn't stop with me.

By Katia Lief

YOU ARE NEXT

Coming November 2010
NEXT TIME YOU SEE ME

KATIA LIEF

You are Next

AVON

An Imprint of HarperCollinsPublishers

This is a work of fiction. Names, characters, places, and incidents are products of the author's imagination or are used fictitiously and are not to be construed as real. Any resemblance to actual events, locales, organizations, or persons, living or dead, is entirely coincidental.

AVON BOOKS
An Imprint of HarperCollins*Publishers*
10 East 53rd Street
New York, New York 10022-5299

Copyright © 2010 by Katia Spiegelman Lief
Excerpt from *Next Time You See Me* copyright © 2010 by Katia Spiegelman Lief
ISBN 978-0-06-180902-6
www.avonbooks.com

First Avon Books paperback printing: October 2010

Avon Trademark Reg. U.S. Pat. Off. and in Other Countries, Marca Registrada, Hecho en U.S.A.
HarperCollins® is a registered trademark of HarperCollins Publishers.

Printed in the U.S.A.

10 9 8 7 6 5 4 3 2 1

For Karenna

ACKNOWLEDGMENTS

Despite all the lonely hours spent writing a novel, no author works completely alone. There is always a push and pull from outside sources . . . in this case my editor, Lucia Macro, who offered just the right kind of supportive feedback as we steered the story toward its final form; my agent, Matt Bialer, whose persistence and encouragement never failed as he read draft after draft; his assistant, Lindsay Ribar, whose editorial skill as a reader was as impressive as it was helpful; all the creative and hard-working people at HarperCollins, among them Esi Sogah, Eleanor Mikucki, Thomas Egner, Pamela Spengler-Jaffee, Shawn Nichols, and Christina Maddalena; and last but not least, my husband, Oliver Lief, an accomplished film editor whose talent for storytelling and editing was a constant guiding light.

PART I

CHAPTER 1

There was something intensely satisfying about digging bare-handed in the dirt. My gardening gloves were soggy so I'd abandoned them on the cracked cement next to the barrel planter I was filling with orange begonias. By late summer these six plants would be triple in size and the pot would overflow with clusters of bright waxy petals. Waiting patiently as they grew and enjoying their beauty was one in a million facets of my therapy, but then everything I did these days was an aspect of recovery. So sayeth Once-a-Week Joyce, as I had secretly dubbed my therapist, recalling as I had a hundred times and with the usual inner tickle how at my initial appointment she had made sure to point out that the word *joy* was embedded in her name. I had smiled for the first time in months, which had been exactly her goal.

I'd been outside doing the back garden all morning and these front pots would take the last of the dozen trays of spring flowers I'd carted home from the nursery yesterday afternoon. One of the planks on the barrel had rotted over the winter and was sagging out. I wouldn't bother my new landlord with it; next spring I would use my own money to buy another one. I patted down the soil, noticed that every one of my short-bitten fingernails was crusted with black dirt, and wiped my hands on the front of my jeans. It was hot out. I was suddenly thirsty and my mind conjured a tempting image of sweet ice tea over a stack of ice cubes. The cool, shadowy inside of my ground-floor one-bedroom apartment beckoned. I bent down to collect my gloves.

A dented gray sedan stopped in front of the brownstone.

A black guy wearing a red baseball cap turned off a Willie Nelson song and leaned partway out of the driver's window. That was when I saw the police radio on his dashboard and knew he was a cop.

"I'm looking for Detective Karin Schaeffer."

"I'm no longer with the police force."

He left the motor running and got out slowly. Smiled. All I wanted to think about was that I liked his perfect white teeth.

"Billy Staples, detective first class."

I stood there. It wasn't nice to meet him and I wouldn't lie by saying it was. I didn't want him to be here because they didn't show up in person to deliver paperwork, and anyway, my medical discharge had already been signed, sealed, and delivered. They only came in person with bad news.

"I'm kind of busy," I said. Standing there in my dirty jeans. Holding limp gardening gloves and a muddy spade. Looking like a retired old lady with nothing but time on her hands, though I was only thirty-three.

"Listen, Karin, I know you don't want to hear anything from us. I got that. But there's something you have to know."

"How did you find me?" Phone book, Internet white pages . . . I had made an effort to unlist myself in every directory.

"Well, for one thing, you sent the benefits department a change of address."

Of course I had; I needed those disability checks to pay my rent, since the sale of my house hadn't netted any profit.

"Right," I said. "Sorry, I'm just a little tired. Not thinking straight today."

"I understand."

I'd heard that too many times by now: *I understand.* So he knew. Everyone knew. All the world had been informed of Karin Schaeffer's tragedy, and then moved on to the next big bad story . . . except for me, of course, having been abandoned to it.

"You know you have an enemy." It was smart of him not to have phrased it as a question. Of course I knew I had an enemy.

"Martin Price is behind bars," I told him.

The media had called him the Domino Killer. In the detectives unit we'd called him JPP for Just Plain Psycho. The judge called him the worst threat to innocent people she'd ever encountered and put him away forever, specifically for the murders of Jackson and Cece Schaeffer, my husband and three-year-old daughter. There had been others before that but it was my family's murders that had put JPP away once and for all.

"He escaped last night. Got a call from your old unit

in Jersey—asked me to find you. Seems no one answered when they called."

"Well," I said, "thanks for telling me. I guess." I wanted to get inside. Wanted the cool of my own private space. Wanted that sweet ice tea. But Detective Staples wasn't finished.

"The thing is, he left a note for you."

"A note?" Please, no. Not another note from Martin Price.

"Well, kind of a note."

I could already see it. I already knew.

"They found three dominoes laid out on his mattress: three, five, and one."

My address: 351 Pacific Street. Brooklyn, New York. A far cry and a different life from the house in New Jersey I'd shared with Jackson and Cece. Ours was such a sweet house, green clapboards and a front porch where we used to sit and watch Cece play on the lawn. I could still see her running toward me across the dandelion-speckled grass, bare-legged in a plaid sundress, brown curls bouncing around her cherubic face, calling, "Mommy, chase me!"

"He also left you another message," Billy said in a lower, softer voice that told me he wished he didn't have to deliver this one.

I closed my eyes. Saw the last message he'd left me almost a year ago, written in lipstick on my bathroom mirror: *You Are Next*. Only it wasn't lipstick. It was my daughter's blood.

"It said, 'See you soon.' "

"Whose blood this time?"

"His own. Must have cut himself. Probably had to

steal some bandages, so every local pharmacy is getting its security footage looked at right now."

I nodded. It would be the logical first step. But knowing JPP, he'd have disinfected and bandaged his wound and moved on by now. He was scary good at this. JPP's thing was to engineer the toppling of a whole group, to watch an entire family fall one by one by one.

He had already murdered five members of a family, the Aldermans of Maplewood, New Jersey—my old beat. Three murders into it the dominoes JPP left behind started making sense. Their face numbers offered a clue. The problem was deciphering it before he came back for the kill. My department and the FBI had already been working the case for a year before I was put on it.

I was a newly minted detective when I found him pretty much by accident. I never would have thought to look in one of those zillion-gallon chemical tanks off the highway. Never realized any of them sat empty sometimes. We'd had a tip and were canvassing the area and I heard an echo that sounded like it was coming from inside the tank. Climbed the side ladder and there he was, way at the bottom, napping on his side with his fists clenched just like Cece used to do when she was a baby. How he could sleep in that fog of petroleum fumes, I never knew. But there he was, superhuman, inhuman, or both.

Because I had found him, his imagination focused on me, and my family became his next target—though I didn't know it at the time. To anyone else it would have seemed random, but to JPP it made some kind of twisted perfect sense.

Two months after his arrest, he escaped off the
prison bus during a transfer to the courthouse to hear
the charges read against him, five separate charges of
murder in the first degree. He nearly killed two guards
with a homemade shiv on his way off the bus. Hid.
Traveled, somehow. Found my family, and the rest was
history.

Now whenever I pictured our lawn I couldn't help
seeing six dominoes sitting in plain view on the
grass—the first three digits of Jackson's and Cece's
social security numbers—though in reality the dominoes weren't found until the grass was cut and my husband and child were already dead. JPP had "warned"
us, his way of giving us a loophole of escape; in his
mind, he had done the right thing before proceeding
with the inevitable. He was chillingly efficient in that
way, like a corporate functionary, following his own
predetermined procedures as he went about his task.
My former partner, Mac, tried hard to convince me it
wasn't my fault we hadn't found the dominoes in time.
They had sunk into the long grass. Jackson and I had
run errands all that last weekend, and the lawn had
gone uncut. We had missed our loophole, our chance.
And then JPP showed up early one morning, after I'd
left for work and Jackson and Cece were alone in the
house. Mac had tried so hard to convince me that there
was no way I could have known the dominoes were
there or that JPP had targeted my family as his next
set of victims. "You would have had to be as crazy as
he is to think that way," Mac had said. But none of
his comfort reached me. Jackson was dead. Cece was
dead. And it was my fault.

I had come to Brooklyn because it was unlike anywhere I had ever lived. I thought of it as hiding in plain
sight; hiding from myself, really, since JPP was locked
up and couldn't get to me. Everyone had agreed it was
a good idea, safer to lose myself in a crowd than suffer
alone in the country somewhere. How did he find me?
I had moved here only four months ago and had spent
hours online and on the phone erasing any trace of my
new location. But the thing about JPP was that if he
wanted you, he found a way.

"Come on," Detective Billy Staples said. "I've got
orders to bring you in."

I heard it two ways at once: Protecting me was the
obvious thing to do, and yet I didn't want to go. I'd been
there, done that. The police could do their best to save
my skin, but the part that really needed saving—my
heart and soul—were very much my own problem. I
had been working on them full-time for months now,
doing nothing but finding any small way to "recognize
pleasure" again, as Joyce would say. She hadn't bothered saying "feel" pleasure or "be happy" because I
wasn't nearly that advanced yet. I was trying to hold
myself together and I had discovered that I had to do it
on my own. If I stepped into a police department right
now, or any place filled with the smells and sights and
sounds of my old life—the life that had brought this
on—I didn't think I could handle it. I needed to stay
quiet and stay home, at least for now.

"Don't I have a choice?"

"I'm not sure what other choice you really have right
now, you know?"

"I'm going to stay."

"No, Karin, you've got to come with me. It isn't safe for you here."

But safety for me, these days, was in the eye of the beholder. "Detective Staples, I don't believe you have the right to compel me."

He jammed his hands in his pockets and stared at me. He was wearing jeans, too, but his were clean. "Okay," he said. "Have it your way. But we'll be out here, just in case. And I want you to call me the minute you change your mind." He handed me his card, white embossed with shiny blue lettering showing his whereabouts at the NYPD.

"Thanks." I slipped the card into my pocket. "I just want some time to think, and then I'll get in touch."

He paused, then asked, "Do we need to worry about you?"

I knew what he was referring to: Nine months ago I tried to take my own life. "No. You don't need to worry about me. I've dealt with that."

A cloud passed overhead and the sun blasted into his face, revealing a map of lines across his high cheekbones and a few gray hairs at his temples. I had put him at about thirty but saw now that he was older by a decade. He nodded and turned toward his car, then looked back.

"By the way, I almost didn't recognize you. You don't look much like your photo."

No, I didn't. In the head shot they took for my employee ID I had shoulder-length reddish hair and a big smile. The photographer had been joking around that day, or maybe he always did so staff photos wouldn't look like mug shots.

"That was taken five years ago," I said.

He nodded, understanding me. "A lifetime."

"Thank you, Detective. I have your number."

He drove away and I went through the locked iron gate most brownstones had at the ground-floor entry, separating a small space from an inner door. Between the two doors there was a cupboard beneath the front stoop that served as a catch-all for stuff I didn't want to bring into the house, like the bag of rock salt I'd bought to melt ice from my entryway in the winter when I'd first moved in, and the dirty gardening accessories I stashed there now. The inner door itself had a glass-paneled upper half and a flimsy lock I rarely bothered turning. I turned it now and stood in my front hall, knowing that even the best of locks couldn't keep JPP out if he wanted to get in.

I had tried to make my new home as comfortable as possible, more like the apartment I'd lived in before Jackson and I bought a house together and tossed our eclectic stuff away in favor of the more mature and dignified stuff of coupledom. I'd sold all our real furniture with the house and started fresh when I came here, collecting castoffs from the sidewalk and buying cheap furniture off Craigslist. I bought what I *liked* and what I *wanted*. It had been one of Joyce's dictates. *No shoulds.* Except for one thing: She specifically asked me to put a mirror near the front door so I could check myself coming in and going out. She wanted me to catch myself if I "zombied-out" again. I'd hung an enormous mirror with an ornate faux-gilt frame on the wall above a shoe caddy. There were four pudgy angels, one at each corner, each aiming an arrow at the image in the mirror, the idea being to make you feel beautiful, chosen by love, when you looked at yourself.

But I didn't feel anything when I looked at myself today. What I experienced was a kind of muted unfeeling I'd gotten used to since after my suicide attempt. It was the best I could do and it was better than despair. I looked at myself, at the long hair I'd colored blond at Joyce's insistence; in the weeks after my family's murder my hair had turned prematurely gray, and Joyce said that, when she met me months later, my faded appearance had shocked her. She said it wasn't good for me to "go around looking like a ghost." Now that I'd dyed my hair, its lack of natural color made me feel like a blank canvas, as if I could be anyone, and in a way I liked that. I wanted nothing more than to be someone else, someplace else, without any of my own memories. I looked at myself. Tall. Thin. Flat. Sinewy limbs like a boy's. Expression a blank wall between memory and feeling. I felt no fear, and I had nothing left to lose.

I knew what I wanted: I wanted him to find me.

Then this could be over, once and for all.

CHAPTER 2

Earlier that morning I had brewed tea in a large cooking pot, sweetened it with honey, and left it to cool on the stovetop. I now ladled some of the sweet tea into a tall glass of ice and took a long drink. My hands were still filthy; I hadn't bothered washing them since I planned to head directly into the backyard to water what I'd planted. Rain wasn't due for a week, and if I didn't baby them, the new flowers would quickly wither. Even as I thought that, I realized how irrelevant—to me, not the flowers—it might soon be. But as long as I was on this earth I was going to care, even if I had to force myself; this was something Joyce had stressed, and she was right.

I drained my glass and refilled it, then sat at my kitchen table to think. So much of what Joyce and I had discussed in the past months swirled through my mind. *Act as if. Keep going. Stay alive. The rest will follow.* She never bothered saying what "the rest" was, never dared call it "happiness," knowing I believed mine had been all used up. Knowing, I suspected, that I still harbored a death wish. That was what I needed to grapple with right now: the fact that I still yearned to join Jackson and Cece on the other side. I actually pictured it that way, a here and a there, a place where I was and a place where they were, a place where I could join them if only I could leap some mystical fence. I wanted out of here. I wanted to *go*.

But six months ago Joyce had brought my family and friends together in an intervention—my parents; my brother, Jon; his wife, Andrea; even my old partner, Mac, was there—and I had vowed that for one year I would not try to kill myself again. "Just one year," Joyce had said, adding, "But it's a renewable policy!" Everyone had chuckled at that, and I loved them, and I was grateful they had gathered together just for me, and I promised myself to honor my promise to them.

The thing was: What if I just stayed here and let JPP come for me? The technical definition of suicide was death by one's own hand, and I wouldn't lift a finger. He would do all the work. And finally I would be propelled to wherever Jackson and Cece were, which was the only place I really wanted to be.

I crossed the kitchen and set my empty glass in the sink. A window overlooked the back garden and I saw that the sun was at its peak. The new flowers were already wilting. Well, I was still here, and for now I would do it, I would care.

Outside I untangled the green hose from where it had snaked into an unruly pile against the fence. As I watered all three flower beds and all seven pots, I looked around at this place that still felt foreign to me and yet was, officially, my home.

The brown-colored sealant on the back of the house

appeared fairly new; brownstone itself was costly and
so was usually reserved for the more elegant fronts of
the attached houses that lined the entire length of the
block. Since moving to the city I had learned that a
block was literally a single square on a grid, usually
with attached buildings tracing an outer edge around
a hollow center of open space for yards. This house
where I now lived was three stories tall and there was
no fire escape. It would be over the rooftops that one
might enter or exit in a fire or other emergency. It was
not a bad design, when I thought about it, and today I
did. It was urban planning that allowed for both conti-
nuity within communities and also individual privacy.

At eye level the gridlike configuration of houses and
yards felt much more personal. The yard where I now
stood watering my fledgling garden was a spacious
rectangle with a brick patio near the kitchen door; it
had come with my apartment and was for my exclu-
sive use. Every house had such a yard and most of the
yards were separated by fences. I had heard that some
of the fences had doors connecting neighbors' yards,
but since my apartment was on the ground floor and
lacked any elevated views I hadn't seen this for myself.
What I had seen was that, in the basement, where I did
my laundry and stored my bicycle, there seemed to be
a door connecting this house to its neighbor.

It looked like a makeshift, homemade door that a
former owner had added for some now-forgotten purpose. Perhaps there were other connective passageways
in other basements on the block. It was something
I could mention to Detective Billy Staples, whose
number was right there in my pocket. My cell phone

was also in my pocket. I could do it right now: put down the hose, take out my phone and Billy's number, and place the call. Tell him specifically how he and his colleagues could protect me—tell them about the connecting basements and yards offering unmapped routes into and out of the block—along with the more obvious net I knew they would throw around me. I knew that before long there would be undercover officers up and down the street outside my house, and probably on all the streets surrounding the hollow square of connected brownstones. There would probably be a SWAT team stationed somewhere, crouched at the ready. And there would be a helicopter searching from above. Martin Price was a dangerous escaped felon, a serial killer with a gruesome résumé, who had effectively given my address as his destination. The police and the FBI would be waiting for him outside and simultaneously guarding me. I thought this over. I could do it: give them more information to help them protect me. Or I could just continue watering my garden.

When all the beds were soaked, I turned off the spigot and piled the hose back up against the fence. Then I went inside, passed through an inner door leading from my kitchen into the common hallway, and checked the lock on the basement door. It was a hollow door, the cheapest you could possibly buy, and the lock was as flimsy as the lock on my front door. I turned the little pinched lock-catch in the center of the knob then double-checked that it was now unlocked. It was. Good. No need to make JPP have to break my landlord's property when he came. And he was coming.

I went back inside my apartment, stripped off my

dirty gardening clothes, and got into my blue-tiled shower. Standing naked under the streaming hot water, I remembered the anomaly of how calm and collected JPP had appeared in the courtroom, costumed in a blue suit and striped tie, in contrast to the vivid images of the murders. The district attorney had urged me to stay home the day he planned to present evidence, which included photographs from the crime scene. I considered not going but ultimately felt I had to be present for every moment of the reckoning of that fateful day. I slipped into the back of the courtroom just as a digital image of Cece's body flashed onto the screen. I hadn't seen it before and it shocked me beyond anything I had imagined. The lawyers and cops had spared me the details but I had inevitably picked some up on the news. I soon learned to avoid all media. But I did know the bare fact that her pink-flowered bedspread had been so soaked with her blood that it had dripped and pooled onto the floor. Nothing, however, had prepared me for that image—the waxen stillness of her beloved body. I screamed, as if I had just that moment learned of Jackson's and Cece's deaths. Every face—judge, jury, attorneys, defendant, spectators—turned to look at me, stunned. After a silent moment of recognition, expression emerged on the faces: tears, empathy, sympathy, pity, even shame. The one face that showed no emotion whatsoever was that of Martin Price.

He looked at me with a blank expression on his unexceptional face, the kind of face one might call average or nondescript. His was the face of someone you wouldn't notice if you passed him on the street. He was the neighbor people thought was *nice*, the guy who no one ever worried about, who paid his rent on time, who never made noise, never complained, didn't bother anyone . . . kind of a nerd, with almost-blond hair parted far to the left and combed far to the right. As my scream reverberated in the courtroom, Martin Price turned to me with vacant almost-blue eyes that looked but didn't seem to see. It was as if he had heard some unexpected noise, had identified it, and was ready to return to his previous activity.

After what felt like long minutes but must have been just a few moments, Mac jumped up from his front-row bench and hurried me out of the courtroom. He wrapped his arm around me and bent his head low, sheltering me with his body as he moved me forward and out. I could still remember the piney scent of the soap he used, how he was so close to me that day that I smelled it for the first time, despite the months we'd spent together at work.

I turned off the shower, stepped out dripping onto the tile floor, and rubbed my skin dry with a towel. Through a small bathroom window looking onto the garden I heard a bird's repetitive melody, and a mother calling her child in for lunch, and the intermittent grinding of a hand drill, and the air-chopping agitations of a helicopter circling overhead. Steam from the shower drifted through the window into the fresh outside air.

From the standalone wardrobe closet in the corner of my small windowless bedroom—an inner, doorless space that was hardly a real room, wedged between the living room and kitchen—I chose a pair of clean blue jeans and a short-sleeved white blouse made of a pretty eyelet fabric. I had worn this shirt the last night Jackson, Cece, and I had spent together, and hadn't worn it since.

Because the bedroom was so small, my double bed was pressed into the corner. Beside it was a bedside table someone had discarded because of a gash on the black-painted wood, a problem I had solved by covering it with a piece of bright Mexican cloth I picked up at a local yard goods store. I had a lamp shaped like an airplane that I'd bought at a stoop sale. It didn't cast much light for reading but I did the best I could with it. I turned it on and lay on my bed with a book. But it was impossible to concentrate. I thought of getting up and going to the front window and taking a look outside, but decided against it. I basically knew what was happening out there. And I knew what was going to happen. My task now was to stay inside, keep still, and wait.

I put the book on my bedside table, got up, and went to the living room. It was normally the brightest room in the apartment, but that morning I hadn't bothered opening the curtains on the two front windows, which faced the street, and so I switched on the overhead light. It wasn't a bad room—it was where I had put most of my slapdash decorating efforts since moving in—and I always felt comfortable here. The walls and painted-over pattern-embossed tin ceiling were white, and above a puffy pink love seat (free on Craigslist) I had hung a vintage French poster of a man bicycling in the sky above a town at night. I had a rocking chair, and a glass coffee table, and a long, low bookcase. I knelt down to reach the red leather photo album I kept on the bottom shelf.

On Joyce's advice I had displayed no photographs of Jackson or Cece around the apartment, and so when I needed to see them this album was my treasure chest. It was devoted to our family's life from the moment of Cece's birth. The first page announced her arrival with a photograph of me lying in the hospital bed holding my scrawny newborn, who was swaddled in a thin flannel blanket and wore a striped knit cap, and Jackson leaning over to kiss my cheek. In silver pen beneath the photo I had written *Welcome Cecilia Elizabeth Schaeffer.* Her peachy skin looked ill-fitted to her tiny six-pound body. We had named her after Jackson's mother who had passed away that same year. I touched my fingertip to Jackson's face in the photo. I could almost feel the roughness of the stubble on his cheek. He hadn't shaved for two days; we had rushed from bed to the hospital early the previous morning. The birth had taken over twenty-four hours and we were beyond exhausted and yet it was the happiest day of our lives. We had created, and had borne, and now possessed our very first child. Jackson's messy brown hair fell over part of his face as he leaned into the kiss. He had decided to let his hair grow somewhat long so he would look "like a real guitarist," he'd said of the band he had just joined for weekend gigs at local clubs. For years he had worked as a paralegal at a large law firm in Trenton, and now he was in law school. He was a responsible man before he became my husband, and as a husband and father he was more than I would have imagined I could reasonably expect. He was easygoing and fun and loving and talented. He was the love of my life, before Cece came along. Every night I would lie in

Cece's bed and read her a book, and then I would slip away and Jackson would slip in with his acoustic guitar and play her quiet tunes until she fell asleep.

The next pages showed early milestones: first bath, first solid meal, first day at the beach, first time at the zoo, walks in the stroller, rides in the car, naps with Mommy, cuddles on Daddy's lap. She grew before our eyes, as children do. Blossomed. Rolled, sat, crawled, walked, talked. And then she was a toddler who could run! And then a preschooler naming colors and counting almost to ten. And then . . .

I stopped on a photograph we had let Cece take of me and Jackson on our fifth, and last, wedding anniversary. In the crooked, blurry picture, we were outside on our porch in late fall, leaning against the railing, pressed close together so we would fit inside the frame. Laughing, of course. As soon as she'd snapped the picture, Cece dropped the camera on the porch and sat down to play with an ant that had caught her attention. Jackson jumped up to see if the camera was broken (it was not). Later that afternoon we had an early dinner together on the porch, put Cece to bed, and made love by candlelight. We had spoken of having another baby.

I closed the album and held it to my chest and lay down on the couch. Overhead I could hear the helicopter making its wide sweeping, chopping movements, diminishing and returning, and repeating, and again. I didn't feel safe, though. In truth I felt very little. Blank, teetering on sorrow. I closed my eyes.

Eventually I realized I was hungry. Got up. Made myself a turkey sandwich and poured another glass of ice tea. Ate alone at my round wooden thrift-store table with its single claw-footed leg in the center. Around the table were three mismatched chairs, one of which I managed to keep free of piles—stacks of mail, stuff I'd bought but hadn't put away—so I always had a place to sit. My chair faced the window and as I ate I gazed outside. The yard was quiet and still. A bird fluttered down onto a branch of an old fruit-bearing peach tree that had recently budded. The bird hopped, sat, flew away.

I cleared my place and washed my plate, glass, and utensils by hand. My kitchen was equipped with a dishwasher but I rarely used it. While I was drying my hands on a dishtowel, the phone rang. I debated answering, let it go five rings, and then the answering machine on the counter picked up. I listened to the click, a kind of electronic gulp, and then the sound of Mac's voice: "Karin, I know you're there. Pick up." A pause. "Listen to me. I got a call from New York. What's this about you refusing to leave your apartment? Karin! Pick up!" Another pause. "Okay, that's it, I'm on my way." If he was in New Jersey and there was traffic, it could take him two hours.

I ran to the phone and lifted the receiver. "Mac, it isn't necessary to come—" I stopped talking when I heard the drone of a dial tone. I held the receiver in my hand a moment, realizing I was glad I'd missed him. I was depressed, and he would have heard that in my voice, and then he would have called someone nearby to come sooner. And save me. Save me from JPP. Save me from myself.

My apartment grew intensely quiet as afternoon settled. My landlord rarely got home until late evening and I was alone inside the building. At least I thought

I was alone. Sitting at the kitchen table with a deck of cards, playing solitaire, I listened carefully for any sound. The hisses and shuffles and clicks of an old building composed themselves into something nearly musical. It was surprising what you could hear when you sat alone in the quiet with nothing turned on.

I decided in advance that when he came, I would simply sit here. I wouldn't get up. I wouldn't say or do anything. I would just continue playing my hand until he made his move. There were moments when I found myself hoping Mac would arrive first, haul me up and out of the deep well of isolation that had swallowed me. And then there were moments when I hoped he wouldn't. The thought that minutes from now I could be released from this mirrored labyrinth of memory and grief felt like a tremendous liberation, and I wanted that so badly. Wanted to be free. Just free.

I won the game, gathered up the cards, and shuffled. Then I lay down seven new cards, faceup, to begin another game. I turned over the top card on the dealing pile and looked to see what I could do with it . . . and that was when I heard the first sound.

A click.

The basement door creaking open into the common hall.

A careful footstep followed by another, and another, and another. Then silence.

The knob turning on my apartment's inner door.

CHAPTER 3

The door creaked open slowly, as if he relished the pleasure of his arrival, as if he was memorizing every moment that brought him closer to me so he could turn it over in his mind later and enjoy it. It was what they did, JPP and his ilk. Serial killers were a special breed that had been extensively studied but little understood. Something was wrong with them, something that evaded our comprehension. They were not like us. I struggled to keep my thoughts trained to the kind of clinical detachment preached in cop school. *Separate yourself from what you see at a crime scene. Do your job. Collect information. Don't take it personally.* Wisdom that sounded impossible until you were on the street in uniform and faced the dark side of the underbelly. Then you had no choice but to shut down.

I forced myself *off*, shut down; pushed back against the electrifying sensations that threatened to force me up and out of the kitchen chair. I looked at the card faceup on the dealing pile: a seven of hearts. It would become evidence. Images of the kitchen where I sat, waiting, listening, flashed through my mind with the crisp efficiency of a high-speed camera. Body slumped over the table, cards flung across the floor, blood spatter on the ceiling and walls.

How the hell did he get in, the cops would ask themselves, *when we had her covered from every angle?* And then they would go to the basement and see the door. The blogs would fill with urban legends of secret passageways. Investigators would sift through it for the gems of fact. Maps would be drawn. And this would never be allowed to happen again.

There was an oozing quality to his entrance that sickened me in the pit of my stomach. Combined in the moment was both the imminence of my own fate, and a visceral emotional memory that this was directly connected to the fate that had befallen Jackson and Cece. Their fate would now become mine and we would be reunited. It was all I wanted. The coroner's report showed that JPP had killed Jackson first, bludgeoning him in the back as he stood at the kitchen counter buttering toast. Waiting in my kitchen now put me, in my heart, back with Jackson. If only I had died then, preferably first, I would never have been tormented with the knowledge of what came next.

I could tell by the stealth of JPP's footsteps that he thought I didn't hear him. He was getting closer. I played the seven of hearts and turned over the next card on the dealing pile: the king of spades. I could hear him breathing, slowly, deeply. What kind of weapon was he holding? He had used ropes, knives, and saws on Jackson and Cece and also on the Alderman family. He wanted to feel it, experience the tearing of flesh and the sharp smell of fresh blood. The kill itself was what mattered to him, not the actual death. The death was a practicality; it eliminated a witness so he could keep on the loose and kill again. Though he wasn't very good at that part: He always got caught sooner or later. And then he always escaped. Obviously he loved this so much it was worth the risk and the trouble.

He crept closer. And closer still. Finally he was so close I could smell him. The powerful reek of his body odor almost made me retch. I held my breath and swallowed. Played the king of spades. His body must have been in overdrive, he must have been sweating profusely to have generated such a foul stench. I swallowed again. He stopped walking.

"Don't pretend you don't know I'm here," he whispered.

I held still. Breathed. Turned the top card on the dealing pile: the two of clubs.

He took one deep breath and then slowly exhaled. He wanted me to turn around and see him. But I wouldn't do it. I wanted him to kill me the way he had killed Jackson, with a single blow to the back. And then this would be over.

I felt him come within two feet of me. Felt the heat off his skin. His smell intensified. Footsteps amplified. And then from the corner of my eye I saw him: his bright red face, short pale hair, agitated vacant eyes, and the glint of a large knife with a curved blade. He dropped a canvas bag on the floor. It buckled over and a coil of rope spilled out.

"Hello." Grinning.

I forced my attention to the cards spread out on the

table. Played the two of clubs. Turned over the top card on the dealer's pile: the queen of spades.

"You can play her to the king," he said.

I held still.

"Do it."

I didn't move. Didn't breathe. Didn't blink.

"Look at me."

Refusal. Stillness. Waiting. Perfecting the effigy of myself.

He moved closer and put himself right in front of me. His face closed the gap between us until the tips of our noses touched.

"*Look.*"

His smell was overpowering and I couldn't control the impulse to vomit. It rose into my mouth. I swallowed it back. And then I couldn't help myself: I looked directly into his eyes.

Which were strangely human. I hadn't expected that. He wanted something very badly. Yearned for it. Staring into my eyes, he pressed the tip of his knife into my sternum. I felt the fabric of my shirt rip. Felt the sharp blade of the knife sever the top layers of my skin. The wetness of my blood gathering on the surface.

"You want this as much as I want this," he said. "I can tell."

I tried to detach my eyes from his but found I couldn't. We were too close. I waited for him to pick up his rope so he could tie me to the chair and get to work. But he didn't. Instead he seemed to make a tactical decision to restrain me with his eyes, my refusal to fear him; his power to control me, my willingness to let him.

His face moved closer, the sides of our noses slid

against each other, and our mouths met. I had sensed him, heard him, smelled him, and now I tasted him: sour, salt, mint. His lips felt rubbery and dense. A dead fish: That's what his body was. A livid, slithering, stinking fish.

He leaned back and, pinning me with the knife, reached into a pants pocket with his free hand. A domino emerged, and then three more. Four dominoes. Of course: After me, someone would be next. My heart pounded wildly. *Someone in my family.*

That was his game. In my fog I hadn't thought it through. He played a game with a series of moves geared toward a single grand finale. He wouldn't stop with me.

"Open wide." Spoken like a dentist. Impassive. Just doing his job.

I clenched my lips. It shouldn't have mattered, since I had already decided to submit to this. Had been submitting. Had waited, welcomed him, allowed the knife and then the kiss. But something in me refused to allow him to put his dominoes in my mouth. Plain stubbornness. Revulsion. An instinctive limit. Something.

Holding the dominoes in his fist, he pried the knuckle of his forefinger between my lips. My teeth parted against the pressure as he forced his finger into my mouth. Another automatic response: My teeth clamped down on his bent finger until I tasted his blood and felt a surprising satisfaction.

He groaned and pulled his finger out of my mouth. His fist reflexively opened and the dominoes scattered on the table. Four dominoes among the cards. Two different games combined. His and mine.

Five. Three. Four. Two. One. Three. Six.

I couldn't stop my mind from processing those seven numbers. Four, six, five, two, one, three, three. Three, six, one, four, five, three, two. Scrambling them in every possible combination. What did they mean? If it was a phone number, it wasn't one I recognized. I didn't know my family's social security numbers. The seven numbers were too long for any of their addresses. What else? *What else?* Driver's licenses. Passport IDs. Account numbers. Personal numbers and codes and sequences I couldn't possibly know. Birthdays. I knew all of them—I was the daughter, sister, and aunt who never forgot a birthday. My mind flew through the calendar, processing the numbers, trying to hit a match.

Nothing.

But it had to mean something.

What did the numbers mean?

Who did JPP plan to kill next?

My mother?

Father?

My older brother, Jon? His wife, Andrea? Their daughter, Susanna?

Who?

I pushed one foot against the table, propelling my chair back and my body away from the knife. Just a couple of inches away, but far enough to force my knee between us; I brought it up hard and fast into his groin. Watched the issue of pain through his body and its release before he gave way to it.

He doubled over. His hand opened. The knife fell to the floor. Easy as one, two, three. But it couldn't be that easy—and it wasn't.

His open hand slammed my face with unreal force, twisting my head sharply to the right. I almost blacked out. But didn't.

His hand reached to the floor for the knife.

I ground my shoe into his wrist, forcing his fingers to splay open.

His free hand wrapped itself around my ankle with a viselike grip.

Struggling, I reached down for the knife.

Once, as a cop, I had shot a man as he ran out of a store he had just robbed. He didn't die because I hadn't shot to kill because I hadn't needed to.

A knife was another thing. And this was a different game.

It was heavy. About ten inches long. Sharp.

He pulled at my ankle, struggling to free his wrist. I felt my foothold begin to give way.

It was now or never. Me or him. And I had changed my mind: It was not going to be me. It was not going to be me because I couldn't let it be someone else next.

I brought the knife down quickly, with all my strength, aiming for his heart. Aiming to kill. To hit. Sink into. Tear through. All the metaphors of forcible death fountained through my brain, aided and abetted my desire to destroy him. Now. Him. Not me.

Because I had changed my mind.

The crime scene was changing shape. Players reversing position.

He released my ankle and his hand struck mine with such force that the knife flew across the room, landing on the floor near the sink cabinet. He pushed me off him and crawled toward the knife.

Sweat must have poured off his face because as I moved to intercept him, I slipped on something wet—and fell.

Just as I fell I heard my doorbell ring. Someone pounded on my front door.

JPP grunted, crawled faster, reached the knife. Had it in his hand. Turned his eyes on me and said, "You can't get away!"

"Karin!" It was Mac's voice. Outside my door. "Open up!"

The doorbell again. More pounding.

If I didn't run, if I just stayed still, he would kill me; he wouldn't be able to resist it. And he probably couldn't work fast enough to evade capture. Mac was outside my door, half the NYPD was out front and circling the sky above us. They would get him and throw him back in prison. But if he escaped again and went for . . . *who? Someone in my family. Someone else would be next.* JPP was an escape artist—I couldn't take that risk.

I scrambled up and ran for the door.

JPP was fast. He caught the back of my jeans but he underestimated me. I back-elbowed him in the face, twisted to see him, heel-palmed him under the chin. He reeled backward then went down with a crash, dropping the knife again. This time I wasn't going to waste seconds trying to get it. I heard him standing up as I ran for the inner door, which was closer than the front door.

I ran into the common hall with JPP right behind me. From my apartment came a crash: Mac and the other cops had broken in.

"Here!" I shouted. But there was no time to consider whether they had heard me.

I ran up the stairs. Passed my landlord's front doorway. Where were the cops? I heard a ruckus in my apartment; why weren't they behind us? I ran up the next set of stairs to the third and final floor where there was a utility closet inside of which an iron ladder rose straight up to the roof.

The utility closet was narrow with a high ceiling that connected to the roof via a hatch. I climbed the ladder, shaking, moving as fast as I could.

And then I heard JPP reach the third-floor hallway. Heard him run its length before realizing he had reached the end. Heard him run back and find the closet, open the door, look up into the narrow darkness. Felt him see me. Smelled him coming closer before I heard him on the ladder beneath me. Climbing. Just behind me. With his knife, I imagined, held between his teeth.

The hatch was impossibly heavy—I couldn't push it open. And then I felt a lift in its weight and I pushed and pushed and pushed and . . . one final push defied gravity and suddenly it was a mere flap falling open. Revealing the night sky, air, stars—escape.

As I scrambled up onto the roof I felt JPP's hand touch my foot. I kicked it away and leveraged myself all the way up and out. Sprang to standing—and ran across the rooftop toward the nearest adjoining rooftop, which would lead to another and another and another until inevitably I would find an avenue of escape. Somehow. Something would present itself. It was how they trained us at the academy: to take action, keep our eyes open, recognize opportunity, and proceed from there.

I heard the SWAT team's sniper fire before I saw men crouched on the rooftops all around me.

Two officers let off shots and then a voice shouted, "Hold your fire! It's the woman!"

Two shots.

I felt one of them burn through my abdomen. And then a floating sensation as I became weightless.

A plane of white.

A relinquishment of mind.

Freedom.

Release.

CHAPTER 4

Jackson came to me, playing a song he wrote on his guitar. Its harmony rose and dipped through my brain, which felt foggy, numb, confused, unable to comprehend exactly what was happening.

And then the smell of something sharp, antiseptic, filled my nose, forcing away Jackson and his lovely song.

And then I heard my mother's voice rise out of distant memory: "She's got a brain like a steel trap and on top of it she's tall, thin, and gorgeous. Whatever she decides to do with her life, she's going to take it by storm." Speaking on the phone to someone. Who? I was ten, had just been returned home by a friend's mother from gymnastics practice. Walked into the kitchen and heard my mother talking about me. I could tell by her overconfident tone that she was in that mode of hers, forecasting her children's futures. Sitting at the table, laughing now, red phone pressed to her ear, connected to the wall by a ten-foot curly cord. I felt betrayed. Also complimented. Didn't know what to make of my mother's interpretation of me, or why she thought she knew me so well when I hardly knew myself. I had just fallen off the balance beam three times in a row because my legs had suddenly grown too gangly and all I knew that day was that I didn't have the goods. Not the goods I wanted. I wanted to make the gymnastics team and now I knew I wasn't going to.

"Karin."

Was she talking to me? She was looking at the wall, twirling the phone cord around her finger. Her nail was pink, shiny; she'd gone for a manicure that day. She didn't even know I was home or that I was standing in the doorway, listening.

"Can you hear me?"

The chemical smell seeped from my nose into my brain. My brain was a sponge, murky, sopping up the smell.

And then my eyes opened, pushing back the dream.

"Karin?"

Why did my mother have Mac's face? Mac's voice?

I blinked.

He smiled. Just smiled and looked at me. The skin of his clean-shaven face looked flexible and soft, arcing upward with his smile. His blue eyes also smiled. His hair was less brown, more gray, and shorter than when I'd last seen him. When? I couldn't figure it out. Weeks or months. Lately real time had passed between our visits. We hadn't seen each other daily since the night I'd swallowed a bottle of pills, my last day on the force, the last day of our partnership. The last time I lay in a hospital bed.

I was in a hospital bed now. Scratchy white sheets. Fluorescents too bright overhead. That smell.

"Mac?"

"Karin."

He laid his right hand over mine on the blanket beside me. His left hand fiddled with something on his lap: a square pink envelope with Hallmark embossed on the back by the seal. His big gold wedding ring seemed looser than usual . . . Mac had lost weight . . . defying an old argument of ours: You needed to be at least fifteen pounds overweight to work at slimming down, and he wasn't. I used to tell him he was too insecure, thinking losing weight would please his wife, Val, always trying to please her, never succeeding.

"I told you not to diet." My voice sounded thin, dry. The effort of speech initiated a throbbing pain deep in my abdomen.

"I told you not to die." His smile melted and his eyes moistened. He blinked, steadied himself.

"Well, I'm not dead, am I?"

"Evidently not."

But he was right in the starkest way: He had told me not to die, they had all told me not to die, and I didn't listen. But I couldn't go there right now; just couldn't. Had to change the subject. Anything safe.

"How's Maplewood?" The town in New Jersey where we had both lived and worked until events led me away and I stopped living and working anywhere.

"Same as always."

"How's Val?"

His eyes fled away from my face a moment, then returned. He shook his head.

"You really want to know?"

"I asked."

"She's divorcing me."

"*Why?*"

"Says I don't love her."

"Enough?"

"At all."

I hadn't been married as long as Mac and Val but I knew that was a pretty harsh accusation for one spouse to level against another.

"She says I'm in love with someone else."

"Are you?"

He paused and then said, "You know Val . . ."

But I didn't know Val all that well. I had met her a few times. Had dinner at their house once. She had struck me as high-strung but in a tolerable way. Attractive. A great cook. Basically, I'd liked her. I didn't know what to say and so I closed my eyes. The pain in my abdomen seemed to reach down many layers, straight through from front to back. And then I remembered why I was here and electricity bolted through my brain, awakened me.

"Did they get him?"

Mac shook his head. "He got away."

I recalled the noise of the cops breaking into my apartment while JPP chased me up the stairs. The clanging of the knife against the metal ladder. The riptide of panic.

"How?"

"Don't know. It was chaos after you got shot. Everyone was focused on you."

"I heard two shots. Where else was I hit?" Besides my abdomen, nowhere else hurt.

"You were only hit once."

"*Only?*"

"They're sharpshooters, Karin. You had to know they were up there."

"I knew."

"And you surprised them anyway." His expression pinched in disappointment, as if he felt personally slighted that I had tempted death.

"I wasn't thinking."

"It's a hell of a way to commit suicide."

"He was after me." Every word hurt. I stopped talking, gritted my teeth against the pain. But I had more to say: "At that point I was just trying to get away from him."

"After you waited for him, Karin. Don't tell me you weren't waiting."

I wouldn't lie to Mac; I respected him way too much. But I couldn't look at him, either. I turned my face to the opposite wall. A second visitor's chair was nestled in the corner. A blue-and-green plaid sweater I recognized as my mother's was spread over the back of the chair. On the long windowsill there was a paperback bookmarked halfway through. Two bouquets of flowers in clear glass vases, one with a yellow bow tied around the vase's neck, sat on a bureau, above which a television was mounted at an angle. I realized I was in a private room, a luxury I was sure I couldn't afford. An upgrade someone, presumably my parents, had paid for. Against my will I started to cry.

"I'm sorry. But you can't know what I've been going through, Mac. No one can. I just thought—"

His hand squeezed mine. "*Shh.* I understand."

I turned back to look at him. "No, you don't." No one

could possibly understand what I felt or what I'd been enduring—trying to endure, failing to endure—these past months.

Mac's forehead tautened, eyes saddened. I knew the look: wisdom, frustration, surrender. We both knew there was nothing he could possibly say to help me.

"How did he get away?" I asked.

"Probably the same way he got in, through the basement."

"The second shot didn't hit him?"

"It might have. They saw him pop up through the hatch a second, but it was dark out and they lost sight of him. They thought they hit him but there was no blood anywhere. Not his, anyway."

So my apartment had become a crime scene after all, the scene not of a murder but an attempted murder. Attempted suicide. A close call, a lost chance, that cut two ways. Images flashed through my mind. The canvas bag spilling rope onto the floor. The table, the cards, the dominoes.

"The thing is," Mac said, tapping the pink envelope against his knee, "no one's been able to find the second bullet, so we just don't know. We know he got away. The question is: In what condition?"

"You're telling me he could be dead?"

"Dead, injured, perfectly healthy. Take your pick."

It was like standing in front of three unmarked doors, no idea which one held the prize or the drop off the cliff, forced to blindly choose.

"What day is it?"

"Wednesday. You've been out of it two whole days."

"Did they figure out the dominoes?"

Mac's eyes narrowed. "Dominoes?"

"They were on the table with the cards. Four dominoes."

"There weren't any dominoes, Karin. Believe me, we looked."

"He must have taken them on his way out."

I didn't understand what it meant, that JPP would take back his dominoes, retract his precious clue. Maybe he *had* been shot. Maybe he had been badly hurt. Maybe he didn't know if he would be able to continue playing his sick game, so he took back the dominoes to buy himself time and space to decide his next move, if any. Or maybe none of the above. Meanwhile . . . two days had passed. Two days! My heart raced when I thought of the possibility that he could be lurking around my family. Lurking, or worse.

"Five, three, four, two, one, three, six."

"You're sure, Karin?"

"Yes." I could still see the four dominoes. They had blazed into my memory in that moment of high adrenaline when all at once I saw them and realized their threat and changed my mind. "Mac, if something already happened to someone in my family, you would tell me, wouldn't you?"

He looked at me and nodded, but it was noncommittal. I couldn't read his expression, couldn't tell if he was hiding something he didn't want me to know.

"Mac?"

"I don't know what I would do in that situation, Karin. But your parents have been here the whole time and I haven't heard anything in the last couple days."

That satisfied me. Mac wouldn't outright lie.

He stood up and dug into his jeans pocket for his cell phone, pulled it out, flipped it open. "The dominoes—tell me again."

"Three, six, four, one, five, two, three."

He typed the numbers into his cell phone and saved them. Then he started to dial a phone number.

"You can't use that cell phone in here," a passing nurse called through the open door.

"See if the landline works," I said.

He picked up the regulation hospital phone on my bedside table and dialed a number. I wondered who he'd report to first. Because JPP had attacked me in New York City, Detective Billy Staples would be working the case now. The New Jersey task force was based in Maplewood, Mac's current and my old jurisdiction. The Feds had also been in on the case for a year before we caught JPP. Obviously this was going to be a collaboration.

"Staples, it's MacLeary." Seamus Cian Benjamin MacLeary had been too burdensome a name for his classmates, and so from kindergarten on he had been Mac. "She's awake. Price pulled out some dominoes when he was with her, must have collected them at some point." He reeled off the seven numbers. I was amazed he had memorized them so quickly, but then again when you're desperate your mind goes into overdrive. For a moment his determination to stop JPP from striking again made me think he could really do it, that Mac of all people could and would stop the monster from destroying one more innocent person. But as soon as I thought it I remembered how often we had all felt that way, about ourselves and each other: *Today's the day* or *You're going to catch him, I sense it* or *I feel lucky today.* And how many times we had been wrong.

Mac hung up the phone and called Alan Tavarese, the detective who had replaced me in Maplewood, and said basically the same thing. Then he looked at his watch.

"I gotta get moving."

He smiled a little sadly and leaned down to kiss my cheek. I breathed deeply, hoping to catch a whiff of his pine-scented soap. I wanted to say something to him but didn't know what. I wanted him to stay. And I couldn't wait for him to go, to hurry back to the task force and make sure things were done right. He glanced at the pink envelope he'd put on my bedside table, on top of a book I'd never seen before, and headed out.

"Mac?"

"Yeah?"

He turned to look at me, really look at me. Something moved in my heart, a feeling I recognized from our old partnership: This man was my true friend.

"Call me as soon as they run all the socials of everyone in my family."

"Will do."

"And thanks for not telling me not to worry."

"Wouldn't be any point." The lines by his mouth dimpled when he smiled. "Just stay alive. That's all I ask."

I nodded.

And he was gone.

When I reached for the envelope I had to pause, the pain was that bad. Like a relentless hot blade. Now I knew what it felt like to get shot and I wouldn't wish it on anyone. Well, maybe one person. I could still see JPP's face millimeters from mine. I closed my eyes to try and blank out the memory but it only intensified. My imagination reconfigured the scene with the nozzle of a gun on his forehead, my finger squeezing the trigger, a blast obliterating him. Cleaning the slate. Leaving behind emptiness. Peace.

A tear rolled down the side of my face; I hadn't realized I was crying. I felt like such an idiot. Torn between regret at having missed my chance to let him finish me off, and shame that I had been such a coward in the first place. But then I remembered why I had changed my mind. I should have thought of the domino game sooner, but it was better late than never. Somehow I was going to have to get over myself and focus on the only thing that mattered now: making sure my family was safe . . . what was left of them.

I didn't know what they'd been giving me to blunt the pain but I wanted more. A call button, connected to the wall by a floppy cord, sat on the bedside table. I took a breath and went for it. Pressed the button. Heard a distant *ding* somewhere out in the hall. While my hand was there I snatched both the envelope and the book, thinking they were probably a gift that went together.

The envelope had been sealed only at the tip and opened easily. A Peanuts card showed Snoopy mummified in bandages lying atop his doghouse on a sunny day. A little airplane curling through a blue horizon had sky-written *Get Well* . . . I opened the card and read . . . *Soon!* A healthy, happy Snoopy hung from one paw off the bottom of the exclamation point while the other paw waved hello. The white space was filled

with signatures. It looked as if every member of the
Maplewood detectives unit had signed it. Then I noticed Billy Staples's signature along with a few others
I didn't recognize, probably FBI. The unit *and* the task
force had signed. Mac had covered all the bases. That
was sweet of him.

I put the card aside and lifted the book. It was a paperback called *Secrets of the Path to the Inner Sanctum of
Buried Happiness*. This couldn't have come from any
cop I knew. I opened the front cover and saw from the
inscription that it was from my therapist, Joyce. In pre-
cise rounded script she had written: *You are forgiven.
You are loved.* Tucked between the front cover and first
page was a business card for another psychiatrist, Dr.
Gordon Weinberg, along with a folded note.

Dear Karin,

*I am extremely sorry that I can't be here with you
now. As I mentioned recently I promised to work
with Doctors Without Borders in China for three
weeks helping earthquake survivors. After deep
consideration I felt I had to honor that commit-
ment. But you are in my thoughts. I'll be back on
5/11 and have given you my first appointment.
See you in my office 5/12 @ 9 A.M. I'll expect you!*

xo Joyce

*P.S. Call Dr. Weinberg in my absence, any time
of the day or night. He's expecting it.*

I laid the book aside, sorry I had missed her visit, feeling like an abandoned child. But at the same time I understood her dilemma. Millions of people needed her in China, and she had to know I'd be watched like a hawk now.

A tiny Polynesian nurse in a white pantsuit came into my room. "You okay, Karin?"

"The pain—"

"So I thought." She stood at my bedside and pressed air bubbles through the needle of a hypodermic filled with something clear. Then she wrapped my upper arm with a rubber tourniquet, watched for the vein in my elbow to grow fat and blue, and slid the needle in.

"What is it?" I asked, already feeling dreamy and warm.

"Morphine, my dear."

"What's your name?" I sort of wanted to know the name of the person who was getting me high and sort of didn't care.

She answered but I couldn't hear what she said. I was under water again. There were sounds in the hall, footsteps in my room, the flowery smell of the perfume my mother always wore, a conversation that to me sounded like deep sea gurgling and swishing and then in my mind I was floating amid brilliant coral reef, fascinated by its beauty, my consciousness penetrating the mysteries of color in the absence of light.

CHAPTER 5

It was a chilly Tuesday afternoon, eight days after I'd been shot, when we drove up to my parents' Victorian house on Upper Mountain Avenue in Montclair. Painted yellow as long as I could remember, the house was three stories tall with a complicated symmetrical design and a wraparound veranda that had always reminded me of the hem of a long skirt blending gracefully into the sloping front lawn.

My mother pulled the car up to the curb and the first thing I noticed was that the dogwood tree was dripping with white blossoms.

The next thing I noticed was a blue windowless van parked across the street at the curb. In the driver's seat sat a young man who watched our arrival. At least one other undercover cop would be sitting in the back of the van monitoring surveillance equipment. I glanced at the front door of the house and noticed the addition of a security camera, a smoky half bubble affixed directly above the door frame. I hoped these cops had some experience with seriously bad guys in case JPP came back for me.

Unless he was dead or injured and didn't come back for me.

Unless he was alive and well and planned to return for someone else in my family. Someone less willing to die, more exciting to kill.

I started up the long path toward the house. My mother was behind me, wheeling my suitcase, which made a racket on the uneven stones.

Which of my family members would he pick off next, if he was still out there? My brain began its compulsive grind, igniting a spasm in my wound. I stopped walking and took a breath while my mother paused to help steady me.

"Okay, darling?"

Mom hovered beside me, tall and wrinkly-soft, emanating concern. Her short rust-red hair was uncharacteristically shapeless and the skin beneath her eyes was bluish and saggy. She hadn't left the hospital at all, except for a trip to my apartment in Brooklyn to pack me some things, and a brief visit home this morning to prepare for my arrival.

I nodded. Took another breath. Proceeded slowly.

Dad was waiting on the front porch, presumably where she'd parked him in view of the cops—sitting on a wicker chair, oddly still, hair and skin the blended gray of quickly advancing age. Having gone into retirement together, facing their golden years after decades of shouldering all the usual adult responsibilities involved in raising a family, she now found she sometimes needed a sitter for my father, whose dementia increasingly left him confused. She hadn't quite figured out what to do about that and I doubted she would anytime soon. At the hospital she had made it clear that her focus now was me.

She set me up in my old room: a soft double bed covered in white chenille, cream-colored wallpaper across which riderless brown horses sprinted all in the same direction. As a girl I'd tried counting the horses but never got much beyond fifty or sixty; after a while they blurred together and you lost track of which ones you'd already calculated into your total. Mom had put a vase of lilacs cut from her garden on top of the dresser. I settled myself on my bed. When she was through arranging my things, she came over and perched on the edge of the mattress.

"Does it hurt when I sit?"

"A little. But stay."

"I love you, Karin. We're going to get through this. I promise."

She took one of my hands between both of hers. Her skin felt familiar and perfect and warm. She leaned down and pressed her cheek against mine and took a deep breath, inhaling me. I remembered doing that to Cece sometimes when she slept: drinking her in, loving her.

"Jon's stopping by in a minute," she said. "Every time he came to see you in the hospital you were sleeping, and he has a flight later today."

"I'm glad he's coming," I said. "I want to see him." In truth I didn't feel up to visitors, but Jon was my brother. We had been close all our lives. I was as eager to see him as I felt guilty for having let him down. Again. After my first suicide attempt he had seemed heart-broken. I worried that this time he would be frustrated with me, possibly even angry.

Moments later Jon walked into the room, holding in his arms his two-year-old daughter, Susanna, who in turn held a cloth baby doll. Behind them was his wife, Andrea, seven months pregnant with their second child, a son. Andrea was as small and dark and fragile as Jon was tall and pale and sturdy. Married four years now, from their first meeting they had been a classic case of opposites attracting magnetically and staying tightly connected through thick and thin. They had weathered bouts of Jon's unemployment followed by long absences when work took him to Hollywood—his career as a special-effects makeup designer toggled him back and forth between the coasts. They had weathered bouts of Andrea's periodic depressions that had deepened with stay-at-home motherhood. Yet through all that, they had persevered. As his career blossomed, moving the family to Los Angeles had begun to seem inevitable. But the decision was postponed after the murders, so they could stay close while I pulled myself together. Which no longer seemed inevitable, at least to me.

Jon set Susanna on the end of my bed, inches away from my feet, where she made herself comfortable, sitting cross-legged in her pink dress and making a cradle in her lap for her doll. The silky blond hair that had never been cut spilled down her small back. Her lack of self-consciousness around her suicidal aunt was breathtakingly real. I adored her for not giving me and my angst the time of day. Susanna would be three years old soon—the same age as Cece when she died. Every time I'd seen Susanna since then I had gone to bed in tears. She was a year younger than Cece, only Cece had been frozen in time, so this year, when Susanna turned three on the fourth of July, they would be the exact same age. I had dreaded Susanna's birthday. Now, looking at her, feeling her scant weight at the end of my bed, I couldn't bear to think of how close I came to missing it.

Andrea leaned down to kiss my cheek. "We'll only stay a minute." Up close, the dark swaths under her eyes appeared purplish. She had once remarked that she hadn't had a full night's sleep since Susanna was born. Looking at her, you wouldn't doubt her exhaustion.

Jon's pale blue eyes settled on mine. All our lives people had said we had the same eyes. Seeing his gentle expression, I felt relieved. Saddened. He wasn't angry, but I could see I had hurt him.

"Jon, I'm *sorry*."

"Don't be, okay? I had to come see for myself—that you're all right." He stepped closer, leaned down until we were face-to-face. "Are you all right?"

How could I answer? I was alive. I didn't know if I was all right.

He leaned down to kiss me. "Take care of yourself, Karin. That's the main thing. It's what we all want, okay? And don't worry about us. Please."

"Don't worry about me, either."

Something about the emotion that suddenly filled the room drew Susanna's attention away from her doll. She looked from face to face, reading each of us, and then flipped to hands and knees and crawled the length of the bed, landing herself in my arms. She was unbearably soft. The perfect size. I held her, burying my face in her hair.

A few minutes later Jon, Andrea, and Susanna left; a disappointment and a relief.

After making sure I was comfortable, Mom bustled around the house, putting things in order, while I lay in bed. My last shot of morphine was wearing off, and as the pain sharpened I relaxed against my pillow and tried to drift off but couldn't manage more than an uneasy half sleep. My mind kept flashing with images of sudden, violent, interrupted life. I couldn't close my eyes anymore without seeing them. All of them. Jackson and Cece, mostly. And the Alderman family. Their parts and pieces mingled together in a puzzle my mind could never complete. Trying to evade the images was useless: They were always there, their sharp edges cutting the surface of my consciousness. Time fragmented, memories raced ahead, or suddenly stopped, or shrank back, like individual scenery backdrops controlled by a mechanical pulley operated by a lunatic. While I, trapped in the nightmare, raced forward yet fell behind. Swallowed by a time warp, a quicksand slowdown, against which I was powerless. Swallowed by memory. Their faces raced through me, past me: Cece, Jackson, and each of the five Aldermans whom I only knew from crime scene photographs. I couldn't stop seeing the images I'd studied and memorized back when I was a member of the team trying to catch JPP the first time. They flooded me now.

There had been five murders, four crime scenes, and the police photographer had captured every inch of every angle of every place where a body was found. Every splash of blood was recorded by the camera, measured and marked, and if the spray extended beyond the scope of the lens, then multiple shots were taken and later joined together. Every fingerprint, every footprint, every hair, every strand of fiber was collected, collated, measured, recorded. If there was a glass on a counter, it was bagged. If there was a used tissue on the ground, it was bagged. If there was a stray button on the floor, it was bagged. Strangely, the gatherings made by a team of forensic specialists could resemble the quirky treasures often collected by serial killers themselves to catalog and relive their crimes. I'd once heard a detective quip, "The psychos build their kit on the way in; we build ours on the way out." It was a cold, cynical remark but it was true. After a while, you started thinking like the creep you were trying to catch. You hated it. But you feared that, if you didn't, you'd never get him.

Working the Alderman case was my first descent into the horrors of a twisted mind. Living the Schaeffer case, Jackson's and Cece's, was my second descent. Surviving my own, a week ago, was my third. With each descent the darkness only got darker, even though each level seemed as dark as things could possibly get. I practically yearned for the innocence of the Alderman case. No: I yearned for the time before that, before my choice of career earned me a front-row seat at the worst show humanity could offer.

Why did I become a cop in the first place? Lately I had often asked myself that. To please my father, I suppose, was the easy answer. He was a military officer, an unambivalent force of nature whom I'd worshipped growing up. After retiring from the army at the age of thirty-eight, he became a cop and later a detective. It had been no secret he'd hoped Jon would follow in his footsteps, but when he didn't, when my brother followed his talents to Hollywood, I anointed myself my beloved father's best and last hope. So I joined the Junior ROTC in high school and eventually headed off to the army. When my tour was up, and I was finally thinking about college, 9/11 happened. I abandoned my plans and on 9/12 applied at the police academy. One year later, I was on patrol. Six years after that, I made detective. Another year, and Jackson and Cece were dead. Now my father barely remembered what day it was, let alone how faithfully I had emulated him.

So why did I become a cop? It seemed like a good idea at the time. For a while it continued to seem like a good idea. I liked the work, the action, the adrenaline when you had to move and think on a dime. At times the work had even inspired me. I remembered how charged up I was to get assigned to the Alderman case. How much I wanted to be the one to crack it. Never realizing that I *would* be the one to crack it, or imagining that it would be pretty much by chance and would ultimately rob me of what I most loved. Never thinking it might not be worth it or that someday I would be lying in a bed wishing I was a magician who could turn back time, or at least turn off the kaleidoscope of images of dead people.

Not just dead people. Loved ones. Strands of a web whose cut ends reached perpetually into the hearts of those left behind.

Jackson.

Cece.

The Aldermans.

Lying in bed, my brain flashing, I recalled seeing

those photos for the very first time. Recalled the initial shock of viewing the documentation of JPP's *work*. Recalled the sour taste of bile my stomach kept regurgitating and which I kept swallowing down. Recalled realizing how stupid it had been to eat lunch before attending my first meeting of the task force.

There were approximately a hundred photographs from each of the crime scenes and I studied them all. They were the worst things I had ever seen in my life but I forced myself to look because it was my job. I had recently been promoted to detective and had just joined the task force. It didn't take long to tap into the collective desperation that had built up among the members over the course of a year to capture the monster that had done this. To stop him before he struck again.

Gary Alderman, the father. He was the first to die. Found in the garage, with the door closed, sealed into a running car with a tube connected to the tailpipe routing in toxic air. Discovered in the morning, before school, by his nine-year-old daughter, Rhonda. Who also noticed a domino she had never seen before propped on the corner of her father's worktable in the corner of the garage.

One domino, two numbers: a one and a two. Twelve. Her sister Zoë's age.

The worktable was always heaped with random things and Rhonda didn't think anything of the domino. In the chaos that day, she added it to her collection of toys, not because she was greedy but because it had belonged to her father, and the little girl ached for any link to him. No one understood why Gary had taken his own life. There was no suicide note.

Zoë, the oldest of the three Alderman children, was second to die. Found in a ditch five miles from home, three hours after she failed to return from school. Half naked. Stabbed and strangled, with a nylon cord so tight around her neck that her eyes bulged to twice their normal size and her face was dark purple. Someone else's skin cells under her fingernails; she had fought hard against her attacker. Two dominoes were found beneath her body.

Two dominoes, two numbers: one, seven. The address of Rhonda's school: 17 Burnett Street.

The dominoes were bagged as evidence but not connected to Gary's death. No one mentioned the dominoes, or any other grisly detail of Zoë's murder, to Rhonda because she was so young. Otherwise she might have thought to mention the other domino, the one she had taken from her father's worktable before anyone else noticed it.

In the space of two months, Gary had taken his own life and Zoë had been murdered. A happy family had been reduced to misery. Not quite reduced. Not yet.

Rhonda died third. Found in the girls' bathroom of her school by the janitor who thought all the students had left for the day. Bound to a toilet, naked from the waist down, with her tights tied around her neck and her skirt tied like a bag over her head. Stabbed multiple times. Three dominoes had been dropped into the toilet. Three dominoes, six numbers. Nine, eight, five, three: the last four digits of a credit card used by Alice Alderman, Gary's wife and the children's mother. Two, four: the number on the baseball jersey of Teddy, age six, who had just joined his first team.

Finally, the police saw the connection. The dominoes. The family members. Killed one by one by one. Gary's death was now ruled a probable homicide and added to the investigation into his two daughters' murders. An investigation that now sought a serial killer.

A task force was born.

Alice and Teddy went into hiding. The police department provided round-the-clock protection: two men sitting in a surveillance van outside the summer home of Alice's sister's boss's friend.

But somehow, he found them. The Domino Killer. JPP. The man who was not yet known to be a twenty-seven-year-old mild-mannered loner named Martin Price. JPP cut the outside phone line to which the surveillance system had been linked. Broke, entered, and killed, quickly, in the minutes the lookout team took to decide that their equipment had not malfunctioned but the house had been breached.

Alice died first. Facedown on her bed. Stabbed. Strangled. While Teddy was locked in the bathroom, weeping, holding on to the stuffed dog that helped him fall asleep at night.

Teddy was next. Strangled. Quickly.

By the time backup arrived and they got inside, it was too late—and the killer was gone.

On the railing of the back porch sat a single domino. One number, covered with a piece of black tape, leaving only the blank second half.

Zero.

The Alderman family was gone.

It was the last time any Maplewood detective would rely on anything but wireless equipment. It was a mistake that cost two lives. Slowly, painfully, we were learning.

No one knew who would be next. But with a serial killer as brutal and systematic as the Domino Killer, everyone knew *someone* would be next. It was a matter of who, when, and where. There was no why. How could there be? There was no possible rationalization for what happened to that family.

We believed we were looking for a man, because of the sheer physical strength required to subdue the father. We had an idea of the killer's approximate age—late twenties, because that was typically when serial killers started their so-called careers. Due to the organized nature of the crimes, we thought he probably had a college education or at least a good mind. He liked games but hated people and was probably active online. There was a good chance he lived in the area, because he attacked and vanished with apparent ease. And the killer was extremely angry and/or extremely lonely. He had killed an entire family. There had to be some reason for that, at least in his warped mind.

In the weeks after Alice and Teddy were murdered, the media worked the story for all it was worth and thereby helped us keep our hunt for the killer alive. Hundreds of calls poured into the task force reporting sightings of people who looked like serial killers. The problem was that most serial killers didn't look like the monsters they were. Most were pretty good at hiding their ugliness beneath an exterior best described as average. They hid inside themselves and then burst out briefly, only to retreat back into hiding.

The task force knew that there was always a surfeit

of reports of suspicious people lurking around right after any brutal crime. But even so, we followed up on every single call, because you just never knew. Everyone went out canvassing. One day Mac and I went out on a call from a driver on the Jersey Turnpike that "a kid" had been seen "lurking around" the industrial corridor approaching the Jersey City entrance to the Lincoln Tunnel. When pressed, the caller extrapolated that the "kid" was probably not so much a kid but "a young man." So we were looking for a male of an undetermined age, but probably on the young side. That was all we knew, and truth be told, we didn't expect much.

It was a blistering hot July morning with enough of a breeze to make you grateful every time a swish of cool air brushed against your clammy skin. I was wearing jeans and a short-sleeved shirt, and my hair was bundled up inside a baseball cap so my neck could catch some air. Mac and I wandered among the mammoth containers where companies stored gas before it went to market, assuming we were on the kind of wild-goose chase that periodically sucked up too much of the task force's time.

A steady stream of cars surged by on the turnpike. The tanks were close enough to the traffic that the noise blotted out most other sounds. The blistering air was thick and wavy with gas fumes—fumes from the cars and fumes from the storage tanks—and the smell was overpowering. I was ready to shout over to Mac that we ought to give this one up, when a kind of echoing hollow moan caught my attention. It intensified every time I neared one tank in particular. I circled the tank and heard it distinctly on one side. The tank was probably empty. And if it was empty, then wasn't there a remote chance someone could be inside?

"I'm checking this one out," I shouted over to Mac, who did not appear to hear me, the traffic was so loud.

A narrow ladder ran up the side of the tank, easily two hundred feet to the top. Looking up from the bottom, it appeared to lead directly into the cloudless blue sky. The higher I climbed, the taller and wider the tank seemed to grow. It was massive. And the ladder rungs were hot, burning the palms of my hands when I grabbed on. So I climbed as fast as I could, just to get this over with, to check out a funny feeling I had about this one empty tank in an otherwise brimming garden of gas.

At the top of the ladder I scrambled onto the flat roof of the tank. I could feel its heat radiating through the rubber soles of my shoes. A huge round hatch twenty feet from the edge was open. I knew nothing about the petroleum business but suspected it wasn't business as usual to leave these things gaping to the elements. I crouched over the hatch. And peered down into the darkness.

It was empty, all right. The sun blazed into my face so I raised a flat hand to shield my eyes. When they adjusted, I saw what at first looked like a shadow down at the bottom of the tank.

"Karin?" Mac shouted from below.

I walked to the edge of the tank and saw Mac looking around for me.

"Up here!"

"What the hell?"

"Be right back."

I returned to the hatch. Crouched. Shielded my eyes again. And watched the shadow transform into a sleeping man.

We didn't know what we were dealing with at first. Mainly we knew we had a man who appeared to be stranded inside an empty fuel container. We didn't know who he was or why he was there but we knew our duty was to get him out. Lucky for him the gas company hadn't decided to fill the tank that morning. That was what I thought when I first saw him. *Lucky for him.* Later, I realized it would have been a godsend if JPP had been drowned in fuel, suffocated in a vat of poison. If only I had known what would be in store for me by saving this man's life, I wouldn't have told Mac or anyone else he was in there, sleeping like a baby at the bottom of the tank. I would have closed the hatch, locked it from outside, left him there. He would have fried in hours in that hot, noxious tank.

But no.

I had to save him.

Because we were looking for a serial killer, we wanted to swab the inside of his mouth. He refused to give us permission. We had to apply for a warrant and wait two days, holding him on a trespassing charge, before we got a chance to collect Martin Price's DNA. The state lab graced us with an expedited result—a clean match with the skin cells scraped from under Zoë Alderman's fingernails.

We had him.

Even so, Price tried denying he was the Domino Killer. That kind of arrogance was textbook-typical of psychopaths. It was amazing how many of them thought they alone were capable of committing the perfect crime and getting away with it, even in the face of irrefutable evidence. We got a good laugh out of his repudiation when the charges were read against him at his arrest, which I was given the honor of making myself, since I was the one who had found him.

The way I remember it, that was the last time I laughed, ever.

Though in reality months went by before JPP came after my family. In the interim I laughed many times—at home with Jackson and Cece, at work with my colleagues, at random times over the course of any average day—before the reality JPP had in mind for me came home to roost.

During the brief time he was in custody awaiting arraignment, JPP finally stopped pretending he wasn't who he was: Martin Price, a loner who had been abandoned young, raised in an orphanage, and upon his independence appeared to live a quiet life until his DNA started turning up on people's corpses. He didn't outright confess to the murders, but he stopped arguing, probably on the advice of his lawyer. He didn't say much of anything, just waited in jail for his case to route itself through the system and probably spent a lot of time plotting his escape. When he killed his way off the bus transferring him between jail and courthouse for his arraignment, he used a homemade shiv. Before he got away, we never found out how or why he had targeted the Aldermans in the first place. My guess was that it was some small connection, a perceived slight one of the family members had inflicted on him and which he deeply felt he didn't deserve. What had one of the Aldermans done in the course of his or her daily business to offend this very disturbed man? In my case, it was because I had had the gall to climb a fuel tank and find him. It might have been anyone who heard that ghostly echo and chased an instinct up a ladder to hell.

But it wasn't anyone.

It was me.

The next day, my mother thought it would do me good to get some fresh air. I was already feeling a little better, so I took Joyce's book and Mom maneuvered me out onto the front porch where I reclined on a wicker chaise longue. I stretched out and rested my head on the back pillow upholstered in floral chintz. My mother liked things pretty. It was a bright spring morning, and the dogwood tree with its white-blossomed limbs looked spectacular and sad.

Across the street the surveillance van was still at its post at the curb; a dark blue van with a different driver had relieved yesterday's unit. At noon there was a changing of the guard when a light blue van took the place of the dark blue van. Twelve-hour shifts, noon to midnight. Waiting for JPP was starting to feel like business as usual. I was starting to wonder if maybe he *was* dead. Or maybe he wanted us to think he was. Maybe that was what he was waiting for: the passage of enough time, to trick you into thinking he wasn't coming.

CHAPTER 6

Three weeks later, every last blossom had fallen off the dogwood tree; dried petals now carpeted my parents' front lawn. Mac held my elbow as we walked along the path from the house to the street, although it wasn't necessary. I felt stronger than I had since I'd been shot. The pain in my abdomen had dulled; my muscles no longer felt as if they would unweave if I moved too fast. But I let him prop me up anyway, because it seemed to make him feel better to think he was helping me. As I folded myself into the front passenger seat of his little car—a green MINI Cooper with a black-and-white checkerboard top and two racing stripes down the front—he hovered beside the open door, making sure I could get in comfortably. He was even taller than I was but somehow we both fit.

It was late afternoon, almost rush hour, and so we took the back roads for the seven-mile drive from Montclair to Maplewood. I was returning to New York later this weekend and had agreed to stop in at the station house for a debriefing by the task force before I left. I dreaded it, but felt it was my duty to help in any way

I could, especially since no progress had been made in the case. JPP's latest dominoes had not been deciphered and there had been no credible sightings of him.

We arrived in the village center and drove slowly past the town's movie theater, small grocery store, café, a couple of liquor stores, and a handful of restaurants. Maplewood was a nice, friendly, family-oriented town, with annual parades and good public schools in walking distance from most homes. The golf tee was invented there. So was Ultimate Frisbee. Which, so said my brother, Jon, when he and Andrea bought their house there two years ago and fled Manhattan, was enough of a reason to move anywhere. Jackson and I had followed suit and bought our own house there. After the murders, when I put our house up for sale, it went in a day. The Aldermans' house, also in Maplewood, still sat empty while their estate languished in probate.

The new station house, the Police and Courts Building, was just outside town on Springfield Avenue. We pulled into the parking lot it shared with a neighboring church.

"Nice," I said, as we walked from the car along the sidewalk that led to the front door of the redbrick building that would have been my workplace had I not left the force. We climbed five steps, passed under an arched entryway, and Mac led the way through a revolving door. I had to stop in my tracks when I got inside and saw the high-tech cathedral the joint branches of local law enforcement had built themselves. "Are we standing on a glass floor?" Gazing down through what looked like translucent blocks, I could make out the blurry shapes of exercise equipment.

"Yup. Lets in the natural light to the basement gym. They built it green all the way."

He led me to an elevator and we were whisked up two flights. The new building had two conference rooms, and our task force had been allotted one of them on a full-time basis. A wall of glass separated it from the hallway and I stood there looking in, struck by what I saw.

I remembered the task force I had worked on: the long hours, the coming together of minds, the urgency we had shared as we hunted for JPP. I remembered thinking I finally knew what people meant by blood, sweat, and tears. On the original task force, no one ever felt good or looked good; we were hungry, exhausted, but we didn't stop. The room was dirty. *We* were dirty. And determined in a way that was exciting for a newly minted detective like I was then.

What I saw now was a different scene in every way. I had expected the new room, the new furniture, the new walls. And, as expected, on the new walls hung the old crime scene photos in all their tragic brutality. But what I hadn't expected was that, instead of the two dozen investigators who had populated the original task force, only three people now worked in the room. They appeared too calm. Too clean. Too rested. Each investigator stared at a computer, tapped away at a keyboard. For a moment I assumed most of the team was out working the case. But Mac had told me that the task force looked forward to meeting with me, and I realized that what I saw through the glass wall was *it*.

"That guy there"—he pointed at a dark-haired man

with olive skin, sitting in front of a computer like the others—"that's Alan." His not-so-new-anymore partner. "Don't think you've met him yet."

I hadn't.

Mac put his hand on the doorknob, ready to turn it and lead me in.

"Wait a minute," I said. "Where is everyone?"

"They downsized us, left us with a core group. Everyone else got reassigned."

"*Reassigned?*"

"We're treating it more as a cyber case now, figuring he won't show his face in the off-line world at this point, that if he's active it'll be online that we'll be able to trace him. He could be dead, Karin, if the snipers hit him, and they may have. The chief and the mayor are well aware of that—and bottom line: They slashed our budget in case we're chasing a ghost."

I couldn't believe what I was hearing. Or that I was hearing it from Mac. "But he *might* be alive and you should *all* be out there breaking a sweat. He's a dominoes freak. You should be looking for him wherever people play games. It's a no-brainer."

"I know. Me and Billy Staples in New York, we're on the same page as you. But without the resources . . ." He trailed off but I knew the rest: *There's only so much we can accomplish on our own.*

I stepped away from the glass so they wouldn't see me. I wasn't going in. "How could they pull so far back?"

"The new budgets just went into effect and we're all still getting used to it." A tremor in his voice betrayed his effort to remain calm, cool, and rational. "Reeling from it, if you want to know the truth. I didn't know how to tell you they took their foot off the gas."

"It doesn't make sense."

Mac's tone hardened. "Sure it does. The city went over budget on the building, so they had to cut out some fat."

"Since when is looking for a serial killer who's been terrorizing a community *fat*?"

He shook his head. Said nothing, because there was no good answer. It was our tough luck.

I turned and walked back to the elevators. Behind me I heard the carpeted foot thumps of Mac following. I was so angry I feared I would explode at him, though I knew it wasn't his fault. Mac didn't control the budget around here. But he was still a part of this . . . *outrageous bureaucratic hypocrisy*. Feeling this way, thinking like this, was an indulgence I had never before allowed myself. But now it hit me full force.

Waiting for the elevator, I couldn't resist snapping, "They've gone *corporate*."

"They'll get over it."

"Who are those *office workers* in there?"

He didn't answer. The elevator arrived and whisked us down. He followed me all the way out of the mega-buck, eco-friendly building into the fresh, real, free, breathable air. The sun had vanished; clouds now filled the sky. I walked ahead of Mac toward his car but he caught up with me and tried to take my arm. I pulled away.

"Karin, wait just a minute. *Stop*."

I stopped but didn't turn around. He stepped in front of me. Forced me to hear him out.

"You forget what it was like. These are good people doing terrible work. And the budgets always mattered. We always had to work around them. We're downsized one day, restaffed the next. It's always been a roller coaster."

"I don't remember that." But was he right? The daily realities of police work, for me, felt like a thousand lifetimes in my past. Had my personal misfortune plunged me into a realm from which I could no longer recognize workaday concerns?

"Nothing's changed," Mac said. "Just the building. That's all."

"I don't know, Mac. That was awful in there."

"It's always awful in there, Karin, one way or another. We're looking for a serial killer, and we can't find him."

"Can we go, please?"

We reached the car. Got in. He drove us out of the parking lot and onto the avenue. Andrea had invited me and my parents to dinner and Mac was going to drop me there. I had been toying with the idea of asking him to stay and join us, but now I wasn't sure if I wanted to.

"Just keep something in mind." Mac glanced at me as he drove. "Martin Price's face is in every post office in the country. He's all over the Internet, newspapers, TV. *America's Most Wanted* ran an update of their profile of him two weeks ago. You know how many people watch that show?"

"Not exactly."

"Millions. That's millions of people roaming the world with Price's face imprinted in their memories. That's millions of eyeballs looking for him. So is it such a bad idea to concentrate the search online at the moment? Why would he so much as go out to the store, let alone game tournaments?"

"Because he's a sick control freak who's obsessed with games?"

"Maybe. But don't you think he'd lay low and get his games kicks online?"

"Fine, Mac. Maybe you're right. But why not look anyway?"

We were back to the same question. Riding beside Mac in his car, feeling lonelier than ever beside this man whom I probably trusted more than anyone in the world along with my brother and therapist and mother, I felt the slow tide of a familiar despair creep up the shore of my consciousness. Joyce's book on happiness constantly reminded me that "feelings aren't facts" and "all true paths are hidden paths" and "hidden paths are always stumbled upon accidentally." Feel-good sentiments to distract you from your misery, trick you into thinking that respite was hovering all around you. It wasn't. There would be no respite. No one was going to save the day. Wait until I told Joyce about *that* discovery when I saw her in three days.

I tried to hide the tears gathering in my eyes by looking out the passenger window, away from Mac, as he drove me to my brother's house on Walton Avenue.

Neat lawns fronted nice houses where good families happily lived. One after another after another. So many happy families, blurring past, like a dream I couldn't touch. It was a world I felt permanently locked out of. I wanted it back. But it was too late for me. Now that my body was all patched up and mostly healed, all I wanted, again, was to stop fighting. Give up. And let him find me. I closed my eyes and prayed Mac would crash the car. Then I prayed he wouldn't . . . because he had come around the corner and now we were driving up Jon and Andrea's street . . . and Susanna was out playing on the front lawn, wearing a yellow sundress that looked similar to one I'd once bought Cece, pushing a doll in her play stroller, back and forth, waiting for me.

A surveillance van was parked across the street, as usual. Their house, like my parents' house and now my Brooklyn apartment, had been fitted with an electronic web meant to catch JPP if he came too close. This obvious precaution gave me a queasy feeling now as I realized how much the denuded task force was depending on cyberspace to snag him. Wireless cameras and communications systems all invisibly hooked together into a system mined with alarms. It wasn't enough.

My parents were sitting out front on white plastic lawn chairs, watching Susanna play, when Mac and I pulled into the driveway. She looked adorable in the yellow dress, pushing the miniature stroller as fast as she could across the bumpy lawn. An unexpected jolt caused her doll to tumble onto the grass. She picked it up by one arm, flung it back into the stroller, and now, having noticed our arrival, turned to look. She broke into a big smile when she saw me. My parents waved hello. Mac and I waved through the driver's window but neither one of us made a move to get out of the car.

"Try to forget about the task force," he said. "Let me worry about all that."

The sky darkened suddenly. "Rain's coming," I said, unbuckling my seat belt.

My mother chased Susanna across the lawn and scooped her up along with the toy stroller and doll. "Come inside!" I heard her call to my father, still seated in his plastic chair, as the rain started. As all three retreated into the house, we heard the first thunderclap.

"I shouldn't have taken you there," Mac said. "I should have realized it would upset you."

I turned to face him. "I'm not upset with *you*, Mac." What I meant was, *Not anymore.* He was still strapped into his seat, staring straight ahead at the heavy rain now pounding the windshield. I was struck by the stillness, the solitude, of his profile. One side of his collar had flipped up and I reached over to flatten it. I wanted him to turn and look at me.

"There's an umbrella in the backseat," he said, facing me. In the shadows cast by the storm his eyes appeared darker than usual. We sat there looking at each other for a moment. This man had been so good to me, above and beyond the call of duty.

"Where are you going now?" I asked.

"Home."

"Nope." I reached over the seat for the long black umbrella. "You're coming in and having dinner with us."

"Thanks, Karin, but I'm tired and—"

"I didn't *ask*."

A spray of fine wrinkles by Mac's eyes turned his whole face into a smile. I wondered how he did that: smiling without smiling. How could his soon-to-be ex-wife, Val, reject this good man? But you never really knew what went on inside someone else's marriage.

"Your family won't mind?"

"They practically invited you." Everyone in my family liked Mac. I knew they would welcome him.

"Practically?"

"Come on." I opened the door on my side and stuck the umbrella out first. Got out and went around with the umbrella to Mac's side. We huddled together and ran through the pouring rain across the lawn to the front door, which had been left cracked open for us.

I tried hard to hide the darkness of my mood because I knew how much it upset my family, but the brief visit to the station house had shaken me. A feeling of bubbling-under-the-surface desolation lingered throughout dinner. My mother had helped Andrea prepare the meal, which was delicious: two chickens roasted to perfection; chopped and roasted potatoes, carrots and onions; salad; warm French bread; pear tart and vanilla ice cream for dessert. It was enough to rouse anyone's appetite. But not mine. I forced my way through most of what sat on my plate. I had lost twenty pounds since Jackson and Cece died. Despite a promise to Joyce to make an effort to put some of the weight back on, I had been unable to manage it. My mother had put considerable effort, these past weeks, into encouraging me with her excellent cooking. And I had tried to eat more than I wanted to. Some days I'd even felt hungry. But now, as usual, appetite eluded me.

When Susanna grew cranky, I volunteered to put her to bed and we escaped upstairs together. I hadn't been in her room for a long time and was a little shocked to see a few of Cece's toys and clothes blended in with Susanna's. Shocked, but not surprised, as I had routinely passed things down to

Susanna as Cece outgrew them, which had been natural when she was alive. A plastic walker with chunky wheels. A wooden shape sorter. A pair of red rain boots decorated with yellow ducks. It still amazed me how little it took to incite an avalanche of feeling and memory, as I stood there with my niece, in her room, channeling my daughter in another house, in another room, in another time.

When I helped Susanna into her pajamas, I was helping Cece into hers. When I helped wash Susanna's face and brush her teeth, Cece's face was being washed, Cece's teeth brushed. I sat her on my lap and gently brushed her long, soft hair, smoothing it after each slow stroke of the brush. Having my daughter back, or a ghost of her, for a brief few minutes. But when she got her favorite book—like many children her age, she liked to read the same book over and over for weeks at a time; at the moment it was *The Velveteen Rabbit*—Susanna was Susanna again. Cece's favorite book at the time I lost her had been *Goodnight Moon*.

We positioned ourselves on her bed and I read the book to her, pausing at each page so she could study the picture. Then we snuggled together under her covers for twenty minutes or so, nose to nose, until she fell asleep. Andrea had told me not to stay too long; they were trying to encourage Susanna to fall asleep on her own so bedtime would be more manageable when the new baby came. But I couldn't resist her warm breath dousing my face with sweetness each time she exhaled. I stayed a few minutes longer, after she fell asleep, just looking at her, drinking her in. When I finally went back downstairs, Andrea didn't mention the time, though she had to realize I'd stayed with Susanna longer than necessary.

Everyone was tired. We helped clean up and then Mac drove me back to my parents' house. Mom and Dad went home in their own car.

It was Friday night, the beginning of my last weekend in Montclair. As Sunday afternoon grew closer, my feelings about leaving grew as mixed as they had been about staying all this time. My body was healed enough to live on my own. My mind was here one minute, there the next. And my soul was simply up for grabs.

CHAPTER 7

It was the first time I had stepped foot in my apartment since the night JPP attacked me. In my absence it had been cleaned and straightened. Any remnants of a crime scene were gone. The only difference was that now, from the corner of every room, a little round camera eye gazed upon me at all times. A manned surveillance van was parked outside my front door.

Mac, who had insisted on driving me back to Brooklyn himself, set my suitcase on the foot of my bed, my toiletry bag on the edge of the bathroom sink, and my laptop on the kitchen table.

"So, how about an early dinner before I head back?" he asked. "Take me to one of those great restaurants I keep hearing about around here."

He meant Smith Street, the neighborhood's burgeoning restaurant row, which I hadn't visited once since arriving in Brooklyn now five months ago. I had had no social life and still didn't desire one. But as I had no food in the house and didn't feel like shopping right away, it seemed like a good idea to go out.

At five-thirty on a Sunday it wasn't hard getting a table anywhere we wanted. It was the end of a warm May afternoon and so we chose an outdoor table at a French bistro on the corner of Dean Street. Mac ordered us a bottle of wine, which arrived while we read the menu. As soon as the wine was poured, he raised his glass in toast:

"To you."

We clinked glasses. I took a sip and put mine down, feeling glad to be here with Mac and at the same time utterly strange to be here with him. I no longer knew who I was in any given situation. *Karin*, I reminded myself, *restaurant, food.* We kept the conversation simple and light as we ate our trout almandine and sautéed string beans. At one point a woman sitting at the table next to ours lit a cigarette and a down-wind breeze carried her smoke to us. Mac waved his hand in front of his face to banish it.

"Val quit smoking," Mac said after a few moments.

"Finally." She had smoked for years, despite Mac's pleas to quit with him.

"We had dinner last night," he said. "Talked awhile."

"And?"

"We're thinking about getting back together."

"That's great news!"

"Just thinking about it. No one's in a hurry to rush into anything."

They had been married eighteen years. No children. I had gotten pregnant with Cece so soon after my wedding that I couldn't imagine marriage without kids. Mac and Val had always seemed like a solid couple, but the internal combustion of all that time together must have been much more than met the eye.

We finished our dinners, drained our bottle of wine, declined dessert, and split the bill. Then we walked slowly back to my place in the gentle spring evening.

When we reached my building, he walked me all the way into the front hall and said good night. But he made no move to leave.

"I don't think I can do it," he finally said.

"Mac—"

"Let me sleep on the couch."

"Why?"

"Just one night, to convince myself you'll be okay."

Had he accompanied me home to protect me from myself as much as to protect me from JPP? Of course. And maybe he was right: Maybe he did have reason to worry. No matter what I thought or said or did, I couldn't shake the deep gloom that had dug its claws into me these past months. It was just as dark and heavy a burden as it had ever been. And I still wanted to be free of it, whatever it took.

"I'll be okay," I told him.

"Karin. Please."

So out came the spare blanket, a pillow and a set of sheets.

I made a pot of decaf and we stayed up late playing Scrabble. It was strange: Sitting in my kitchen felt completely normal. There was no sense that JPP had ever been here. My hazy recollection of the attack was beginning to feel like a dream.

"Maybe he *is* dead," I said.

Mac looked up from his lineup of letter tiles. "Maybe. But I wouldn't count on it."

"Right, that would be too easy. But . . ." But what? How far from reality could wishful thinking take me?

Ignoring the fact that it was his move on the Scrabble board, Mac looked at me for a long moment. "It's anti-climactic coming back home and finding—"

"Nothing." Nothing at all. A clean apartment and no trace of the fact that my own personal devil had visited me here.

"What did you expect to find when you came back here?"

I thought about it. "Memory."

He looked at me. Listened.

"Something clear. Like polishing fog off glass. A way to remember exactly, precisely, what happened so I can read the clue and know what's next, if anything. So I can stop wondering."

"Well, that would be handy, wouldn't it?" He leaned in to consult his letter tiles, picked up a Y and placed it at the end of TREMBL on the board. "It's every detective's wet dream: You come home after a bitch of a day and everything you need to know is laid out on your doorstep."

What *had* I expected upon returning home? Although I hadn't really contemplated it, I realized that deep down I must have hoped for something.

As we continued our game in silence, I thought about it. What did I want to happen now? Did I want JPP to come back again and this time let him put me out of my misery? Or did I want him to have died? Of course that would be the best thing: *JPP gone, over, erased.*

But what were the odds? And why would it even occur to me that that wouldn't be desirable?

Later, awake half the night lying in my bed, I knew the answer: Because I still wanted to die. And I feared I lacked the courage to try again to kill myself. I felt I needed him to do it for me. Part of me wanted him to come back and try again. The other part, the part that wanted him gone from the earth for good, also wanted to turn back time and erase him before he erased my husband and child . . . and that was simply not possible.

If he *was* dead now, he wasn't dead enough for me.

Before I finally fell asleep, I thought of Joyce and our early morning appointment. She was going to have a field day with me—a thought that made me smile a little bit, momentarily banished the other thoughts from my mind, opened a mental door to release and finally to the floating away of consciousness. Rescue from awareness. And a short, fitful sleep.

"And then I walked all the way up the hill in the dark. It was the kind of darkness you could see through. Kind of silvery. Then the hill turned into a kind of a ride, a loopy, swingy kind of ride. Like a roller coaster, I guess. And I felt the feeling of riding in a roller coaster, up, down, around, too fast, exciting, scary, all of that, but I wasn't actually in a roller coaster. And then I was sitting cross-legged at the top of a long staircase and down below a front door opened, so I was in a house, I guess. And then you walked in. And I waited for you at the top of the stairs and you flew at me so fast it was like time melted. You smelled good. That's the last

thing I remember: your smell that was like perfume but wasn't perfume. It was just you."

Jackson's words haunted me; that time he told me the dream, shortly before we got engaged. I immediately knew what the dream meant. It was our coming together. Our happiness. Our arrival. The beginning of our lives together. That was the moment I realized we would stay together. His dream didn't make any real sense and yet it made perfect sense. And he had trusted me with it, which meant as much to me as any element of the dream itself.

I woke up the morning of my appointment with Joyce, having redreamed Jackson's dream. Again. For a moment not remembering that he was gone. For that one sweet instant, expecting to see him across from me in our bed when I opened my eyes. And then the awful ascent through semiconsciousness into consciousness. Remembering. Again.

And now, sitting on Joyce's couch, I told her about the dream for the third or fourth time in the months I'd been seeing her. She had told me it was okay to keep telling her the dream, that I should tell her every time I had it. That repeating it to her was fine. She said that after a while the dream would lose its potency and eventually I would stop redreaming it. But it hadn't lost its potency. And I couldn't stop crying.

She sat across from me on her brown leather armchair, leaning back with her hands folded together in her lap. Listening, once again, to the retelling of the redreamed dream of a dead man. Watching me cry. *Letting* me cry, with no sign of uneasiness on her part. On

the coffee table between us was a box of tissues from which I liberally helped myself.

"Everyone's been trying so hard to make me happy. And I try to be grateful. But the truth is, I don't feel anything, and I want them to leave me alone."

"Alone," Joyce repeated, "so you can . . . ?"

I took a breath. Shook my head. Looked away. "Be alone."

"Alone *how*?"

"By myself. To feel whatever I need to feel, without guilt."

"And?"

She tipped her head forward, listening with expectation. While she had been away in China her shoulder-length brown hair had grown, evident by the half-inch stripe of gray in her slightly off-middle part. While she waited for my answer, she sipped from a red ceramic mug of coffee, which she then replaced on a small table at her right. Also on the table was a copy of the same book she had given me, with ripped-in-half green Post-it notes sticking out from between some pages. Atop the book was the diamond and sapphire ring she always removed during our sessions. I had asked her about that once and she had smiled and said, "You noticed," without ever answering. She didn't wear a wedding ring but I knew someone lived with her in the apartment because I'd often heard comings-and-goings behind the closed door.

I didn't answer. Couldn't. Anyway, she knew.

"I've been wondering," she said, "about your impulse to stay back in your apartment when you knew he was probably going to come."

I noticed her choice of words: *impulse*, not *decision*; *probably*, not *certainly*.

I shrugged. Propped my feet on the coffee table, pressed my bent knees together, cupped my hands over my knees, glanced at my skin, which looked dry.

"Sometimes, when I'm home by myself, I still wear my wedding ring," I said, staring at my bare fingers splayed open on my angled knees.

"Of course you do," she said. "So would I, in your situation. But Karin—"

"No. Please, Joyce. Don't explain it to me, because I already know what it means."

"Okay. What does it mean?"

The sound of a horn honking, long and loud; a frustrated driver outside on the city streets. Joyce lived and worked in a first-floor apartment, and the room's only window, cracked open to let in the fresh spring air, also let in every noise. Sitting on this couch these past months I'd heard begging children, quarrelling lovers, nascent dinner plans, chitchat about the weather.

"It means I can't let go."

"Is that what you think?" Joyce smiled warmly. "That you need to *let go*?"

The way she repeated my words, with emphasis, made them seem small-minded.

"Maybe instead you can think about learning to co-exist with your feelings about what happened. If you try really hard to let them go, the way someone might let go of a balloon and watch it float away in the sky until it's completely gone, then you're going to fail. Right?"

"Right."

"I don't think anyone would expect you to let go of your feelings or your memories."

"I'll *never* let them go. It wasn't really what I meant. I meant that the feelings won't stop."

"The pain," she corrected.

"It's always there and half the time I feel like I'm drowning in it. And I want it to stop."

"It's hard to take."

"Very hard."

"So when you chose to stay behind in your apartment that day, you were really making another choice, as well."

I looked at her. It was no revelation what I was up to that day. Why, then, did I have to spell it out?

"Karin?"

"You really want me to say it?"

"Why not?"

"I don't really want to say it."

"Have you said it to anyone?"

"Everyone knows. It was kind of obvious."

"Then say it."

"I wanted him to kill me. I wanted to die." I paused. Breathed. "There, I said it."

"And then you fought him off because . . . ?"

"I realized he still had his agenda. I was terrified for the rest of my family. And so I changed my mind."

"And now?"

I pulled my eyes away from hers. Glanced around her office. White walls. A framed museum print from an old Rauschenberg show. Shelves crowded with books. Trinkets collected on her travels, including a new one: a two-inch-tall Chinese straw doll holding a parasol.

In the far corner of the room, on the floor, a neat pile of old magazines tied with twine, ready for recycling. I resisted a strong urge to look at my watch in the hope that our hour was up.

"I don't really want to talk about it," I said.

"Because if you talk about it, it takes away the energy you might need to actually do something about your intolerable pain."

"Maybe."

"Karin, I think we've reached a place where we need to take another look at the idea of medication."

She had broached it once before, three months ago, and I had refused. Drugs seemed like such an escape, a thought that now struck me as ironic, given my deep desire to flee.

"What kind of medication?" I asked, mostly because I couldn't keep up this conversation. She wanted me to give her the stats on my suicidal thinking: what, where, how, when. She wanted to pin me down and make me feel responsible for my actions, or potential actions. I didn't know what she wanted, exactly; but those thoughts, these feelings, were *mine*. I had been orbiting in them for so long that they had become my comfort zone. I wasn't sure I wanted to give them up. Sitting there, across from her, I felt flat and empty, exactly the state of mind she wanted to banish.

"An antidepressant. We'll try Prozac first. Everyone reacts a little bit differently, and there are other options, but it's a good place to start."

"Joyce, I don't know about this."

"Have you ever taken it?"

"No."

"Do you know anyone who has?"

"Doesn't everyone?"

She sighed. "We need to find a way to move the dark cloud off to the side. I don't think talk therapy alone is going to do it for you. We've given it a good long try and now I think we've got to push forward. Depression can be a treatable illness."

Can be. Not *is.* She wasn't even promising anything. It was the first time she had spoken to me in such a definitive tone about medication. She was my doctor and I felt in my heart that she genuinely wanted to help me. But I had to ask her something.

"Since when is grief an illness?"

"It isn't, not the way genetically inheritable depression is an illness. But when grief doesn't abate, when it undermines your ability to find even an iota of pleasure in life, when it interferes with everyday functioning, then we worry."

"I function day to day."

She leaned forward and looked me straight in the eye. "You're suicidal, Karin."

That silenced me.

"Promise me something."

"Okay."

"Fill the prescription. Take the medication as prescribed. See me this Wednesday and Friday. We'll do three times a week for a while, and then we'll reassess. Frankly, I regret we didn't do this months ago. Trust me, please?"

And that was that. Our time was up. Joyce was now the captain of my ship and I was the passenger. I left her office with a prescription for Prozac in my purse

and a promise to keep. I had to hand it to her: She knew
what she was doing, or at least she acted as if she did.
When you felt helpless there was nothing like someone
telling you exactly what to do.

Mac was waiting for me on the corner of Cornelia and
Bleecker Streets near an Italian café where a handful of people lingered at outdoor tables over breakfast, coffee, newspaper. It was just past ten in the
morning.

When he saw me he walked in my direction, and
when he was within earshot he asked, "Everything
okay?"

There was possibly nothing more awkward than
being met by a coworker (*former* coworker) outside
your psychiatrist's office. If I answered politely and
said, *Yes, okay*, it would be a lie. If I said, *No, not okay*,
it would be alarming. Instead I said the first thing that
came to mind.

"All cured." I grinned.

He chuckled and the tension evaporated.

"Do you have time for a coffee?" I asked him.

"Wish I could, but I should get back to Jersey."

Work. Of course.

We rode the F train back to Brooklyn, where he had
parked his car. But before leaving he insisted on ac-
companying me to the pharmacy so I could fill my prescription. I had mentioned it to him on the way back.
Mistake. I had wanted to think it over a little more
before joining the Prozac nation. Now I had no wiggle
room.

He waited twenty minutes with me at the counter.

Then he waited while I took the first pill, without water, before leaving the store.

"There," I said, smacking my lips. I dropped the bottle of clattering pills into my purse. I had done it: taken the medication. Was doing it: keeping my promise. Trying, anyway.

"Good woman." He winked. He held the pharmacy door open for me as we went back out onto Smith Street. An employee of the store, a young man in a blue smock, stood outside with some kind of machine that scraped chewing gum off the sidewalk. The dried-up flattened blobs were everywhere.

"Looks like a losing battle," Mac said as we passed the man, who shook his head and sighed as he repositioned the machine along the concrete.

Mac and I walked slowly along Smith Street, turning when we reached Pacific, where I lived two blocks down between Hoyt and Bond.

"Want me to come back tomorrow night?" he asked. "Go with you into the city for your Wednesday appointment?"

"Thanks, but no. I think I'll be okay." I didn't feel I needed an escort; but in my heart I was grateful for his offer.

"Let me know if you change your mind."

His car was parked across the street from a school one block from my building. I stopped, which seemed to surprise him.

"I'll walk you all the way home."

"Not necessary, Mac. I really appreciate everything you're doing for me. But I have to be able to walk down the street alone now and then, don't I?"

"Not at the moment, you don't."

"Honestly, I don't feel him anywhere. I don't think he's even in this world anymore. I mean it. I just don't feel afraid."

Mac cocked an eyebrow. "All right. But will you at least call me the minute you get inside?"

I agreed to that. We stood there in front of his car, figuring out how to say good-bye. Finally I reached up and patted his shoulder the way guys did with each other. A quick pat, maybe a little punch. But I wasn't a guy and an awkwardness descended between us, something different and new. He reciprocated by patting my shoulder. Then he unlocked his car door and got in.

I watched while he parallel un-parked and drove up Pacific Street in the direction of the highway that would lead him back to New Jersey. Just the thought of him returning to the place I had once called home, the place where I had been useful and busy and loved, made my heart ache. I would rather have been there with the people I loved. With my parents. With Andrea and Susanna. And with Jon, when he got back from L.A. But everything in Maplewood and Montclair resonated with Jackson and Cece. I couldn't face it. I *had* to stay here, distanced, geographically at least, from the constant torture of associations.

An entire day stretched ahead of me now. An entire life. Minutes, hours, days, weeks, months, years to fill with distraction from the torment that ate at my soul. From the vantage point of this moment, it felt like the kind of uphill journey I didn't think I could manage. Even with the little pill now dissolving in my stomach, worming its way into my bloodstream, infiltrating the system of my unhappiness. The chemical army of sunshine bearers Joyce hoped would push my dark cloud off to the side.

I picked up a few groceries, then spent the day in my garden, weeding and generally trying to resuscitate anything that hadn't already died. After a small dinner I read a little on my bed. Fell asleep early. Slept late. In the morning I was so overfed on sleep I could barely keep my eyes open over breakfast. As I took my second forty-milligram Prozac, I wondered if it contained a sedative.

And then, suddenly, I was completely awake. In fact I couldn't sit still.

I cleaned my breakfast bowl, glass, and mug. Took a quick shower. Dressed in jeans and a T-shirt. And decided that, instead of mooning around inside, I would *do something.* But before I had a chance to figure out what a thirty-three-year-old suicidal ex-cop from New Jersey did alone in New York on a workday, I was summoned by the bleating sound of Skype.

I hadn't heard that chirpy ring for nearly a year; no one contacted me this way. The Skype account had been Jackson's thing . . . Mac must have accidentally turned it on when he set up the computer yesterday. I went over to the kitchen table, where my laptop sat open with its built-in webcam eye always peering out of its slit along the top edge of the screen, and clicked the mouse to accept the incoming call.

And then my heart stopped. I didn't breathe. Didn't move. Didn't think.

He was on my screen, grainy, distorted. *Alive.*

Martin Price.

JPP.

The Domino Killer.

"*Hello.*"

I sat down at the table, in front of the laptop. Shaking uncontrollably. Staring into the cold eye of the webcam. At his face. Or the facsimile of his face. The grayish facelike living ghost of him that floated on my screen.

CHAPTER 8

"Where are you, Martin?"

"Wouldn't you like to know?"

"What do you want?"

"What do *you* want?"

His thin blond hair was neatly combed, parted far to one side, as always. Each small movement he made looked mechanical, like bad animation. But he was real. Alive. Out there, somewhere. Talking to me.

I didn't answer. It made me sick to think he felt he knew something about me. He had tasted my yearning for death, and it had increased his sense of power. I could see it in the smug expression on his face, waiting for my response.

"How did you find me?" But as soon as I said it, I realized it didn't matter. He always found you. He found whomever he wanted. Did whatever he wanted. Moved on. Did it again.

"You really want to know?"

Again, I didn't answer.

"You know, Karin, you shouldn't ask for things unless you're sure you really want them." A grin spread across his face like the slow slash of a knife. I reached a finger to touch his image, to see if anything happened. His grin broadened, lips parted. For the first time I noticed there was a slight gap between each and every one of this teeth, which registered here as blackness.

"You forgot," he said, "didn't you." But it was more a taunt than a question. His hand reached in front of his face and he adjusted his webcam to focus downward, onto his keyboard. He had laid out four dominoes horizontally along the front edge. The same seven numbers: three, six, four, one, five, two, three.

"No, I didn't forget."

"*You forgot.*"

He was giving us—me and the task force—a lot of credit: as if, had I not forgotten the numbers, we would have found him out by now or at least come tantalizingly close. Did he believe we understood him that well? Or did he *want* us to? Did it make him lonely, playing his twisted game without a capable opponent? Had it frustrated him, last time, to learn we had not found the dominoes buried in the grass of my Maplewood lawn until after the murders?

"We don't know what the numbers mean."

He refocused his camera on his face. Seemed to think something over. His smile dissolved into a grimace and he said, "Read any good books lately?"

And then he was gone. A fuzzy square hovered where his face had been. I stared at my laptop screen in shock.

Read any good books lately?

What was he trying to tell me? What did it mean?

Something sizzled inside my brain. Maybe it was the medication trickling into my bloodstream. Or the sight of JPP in my home again. Making his third visit into my life: first to obliterate my family, then to try to destroy me, now to make sure I hadn't forgotten him. Because he was still hungry. Wanting. Out there. Waiting impatiently for us to interpret his clue. But how did he know we hadn't? How could he possibly know we had failed at deciphering those seven numbers?

I pushed away the laptop, propped my elbows on the table, and settled my face into my hands. *Read any good books lately?* What did he mean by that?

Each time he selected his next victim, he conveyed his intentions a little bit differently. The dominoes would spell out a special kind of clue. Part of an address. A social security number. Someone's age. But those seven numbers had been run through every kind of sieve to try and rattle out some meaning, with no result. And then something occurred to me.

Maybe this time, the dominoes weren't the clue.

Maybe they were a map to the clue.

I wondered if anyone on the task force had thought of it. I called Mac and told him everything. I could hear traffic sounds, a long horn in the distance. He sounded impatient, as he always did, talking and driving simultaneously.

"When?" Mac asked.

"Just now."

"Okay. I'll call Alan and we'll get the task force together, try and track where Price made his call from. Meantime, Karin, stay put." He abruptly signed off.

Stay put. It sounded a little patronizing. And it felt wrong. How could I just sit in my apartment? While the paltry task force sat around the table in their spiffy new room and searched for online clues?

Well, I wasn't part of the task force. I wasn't even a cop anymore.

And this wasn't a *game*. It wasn't a *case*. For me, it was deeply personal. As personal as it got. *It was about my family*.

I felt too restless just to sit here—restless in a way I hadn't felt in a long time. I felt anxious to figure this out. To *get* out. Get on the *move*.

I paced my apartment, room to room to room, back and forth from the kitchen, through my bedroom, into the living room, and back again. Thinking. Deciding where to begin.

Read any good books lately.

There were millions of books, old and new. And books were part of everyday life for so many people.

Where did people do their reading?

Bookstores.

Libraries.

Schools.

Cafés.

Bedrooms.

Beaches.

Park benches.

Focus, I told myself. Narrow it down.

Bookstores and libraries: a logical starting point.

First I went to the Library of Congress's online catalog. Plugged in the seven domino numbers in various configurations. Plugged in segments of the full strand of numbers. Tried and tried.

And came up empty.

Next I tried the annual compilation called *Books in Print* detailing every book published in any given year, including the unique identification number for each book. I went online and found their Web site. Shaking, I went through the paces of registration before being allowed onto their search page. Again, I tried different groupings of the seven-digit number. Then I repeated the exercise for every year for the past five years.

Nothing.

The next obvious step was to do the same searches on the online catalogs of libraries. Not knowing where to begin, I started with the New York Public Library's main branch—it was one of the world's biggest library systems. Plugged in the seven numbers in varying order and soon realized that not only did they trigger library call numbers, but in such a vast system the various combinations led to too many places. Too many books. JPP's clue wouldn't have been so chaotic. He was insane, yes; sloppy, no. Still, because so many call numbers were seven digits long, I thought I might be on to something.

Next I tried the Maplewood library's catalog. Nothing.

And then I moved on to Brooklyn's.

Within a millisecond of hitting go on the search page, I struck gold.

I had read the map.

Now I knew where to go. What to look for.

For a split second, I paused. Shouldn't I call this in to the task force? Yes, of course. But I was too eager to *get there*. So I decided on a compromise: I would call Mac and be on my way.

This time Mac didn't answer so I left a message.

Then I hauled my bicycle up from the basement and
rode to Brooklyn's Central Library at Grand Army
Plaza at the edge of Park Slope. The ten minutes it took
to bike there would have easily doubled if not tripled
had I called and waited for and taken a car service. By
the time I saw the huge building looming ahead, I had
worked up a sweat. The library sat at a fork between
two major avenues that spun off the most frenzied five-
pronged rotary I had ever encountered. But, crossing
it, I felt no danger, just a keen determination to get into
the library and up to the second floor where the online
catalog had directed me.

I parked my bike at a bike rack off to the side of the
main entrance. I didn't lock it up because I didn't have
a lock or chain. And I hadn't worn a helmet because I
didn't own one. Jackson and I used to bike sometimes
around our calm suburban streets where there had
seemed to be little threat of injury. Those sleepy streets
had been the polar opposite of these, with their traffic
jams and car doors swinging open into bike lanes and
lack of bike lanes and drivers not noticing you when
they made a turn. But I didn't care; I couldn't bring
myself to step into a bike store. Whenever I thought
of helmets I pictured the orange-and-pink flower-power
helmet I had bought Cece but not yet taken out of the
box before she was killed.

I ran up the wide front steps leading to the library's
front door. Pulled open one of the heavy doors. Raced
in. Found the escalators off to the right and hurried the
ride by taking the moving steps two at a time.

My heart pounded. But my head felt clear. Clearer
than it had in a long time.

I walked into the large room and looked around. Just past an information desk, to the right, people sat at tables quietly reading. To the left were rows and rows of bookshelves. I walked along, scanning the end-of-aisle placards listing ranges of call numbers. The range I was looking for was nine aisles down. I turned in and began looking for the first three numbers: three, six, four. If I was on the right track, then JPP had laid out his dominoes in precisely the order he wanted the numbers to be read. No mixing them up. No segments. He had sent his message loud and clear. He could have just come back and killed me; he would have found a way. But that wasn't what he wanted now. He wanted me to play his game.

I moved quickly but carefully along the aisle, reading call numbers taped to the spines of books. The clammy layer of perspiration that had collected on my skin from riding my bike hadn't cooled or dried. A drop of sweat fell into one of my eyes, momentarily blurring my vision. I wiped it away. And saw the seven digits we'd been searching for: 364.1523.

I pulled the book off the shelf and read the title I already knew from the online catalog. But seeing it in person, holding it in my hand, sent chills through me. *Inside the Mind of BTK*, by John Douglas, the famous criminal profiler who had once worked for the FBI, heading their Behavioral Science Unit, and coauthor Johnny Dodd. The cover was bloodred and beneath the large block letters was a gritty photograph of the eyes of BTK. Dennis Rader. The family man, Boy Scout leader, and church president who for thirty years terrorized his small Kansas town with unthinkable brutality.

Was the book itself the message? Was JPP communicating to us that he aspired to BTK's awful accomplishments? If so, it was an ambiguous clue.

I opened the book, and right there, tucked beneath the front cover, was a piece of white paper folded in thirds. As I unfolded it I wondered how long it had been sitting there, waiting. A stamp in the back cover told me the book hadn't been checked out in over two months.

It was a photocopy. No words, just an image.

Two dominoes laid out and reproduced in two-dimensional black and white.

One domino showed two numbers: four and seven.

The other domino showed the number six.

Three numbers. There weren't many ways these three numbers could be rearranged. Four, seven, six. Seven, six, four. Six, four, seven. Six, seven, four. Seven, four, six.

Seven, four, six.

7/4/6.

07/04/06.

July 4, 2006.

Susanna's birthday.

My head spun as the awful realization sunk in. I braced my hand against the edge of a shelf. Closed my eyes. Tried to breathe. Couldn't. And heard what sounded like someone else breathing heavily on the other side of this bookcase, directly opposite me, one aisle over.

I righted myself, replaced the BTK book, slipped the photocopy into my purse, and slowly walked up my aisle. The heavy breathing seemed to shadow me step-for-step. I sensed that whoever it was knew I was there. Knew I had found what I was looking for. Possibly wanted to share in my reaction. My shock. And there was only one person who could possibly want that. One person who thrived on your fear. Your terror of being next.

I reached the end of the aisle. Heard him reaching the end of his aisle. And then I paused, waiting for him to make the next move.

He also paused.

It was him. I felt it.

JPP was right there. Watching me. Lapping this up.

My mind raced. This time I wouldn't just fight him off. I would capture him. Again. Any way I could. Screaming at the top of my voice, pinning him down with all my strength. Letting him kill me in the process. I didn't care how.

Gathering my courage, I took two more steps, slowly, to the end of the aisle. And stopped. And watched, heart pounding, as he stepped around the end of the two aisles.

But it wasn't JPP.

It was Mac.

His expression of shock, followed by quick relief, mirrored my own reaction. My chest felt as if it would explode. Heat surged through my limbs. My brain, supercharged, repositioned the pieces of what I had known was about to happen.

"Karin." Mac exhaled.

"What are you doing here?"

"Same thing as you."

"But you—"

"I was on my way in to meet with Billy Staples when you called me the first time. I was practically in the city already."

We stared at each other a moment. I wasn't all that surprised Mac hadn't mentioned his whereabouts on the phone; it was his habit, when talking and driving, to keep things to a minimum.

"You were in the wrong aisle," I said.

"I knew where I was. I wanted to see who showed up for that book. Something told me Price wouldn't want to miss this."

"I had the same feeling; that's why I thought—"

"I was him?" Mac shook his head. "No such luck."

I reached into my purse and pulled out the photocopy. "This was in the book, right under the front cover."

Mac unfolded the paper and looked at the copied dominoes.

"Susanna's birthday," I told him.

When he heard that, his eyes flashed at me and his face turned red. I had seen him this way before, when he was overwhelmed by anger. It was the same shade of crimson he'd turned when I first saw him after Jackson and Cece were killed. Silent rage. And now, as we stood dumbstruck in front of each other in a Brooklyn library, my terrified mind tumbled me backward into a memory I'd long forgotten: Susanna, when she was one, sitting on Jon and Andrea's living room couch beside her cousin Cece who was just a year older, while the family paparazzi surrounded them with cameras, imploring the tiny bewildered girls to "Say cheese!" Now that I thought of it, I hadn't seen that photograph since before Cece died. It had been right there in the photo album I'd carefully assembled; but it wasn't there anymore. Had JPP taken it when he was in my home? Butchering my family? Had he kept it all this time as a souvenir?

My knees buckled and I collapsed to the floor, sobbing. Mac crouched in front of me and put both his arms around my back. He placed his dry cheek against my wet one. I smelled the pine soap again and my heart rate began to slow. After another minute, he helped me up. Trembling, he handed me the photocopy, which I slipped back into my purse.

Mac wove his arm through mine and led me downstairs and outside. His green MINI Cooper was around the corner on Eastern Parkway. My unlocked bike was gone—no big surprise—so I got into his car and took off with him to see Detective Billy Staples at the Eighty-fourth Precinct in downtown Brooklyn. On the way Mac called his partner, Alan, in Maplewood and filled him in. While he talked, driving with one hand and holding his phone with the other (violating a law in the service of the law), I tried to reach Andrea.

She didn't answer her home phone. Nor did she answer her cell phone. So I called Jon's cell, aware that he was still in California.

"It's Karin," I said, as soon as he answered. "Is Susanna all right?"

"Susanna? Sure. Why?"

I didn't know how to tell him. But there was no choice.

"You're going to hear from the police soon. JPP left a new warning. Andrea has got to take Susanna away."

His shocked silence saddened me more than I could

bear. A deep exhaustion swept through my body, and my hand holding the phone began to shake.

"Oh my God," he muttered.

"Jon, I'm *sorry*. Please just get her someplace safe."

"Where?" There was a warble in his normally solid voice. "Where is safe, Karin?"

"I don't know. But Jon, listen: Tell Andrea to lock up the house and pack a few things. When the police come they'll tell her what to do." I knew how much this was going to frighten Andrea. But time was of the essence.

I could tell by Mac's reserved expression that he didn't like how I'd handled that, calling my brother to deliver such a shock before the police had a chance to get there and make Andrea and Susanna feel safe. But in my experience safety was just an illusion and nothing substituted for hard fact.

Though we were getting close to Gold Street and the precinct, Mac decided to phone Billy Staples and give him a heads-up. Every minute counted.

"Seven, four, six," Mac told Staples. "It's Karin's niece's birthday. She's only two.

"Her full name is Susanna Roth Castle. We're pulling up to the precinct now. See you in a minute." He hung up, with one hand dropped his phone into his shirt pocket and with the other hand steered us into one of the parking spots reserved for cops in front of the precinct. We hurried out of the car, up the steps, and into a gritty urban police lobby. A receptionist behind a scratched bulletproof divider pointed us in the direction of the elevators, where we waited impatiently for one of two old creakers to make its way down.

"We need to get them into hiding somewhere," I said to Mac.

"Or we'll keep them at home with a shitload of protection. Gotta think this over, run it by the task force."

"Hiding is better."

"You're not officially on the job, Karin, so please—"

"I *am* the job, Mac."

The elevator arrived and took us up three flights to the detectives unit. We parked ourselves at either side of Billy Staples's standard-issue desk in a big low-ceilinged room surrounded by a buzzing hive of other detectives working their cases from antiquated phones spewing curly cords attached to boxy bases. Now *this* was a police station; I felt more comfortable here than in Maplewood's new overpriced monument to good intentions. Here, you could practically smell investigation burning in the air.

I handed Staples the photocopy. He immediately took it across the room and faxed it to Maplewood. While he waited for the paper to scroll through the machine, my cell phone rang with a call from Jon.

"I just remembered where Andrea is today: She had a noon appointment with her ob/gyn, in Manhattan—Dr. Ana Rodriquez, her office is at New York–Presbyterian Hospital, I just called over there but they haven't arrived yet." Jon was talking so fast his sentences blurred. "They must be in the car or on the train; I don't know how they went."

"Okay, sweetie. You hold tight. I'm with Mac and Detective Staples in Brooklyn right now. They'll get someone over to the hospital right away."

"I'm on the next plane home," Jon said, choking back tears.

"Okay." I blew him a kiss and we said good-bye.

I told Mac and Billy, who had returned from the fax machine.

"Wouldn't it be easier to see a doctor in Jersey?" Billy muttered as he dialed in a request for an all-points bulletin to be broadcast to units patrolling Manhattan.

"They haven't lived out there very long," I explained. "She had Susanna at that hospital; it's where she's comfortable."

Someone answered Billy's call and he put in his request, giving all the pertinent information. Then he hung up and stood up. Grabbed his baseball cap and pushed back his chair, which rolled against his neighbor's desk and landed with a *clunk*.

"Your car or mine?"

"Better take both," Mac said, "in case I have to head back to Maplewood in a hurry."

I rode with Mac, speeding up the FDR Drive behind Billy's gray sedan. Since it was midday the traffic was light and we zipped up the edge of Manhattan beside the East River, which glittered in the noon sun, snaking between the city and New Jersey on the opposite shore. It was fourteen minutes to the East Sixty-third Street exit, three more minutes cutting red lights uptown to Sixty-eighth Street and into the looped driveway that led to the entrance of New York–Presbyterian.

Seven or eight patrol cars had arrived before us and were parked at haphazard angles along the curb. Billy dumped his car in the first available spot and Mac followed suit.

We ran under a long awning that stretched from curb to rotating door.

Pushed our way inside, one after the other. And entered a scene of chaos.

Cops, everywhere.

Doctors. Nurses. Administrators.

Patients and visitors had been shunted off to the side where some remained, eager for a glimpse.

Everyone was huddled around something impossible to see.

A woman was screaming. A familiar voice.

Mac, Billy, and I pushed our way through the crowd.

Three nurses were on their knees, trying to calm Andrea, whose body appeared rigid. She held fiercely on to Susanna, who was still as a doll in her mother's arms. Andrea's face was bright red. Ropelike tendons stood out on her neck. Her screams echoed through the large, high-ceilinged lobby, ricocheting off all the hard surfaces. The marble floors. The painted walls. The dome skylight above our heads. Resonated as in an opera, with a force I wouldn't have thought could emanate from the slight body of my sister-in-law.

A doctor leaned down and gave her a shot of something. A sedative, I assumed.

"You're in labor," he told her in a forced-calm voice, trying and failing to reassure her that she'd be safe in their hands. Her baby boy wasn't due for another seven weeks.

"Please, let me through! I'm family!" I pushed my way past until I was near enough to crouch down. I put one hand on Andrea's cheek, and whispered, "Shh." And the other hand on Susanna's back.

The rise and fall of a single breath. That was all I wanted.

"SusieQ," I whispered, "it's Auntie Karin."

And then her lungs inhaled. Exhaled. And she twisted in her mother's unrelenting embrace to face me with an eerily calm expression that told me she understood that something about her life had just radically shifted.

PART II

PART II

CHAPTER 9

"David did *this* to me!" Susanna tried to squeeze shut one eye but ended up closing both.

"He winked at you?" I suppressed a smile. Reached over and flicked an errant curl of macaroni back into her white bowl.

Eyes wide on me, she nodded.

"I said, 'Hello, DavieQ!' " She laughed uproariously at how she had loaned her new baby brother a variation of her own nickname.

"What did he say back?"

"He said, 'Gurgle gurgle gurgle, waah waah waah!' "

Jon turned from the sink, where he was doing dishes, and we smiled at each other. The mirrored kitchen cabinets behind him reflected the brilliant sky swallowed almost whole by the wraparound windows of this city-owned safe house to which the family had been transferred after two weeks in the hospital, when David was deemed ready enough to leave neonatal intensive care. Well, it wasn't a *house* so much as a penthouse bubble securely removed from the urban ant farm twenty-three flights below. We were in Manhattan but might as well have been in the countryside somewhere, away from it all. Away from anywhere JPP might come looking for Susanna . . . yet close to New York–Presbyterian in case David needed to be whisked back for urgent care.

"I miss Mommy," Susanna said, as she spooned some mac and cheese into her mouth.

Jon stared at his daughter, speechless a moment. Then he shut off the water, dried his hands on a dishtowel, and came around the counter to kneel beside her at the table.

"Want Mommy to read to you tonight?"

Susanna nodded.

"Finish eating and we'll choose a book."

She finished quickly and as usual selected *The Velveteen Rabbit*. It had been read so often its covers were soft and tattered at the edges, much like the well-loved bunny itself. Jon hoisted her onto his hip and carried her through the dining/living room into the long hall. Susanna gripped the book in both her little hands and stared ahead, toward the closed door that was her parents' new bedroom. I heard the door open, and click shut.

Before I had crossed the living room—hotellike with its tan leather couches, matching lamps, patterned wall-to-wall carpeting—Susanna was shrieking and the door to the master bedroom opened to release Andrea's raw, convulsive sobs. Jon had told me about this—that Andrea couldn't "deal with anything"—in explanation of her refusal to see me. But nothing had prepared me for the harrowing sound of my sister-in-law's weeping response to a simple request from her own child.

In moments, Jon and Susanna were back in the living

room, she writhing in his arms as he strained to hold
her. She threw the book on the floor and tried with all
her might to push her father away. The agonized expression on her little face pained me to the core, and
in moments I was crying with them. I wrapped my
arms around them and we stood there while Susanna
thrashed. After a few minutes, she collapsed against
Jon's shoulder, pressed her face into his neck, and
sighed.

"Welcome to my world," he whispered to me over
Susanna's head of pale, disordered hair, which he
gently stroked.

After a few minutes, they settled into the couch. She
burrowed into his side and furiously sucked her thumb
as he read to her. I couldn't just sit and watch them as
they reestablished their emotional balance together; in
fact I worried that if I said the wrong thing or made the
wrong move I would throw them off. So I picked up
my purse and walked toward the front door to quietly
make my exit . . . but then thought better of it. I had suspected that it was *me*, specifically, Andrea didn't want
to see—me and the cloud of danger I had dragged into
their lives. But it occurred to me that, with her history
of depression, she could be suffering in a larger, more
amorphous way. So instead of leaving, I headed down
the hall to the master bedroom.

I knocked lightly, unsurprised when there was no response. Turned the knob and slowly inched open the
door. Shadows poured like liquid into the hallway. I
stepped inside and shut the door behind me.

Andrea lay on the bed, propped up by pillows, cradling her tiny newborn. In the gloomy darkness the

rumpled white sheets seemed to blend with her skin, and the color appeared to have bled out of her once-blue nightgown, which was unbuttoned and splayed open to reveal the massive breast into which David's face was buried. He looked a little better every time I saw him now. A little less pink. A little less skinny. A little less small. He suckled at her breast and squirmed in her arms, issuing the sweet familiar noises every baby makes when nursing. Lisette, their live-in neo-natal nurse whose résumé was stacked with experience in preemie care, sat on a chair in the corner. A tidy Jamaican woman of about forty, wearing a white pant-suit-uniform, she was adept at making herself invisible. She pretended to leaf through a magazine even though it was too dark in the room to read.

I went over and kissed Andrea's damp cheek. She didn't move except for her eyes, which lifted, grazed me, and fell again to some vague space above her blanket.

"Hi," I said.

"Sorry."

"Don't be."

I didn't particularly get the sense that she was angry with me, or that she wanted me to leave, or that she wanted me to stay, either. Wanting anything seemed beyond her at the moment, as if her emotions were too insatiable and unremitting to interfere with. Depression feasted on her; you could almost see it gobbling her up.

I crossed the room, pushed aside the heavy drape, and faced the bright, undulating ribbon of the East River. On the edge of the river sat the United Nations, its membership flags fluttering atop evenly spaced poles. It was the same view as from the living room, but angled from this bedroom it looked almost like a different place.

"What if I moved in?" The impulsive idea felt like a stroke of genius. "I could help out with Susanna . . . and cooking, laundry, all that stuff."

"You?" She didn't have to explain herself. In our family, until the day I lost Jackson and Cece, I had often been the butt of jokes for my lack of domesticity. Given my love for family, and the service I'd paid to society as a cop, no one held it against me that I didn't tidy up before someone came over or bake cookies just for fun. And then, not a moment into widowhood, the jokes stopped—a kind of death unto itself. Now Andrea's careless irreverence was a relief.

"Jon could use some help," I said.

"Lisette?" A shuffling sound; the magazine closing. "Could Karin and I be alone a minute, please?"

"Of course." Lisette's voice was deep for a small woman, and comforting. She got up and left the bedroom.

"I can't take this anymore," Andrea hissed, as soon as we were alone, "being a prisoner in this place, for God knows how long, waiting for *him* to find us, while David is trying so hard to stay alive and what if he doesn't? Or what if he does and Susanna doesn't because—"

"Shh." I sat on the bed and reached for her free hand. Wondering if the other hand, the one cradling David's tiny head, was as cold.

"I can't take this anymore," she said again. "I'm a terrible mother. I—"

"*Shh.*"

It took all my strength not to remind Andrea that she had two living children. A threat hovered over Susanna's life, yes, *but Susanna was alive and well.* David's life hung on a thread, yes, *but David was alive and well.* She had two children who were alive. And she had a husband who loved her, *who was alive.* But I didn't say any of that. Putting it into words would be heartless, even cruel. I squeezed Andrea's hand, trying to warm it. What I wanted was to get across the idea that we *all* had to find a reason, and a way, to latch on to life.

"I've been feeling so much better lately." I paused, deciding how much to share before diving in. "And then the other day, sitting in Mac's car on the Brooklyn Bridge—on our way to the hospital to see you—I surprised myself by imagining jumping off."

She stared at me, obviously shocked by my confession.

"How can I explain this"—I searched for words—"so it makes sense?"

"Try."

"Maybe it's the medication," I began, and then I talked and talked.

I had researched Prozac online and learned that forty milligrams, my daily dose, was on the high side but nothing out of the ordinary; eighty milligrams was the maximum dosage. I had also learned that there was a range of reactions, and mine was a bit unusual but not off-the-list. Lately I had begun to feel faster and stronger in a strange way, and sometimes I felt a kind of inner twitching—an irresistible restlessness.

Sitting in stalled traffic on the bridge's middle span far above the sparkling East River, listening as stuck cars uselessly rebelled by honking their horns, an old cliché had fled through my mind that day in Mac's car: *If someone told you to, would you jump off the Brooklyn Bridge?* The correct answer was no. But there I was, ominously, presented with an opportunity. It would be the easiest thing to do. Unlatch my seat belt. Open the door. Dash across the far right lane. Climb up the fence. Hurl myself over. For a split second I pictured myself flying through the air on that glorious day, skydiving with my chest out and my arms wide. Soaring, weightless. Then plunging. The water would be icy. Death would come quickly. The appeal was delicious. And then the car in front of us moved. Mac put his car into gear and we rolled forward, on our way. I closed my eyes, wondering where the impulse to leap had come from. I hadn't contemplated ending my life since the meds had kicked in. What struck me then was how empowered I felt, as opposed to weeks and months ago when I had felt helpless to lift my own hand against myself a second time. Although I no longer felt consciously suicidal, I realized that I was more capable than ever to launch myself into oblivion. That maybe I still wasn't safe. From JPP, of course. But also from myself. As we buzzed up the highway, I realized with a new clarity how lost I had become in the gray area between us . . . how unable to distinguish the true danger.

"Anyway," I told Andrea, "obviously I didn't do it. Later that day I thought of something Joyce once said to me. She said: 'Balance can be a razor's edge.' "

"Did you tell *her* all this?"

"No. I couldn't. I'm afraid she'll take away my happy pills. Can you believe that? After I didn't want them in the first place."

Andrea cracked a little smile. And then, suddenly, she was forcing back tears, whispering, "I don't know what to do."

"Let me help you. Please. You can't imagine how guilty I feel for putting all of you in so much danger."

She looked at me, and I sensed she now understood the tacit bargain in my suggestion that I move into their temporary home, their bubble of safety: The help would go two ways.

Finally she said, "Okay," before closing her eyes and thereby ending our visit.

Later, after Susanna was finally asleep in her provisional bed, and while Andrea, David, and Lisette continued their dance-of-darkness in the rear bedrooms, I sat with Jon on the terrace. It was just past eight o'clock. The sun was setting behind us, pulling the brightness out of the day, leaving behind a tender bluish sky that steadily darkened. The air was soft, a little chilly. We drank white wine . . . a no-no in combination with antidepressants. I did it anyway.

"I was on the Internet just now, while you were putting Susanna to bed."

He nodded, gazing across the river at the New Jersey side.

"Andrea's depressed."

"You think?" One side of his mouth pursed in sarcasm.

"It could be postpartum depression, even though

she didn't get it with Susanna. The next step for some people is postpartum psychosis."

"I probably read all the same Web sites."

"There are a few antidepressants you can take when you're nursing."

"Zoloft, Paxil, and Luvox." He nodded, decisively, once. "She doesn't want to hear about it. She won't put chemicals into her body, period; especially now, when she's nursing."

"Maybe talking about medication first isn't the right approach. It took Joyce months to convince me to pop a pill, and I was suicidal."

He looked at me. At my *was*. Seeing if I really meant it. I kept my eyes steady on his, our same-blue-eyes blurring into each other, silently convincing my brother that I wouldn't add to his troubles now.

"She'll be okay," I said.

His forehead crunched, revealing deep lines that were brand-new. Sipped his wine. Looked back at the sky, which was now streaked with night. "This whole thing is un-fucking-believable." He lurched forward and dropped his face into cupped hands. I hadn't seen Jon cry since we were children. In eighth grade a girl had deliberately handed him a paper smudged with charcoal. He had walked around all day with a blackened face, and no one had told him. When he came home and saw himself in the mirror, he realized why kids had been laughing around him all day. Now, as an adult, I understood what those adolescent tears had meant: It was his first brush with existentialism, when he knew he was all alone. But at the time, when he was thirteen and I was eleven, and he refused to let me into his room while he wept on his bed, I had misinter-preted his feelings as personal rejection.

"If Andrea's shutting down right now," I said, "you shouldn't take it personally, you know."

"It's hard not to."

"I know. But this isn't about you. It's hormonal."

"It isn't just *hormonal*, Karin." He shook his head, refusing to look at me. And I knew he meant the latest dominoes.

I drained my glass of wine. Poured us both another.

It had been two weeks since we'd last heard from JPP. The task force had succeeded in identifying the origi-nation point of his video call to me as a schoolhouse in the remote Kenyan village of Murungurune. It was quickly determined by local officials that no one in the area had seen anyone who looked anything like Martin Price. Being white and a stranger, he would have stood out in the small African township. It was also deter-mined that the Murungurune school had failed to acti-vate the security features on its new wireless Internet router. They did so promptly, meanwhile entertaining a few teams of intrepid reporters who visited in a dra-matic gesture to show the world just how many lives, near and far, a criminal can touch. The underlying re-minder being that no one is safe. Anywhere. Not even the gentle folk of Murungurune. Who appeared more mystified than frightened by their brush with the ma-nipulations of an American serial killer. I had watched them on the television news, and clearly they weren't afraid of JPP. One toothless elderly man even laughed at the absurdity of the idea that his village would be drawn into the broader world's story. When asked, he admitted that he had not yet visited the school to see its new computer, nor did he know what a web was unless it was generated by a spider.

JPP wasn't in Murungurune. Nor was he in Moscow, Jakarta, or South Bend, Indiana—or any of the other places where there were Internet servers he'd managed to infiltrate in order to disguise the true origination point of his Skype call. Which remained a mystery. And so, after all that, no one knew where he was.

"He can't get to you here," I said to Jon.

Night had gathered in the sky and the balcony grew instantly chilly. Jon looked at me: specks of bright-white glimmering in his bloodshot eyes. "I hope you're right." Then he reached across the space between our chairs and took my hand.

The next afternoon Mac drove me to Brooklyn to pack a bag—part friend, part bodyguard. It was the first truly warm day of the season, about seventy-five degrees, basking in the kind of golden sunshine you hope for all winter long. People were out sitting on their stoops. There was no sense of urgency in the air, just communal pleasure that the weather was so perfect.

We found a parking spot a block from my building and stopped at an Italian ice vendor on the sidewalk in front of the local elementary school where children impatiently waited their turn. The air was filled with their chatter. The littlest ones looked about four years old, the oldest about eleven. Cece had never grown old enough for school but even so I saw her everywhere in this scene, recognized her bubbly happiness, her being-here-now-ness, in the face of every single child as they received their colorful ices and ran to friends or mothers or fathers or babysitters, ready for the next event.

"Two small lemons," Mac told the woman, who scooped the soft yellow ices into pleated paper cups and handed them to him. He paid, and handed me mine. The frozen sweetness, slightly tart, melted on my tongue. We licked our ices and walked without speaking until we reached my building, then sat on the stoop, upending our cups and squeezing the last lemony drops onto our tongues.

"I could live in a place like this," Mac said. "Never thought I'd say that about the city."

"It isn't really *the city* out here, not like in Manhattan."

"Feels like more of a small town." He stood up. "Well, I hate to say it, but I have to be back in Maplewood for the night shift. Or should I call it the never-ending shift." When he swiveled his wrist to check his watch, I noticed a white line of skin on one of his fingers.

"Where's your wedding ring?"

"We tried, but we couldn't make it happen."

"I'm sorry."

"Me too."

I unlocked the iron gate and immediately noticed, on the square of dusty ground in front of my apartment's front door, yesterday's mail bundled in a rubber band. Beside it lay a shiny flyer creased strategically as if someone had tried to make it into a paper airplane before slipping it through the mail slot.

"That's funny." I picked up the flyer and flattened it. The single page danced with cartoony superheroes in primary colors.

"Some kid playing a joke."

"Probably." The ad was for an upcoming convention in Manhattan. "ComicsCon," I read aloud. "At the Javits Center, June eleventh."

"That's my birthday."

I looked at Mac. "I didn't know that."

"Well, now you do."

It occurred to me that he would be alone this year, since he and Val had split up, apparently for good.

"I'll take you out for your birthday," I offered. "Lunch or dinner? Your choice."

"I'll think about it."

"How old?"

He winked and didn't answer. Early forties, I guessed. His skin was weathered but not wrinkled, his hair only dusted with gray.

As I put the flyer on top of the pile of mail, so I could unlock the inner door with my free hand, I noticed that someone had circled the date of the convention in black marker.

"That's weird." I showed Mac.

He glanced at it, shrugged. "So what?"

I looked closely at the black circle: Its start and finish blended perfectly so there was no break whatsoever in the line. "I wonder if someone left this here on purpose."

"Yeah, the people doing the convention—they want your money."

"No, Mac, *really*. Think about this a minute."

I unlocked the door and we entered my apartment, which as always felt cooler than outside. I put the mail down on the small table in front of the mirror in the entry hall and picked up the flyer again. Mac went straight to the kitchen, where I heard him open a cupboard, and then the flow of water into the kitchen sink. I found him drinking thirstily, standing in front of the garden window.

"I think he left it here."

"Karin . . ." Mac's tone, so familiar by now: tolerant, regretful.

"He's antsy. We're too slow finding him again. He wants us to play his game—"

"His game is dominoes, not superheroes. That doesn't fall inside his m.o.; you know that."

I looked at the flyer again. Maybe Mac was right; this seemed to be mostly about comic books and all things comics-related. Not games. Not dominoes. And JPP had rarely veered from his theme. When serial killers did revise their modus operandi or the signatures they left behind, it was usually a subtle variation, rarely a big leap forward.

"It's nothing like his other clues," I said. "That's true. But I have such a strange feeling about this."

"It's a stray piece of paper. A wind could have pushed it under the gate. I wouldn't read too much into it." Mac turned to the sink, washed out his glass, and set it upside-down in the drainer.

He was probably right. My feelings these days were a roller coaster of unreliability, which was half the reason I had come home to pack myself a bag.

I filled a medium suitcase with clothes, books, and toiletries, making sure to collect my bottle of Prozac from the bathroom . . . and to take my daily pill, which I had missed, as I'd slept at the penthouse last night.

Almost immediately I felt the uplift, a lightening in my brain, a kind of airiness that made worries peel away.

"It feels a little like I'm going on vacation," I said, closing and locking the door behind us.

"In a way you are, but without the beach."

Mac carried the suitcase back to the car. It was a swift drive up the FDR, back to midtown, where my family awaited me. He pulled up in front of the building and, in parting, made sure I was clear about certain limitations now that I was joining the safe house.

"You have to stay inside."

"I know."

"If you want to go somewhere, call me or Billy Staples."

"Got it."

"I mean it, Karin. The guards will have orders about that." His expression was as serious as I had ever seen it. Obviously I cared at least as much about my family's safety as he did. But he knew me.

"Mac"—I kissed his cheek—"*don't worry.*"

I quickly learned what life in high-tech captivity was like. Anything we needed was ordered and delivered. Groceries. Drugstore items. Clothes. We never left the so-called house, which grew to feel more like a spaceship after a few days of constant confinement. It didn't take long to understand how pent-up Jon, Andrea, and Susanna had felt—waiting for David to grow, and for JPP to strike—or why Susanna tended to throw fits, or why Andrea kept falling into the quicksand of herself. At my urging, she was escorted out of the building three times a week and driven downtown to see Joyce at her office. The outings themselves probably did as much good as the therapy. As for me, my sessions had been reduced back to once a week. Sometimes, when Andrea left the apartment, I found myself feeling a little bit jealous. But I had committed myself to staying until I was no longer needed, and that day was not yet visible on the horizon.

I told Joyce that everything was fine. I was coping. My meds were working wonders. And it made me feel much better to be of use. What I kept to myself was the sizzling sensation brewing inside me. The sense that by including myself in Jon's family's confinement I was forestalling some inevitable rebellion. Cloaking my grief and rage in domestic activity looked good on the outside—it was acceptably therapeutic for me, and this family needed an extra pair of listening ears and help-ing hands—but my volcanic emotions, if subdued at the moment, felt not vanquished so much as dormant.

I cooked. I cleaned. I played with Susanna. Spent hours talking with Jon and more hours talking with Andrea, who, hour by hour, day by day, spent more time in the sunny living room and had even started getting dressed in the mornings and opening her bed-room curtains. My parents visited a few times a week, and Mom always brought a bag of puzzles and crafts. We sat together building birds and butterflies from the colorful squares of paper that had come with an ori-gami kit . . . so many that we strung them together in a large mobile we hung from the ceiling in the living room. We all kept one another company in a variety of ways. And yet the boredom could be intense; our lives were living proof that it was not a vacation to stay home doing nothing indefinitely. Nothing happened

here. Instead we hovered, waited, in case it appeared
something might happen. Our strange goal was to pre-
vent that.

And so one morning, a couple of weeks into my
stay, when David smiled for the first time it was a huge
event. We celebrated with a bottle of champagne Mac
brought when he heard the news—he had been on
his way into the city anyway, though he didn't mention why. He popped the cork and poured the foaming
champagne into wineglasses Lisette, Jon, and I held
up. Andrea and Susanna toasted with glasses of apple
juice. We drank and talked about how well David was
progressing and wondered aloud what he would be like
when he was a full-fledged little boy. As if enjoying
all the attention, David smiled again. And again. Smile
spreading across the small face like a blooming flower
in fast-forward. Blue-gray eyes lighting up. Causing a
contagion of happiness, each and every time.

That afternoon, when David was napping, Andrea
was reading to Susanna in the master bedroom, and
Jon was on the phone talking to someone about yet another movie offer he felt unable, unready, to commit
himself to, I leaned close to Mac's ear and whispered:
"Get me out of here."

A smile of collusion crinkled across his face.

I gestured to Jon that I would be back soon, and Mac
escorted me outside.

At times, during my stay, I had sat out on the balcony
just staring at the cityscape, which from that height
was mostly a horizon of rooftops. Or staring at the sky,
watching the clouds change shape as they drifted past.
Sometimes I stood at the railing and looked down at

the distant sidewalk where people looked like ants and cars looked like toys. It had surprised me how confined I had come to feel in a relatively short period of time. It was partly being sealed into a high-rise apartment building. And it was partly psychological, knowing that, for our own safety, we were supposed to stay put. It was also the Prozac, which had supercharged me, making me yearn for more movement than my life right now could accommodate.

Joyce and I had lately spoken about the meaning of happiness; that happiness was to be found not in other people but within yourself; that happiness was discovered spontaneously in experiences, not things; and that you couldn't plan it or control it, but had to be prepared to recognize it if and when it came your way; and that happiness, or satisfaction, as I had recently learned, could also be found in being of service to others in the most basic ways.

One day she had asked me to free-associate, to not-think when I answered her next question: "What would make you happy right now?"

"Taking a long walk, all alone. Not that I mind being with Jon and his family. I don't. It's just that . . ."

Joyce had smiled. "I understand." She nodded deeply, like a teacher whose lesson was finally sinking in.

Being with Mac wasn't quite like being alone, wandering, following my nose. He packed a gun and was bodyguarding me, after all. But still. It was good. The moment we stepped onto Second Avenue into the bright afternoon, I felt liberated.

To hear the up-close rush of traffic surging along the avenue, the dissonant blasts of horns at a gridlocked intersection, the steady tapping of high-heels as a businesswoman hurried past, the *whack-whack-whack* of a basketball being dribbled along by a teenage boy.

To catch whiffs of sweet perfume, of meaty hot dogs, of acrid gas when a taxi idled near our *Don't Walk* sign.

To walk without meeting a wall or a door or the edge of anything more restrictive than a curb.

"Stop for a coffee?" Mac asked after twenty minutes of just walking that had brought us to Twenty-third Street and Park Avenue South.

"Sure."

There was a café halfway down the block on a side street. We sat at an outdoor table and ordered cappuccinos and an apple muffin to share. I had walked off any wooziness from the champagne and now felt relaxed and a little bit tired.

"So," Mac said, stirring the white froth atop his cappuccino into the coffee beneath it, mixing them until there was no separation, "thought you'd like to know what Billy Staples and I have been up to lately, while Alan and the other guys sit at the computer." He grinned into his coffee. He had drunk two glasses of champagne to my one, and the walk might not have cleared his head quite as it had mine.

"What?"

He raised his eyebrows conspiratorially and paused a moment as if deciding whether to tell me. Then he said, "Looking."

I didn't have to ask if he meant looking for JPP.

"Where?"

"Anywhere off the cyber grid. We decided on our own to, you know, just get *out there*."

Mac hadn't let his guard down around me for weeks; I would have to feed this man champagne more often. Ever since I'd reacted to the ComicsCon flyer found beside my mail as if it was a message from *him*, he had avoided discussing anything that might trigger my intuitive leaps, or paranoia, or whatever you wanted to call it. My *oversensitivity*. Mac's treating me like fragile glass irked me whenever I ventured to think about it. And so I tried not to, investing myself instead in the hard labor of taking one day at a time.

"Tell me more," I prodded.

"Tournaments. All kinds of games. Cards—poker, blackjack, and the new ones: Yu-Gi-Oh, Pokemon, stuff like that. Ping Pong. Chess. You name it." He sipped his coffee to test its heat, then drank.

"So you've branched out from just dominoes." It felt like a small victory, considering our last conversation about it.

"A little, yes, but we're not covering any of the sports stuff. Don't think that's what he's into, you know? We're concentrating on just the games. The *crowds* that show up—these people aren't just fans, they're . . ."

"Fanatics."

He chuckled. "Yeah, that's exactly right. They're real fanatics, most of them. Like Price, but without the killer instinct."

Though he'd said it lightly, I cringed. Sipped my coffee once, twice, to push back the riptide of feeling. Broke off a piece of the muffin's edge. It was too sweet. Sat back and looked at Mac.

"Wouldn't he recognize you?" I asked. "Take off before you saw him?"

Like me, Mac had been part of the news story each time it had appeared in the media. If Price was like most serial killers, he kept every clipping in a scrapbook. He probably had Mac's face memorized alongside mine.

"If he was there, maybe. Probably. But we figured it couldn't hurt to give this a shot even if we don't expect much. We realize it would be risky for Price to show his face anywhere now, but Billy and I were both feeling—"

"Impatient." I cut him off. "Frustrated. Restless."

He stared at me. He knew I was talking about myself.

"How many have you gone to so far?" I had both my elbows on the table now. Leaned forward. Eagerly.

An unmistakable reserve swept his expression as he seemed to instantly sober up.

"No," he said. Reading my mind.

"I could help."

"Karin—"

"If Price saw me, he might not be able to resist. I could draw him out."

Mac signaled the waitress that he wanted the bill. She brought it swiftly and he dug into his wallet for money, refusing mine.

"Let's get you back to the apartment."

"You're going to one tonight, aren't you?"

"Stop."

"That's why you were able to come see us today. You were coming into the city anyway."

He stood up. His tone was warm, exasperated: "Your family needs you."

"Need*ed*. Andrea's up and around now. David's

doing so much better. Everyone's sleeping more. What is my life worth if I can't help out where I'm needed *now*? I lost Jackson and Cece to this creep. I have nothing left."

"Your parents," he reminded me. "Jon, Andrea, David, Susanna."

"Yes. Right. *Susanna*. But if we sit there, waiting, and he finds a way to get to her—"

"You can't come with us, Karin."

"I found him once before."

We were walking now. When we stopped to wait for a traffic light to change, he slid his arm through mine and tugged me close. Shook his head. "It would be too dangerous. And do I really need to remind you you're not a cop anymore?"

"Just tell me one thing: Are you planning to surveil the ComicsCon convention? If you're branching out, why not—"

"On my birthday? Are you kidding me?"

I knew how stubborn Mac could be so I let it drop. He deposited me back on the twenty-third floor, where before even entering the penthouse I felt the tentacles of confinement surround me. I was itching to continue discussing the convention—why *not* go? Worst-case scenario, you waste a little time—but we said good-bye as if the matter was closed. He lightly kissed my cheek and turned to walk back to the elevator.

"Wait! Your birthday's this Thursday. You never told me: lunch or dinner?"

He smiled. "Okay. Let's make it lunch."

The doors to the elevator, which had never left the floor, dinged open the instant he pressed the call button.

The first thing that struck me when I walked into the front hallway was the delicious smell of cooking. I found Jon and Andrea together in the kitchen, working on a meal of cornmeal-crusted salmon and salad. A baguette warmed in the oven. Susanna colored on the floor, David slept, and Lisette did a crossword puzzle in the corner of the living room. Entering this peaceful family scene clarified my sense that, while I was welcome here, my help wasn't really needed anymore.

"Have fun?" Andrea asked. Her cheeks were pink from the heat of the kitchen.

"It was nice to get out."

"I'll bet." Jon clapped his hands and cornmeal came off him like dust. Andrea laughed.

"I think I'll lie down for a few minutes before dinner."

I went to the guest room, where my suitcase was open on a chair, spilling clothes. Sat on the bed, leaned against the wall, cradled my laptop between my knees. Typed into the search window: *ComicsCon New York*. Read through the convention's Web site . . . my skin growing clammy . . . my heart beating a little too fast.

Keep still, I admonished myself, *resist the temptation to take action when maybe Mac was right*. Maybe the best thing for me to do right now was nothing. Stay with my family. Let the professionals deal with it. With JPP—*that monster*.

But how could I sit still, dutifully tending my damaged family like a Victorian spinster, while the man who had put us in this sky-high tomb was out there? How could we just wait? For JPP to sharpen his knives. Or for nothing to happen so we could spend the rest of our lives looking over our shoulders.

CHAPTER 10

Mac arrived a little before noon on Thursday, smelling of clean laundry and pine soap and carrying a bouquet of African daisies wrapped in a cone of zebra-striped paper. He handed the flowers to Andrea, earning a huge smile, and perched himself on a kitchen stool to watch her arrange them in a vase while I went to my room to grab my purse.

"Flowers for *me* on *your* birthday?" I heard Andrea say.

"My wife always liked them"—Mac avoided any reference to himself, which I had learned, especially lately, was his way—"so it seemed like a good . . ." And then I was out of hearing range.

I removed whatever I didn't need from my purse, in case I couldn't find a safe place to stash it at the Javits Center, and hid it under the pile of socks in the top drawer of my dresser. Brought some cash and my cell phone. That was it. I would have liked to leave the purse home altogether but that might have looked suspicious: a woman going out to lunch without her purse. Mac would have noticed. And kept a closer eye on me, which was exactly what I didn't want.

I realized he might hate me for this later. But the buzz in my head was so loud, I was so charged up to do this, I couldn't think beyond my plan.

We ate at Marie-Therese, a small restaurant on East Eleventh Street off Fourth Avenue I claimed to have selected for its interior open-air courtyard. I had been there once before, with Jackson, which was how I knew about it. Normally I avoided any place I had been with Jackson or Cece, if I possibly could, but today was different. Today I had something specific to accomplish. And I felt focused. Determined. Marie-Therese fit the bill perfectly: It was a lovely place, relaxing, charming . . . and well situated, just around the corner from Halloween Adventure—the biggest costume store in the city. I had done my research and learned that it wasn't unusual for people to attend ComicsCon in costume. Once I'd found out it would be that easy to surveil the convention incognito, it was as good as a permission slip to follow my instinct; not that I was about to ask, knowing Mac would only stop me.

We ordered salads, omelets, wine.

"Still on your first glass?" Mac asked, as he poured himself a refill.

"Not supposed to drink, really, with the meds."

"Hasn't stopped you before."

"When in the last month have you noticed me drink more than one glass?"

He paused, considering it. "Well—"

"Okay, two."

"Never." He smiled.

As he grew mellow, my stomach growled and my heart hammered. I felt a sheen of sweat accumulate on my face, though it was not a particularly hot day. I began to feel animalistic, uncivilized, as if my body was preparing for a hunt. Which it was, of course. Pumping adrenaline, gathering energy for the possibility that I might spot my prey. Despite the probability that I wouldn't. I held on to that, to Mac's good common sense, a buoy against my inner tides of suspicion and determination.

"You okay?" Mac asked.

"*Starving.*" I sopped up salad dressing with a second slice of bread. It was delicious. I was hungry, yet not hungry. But I knew I'd do better if I ate.

And so I did. Everything: cheese and spinach omelet, roasted asparagus, more bread. I forwent dessert and told Mac that my stomach was so full it felt like it would burst.

"Be right back," I said, leaving my cloth napkin on my chair, hoisting my purse to my shoulder and heading to the ladies' room. I left him in his seat—groggy, relaxed, sated. Amid potted vines hanging down a brick wall. Beneath a watercolor of a French landscape. Awash in sunshine. I felt more for him now, at this very moment, in a deeper and more personal way, than ever before. It was the sight of him as I turned and left: this familiar, caring man for whom I in return cared more and more all the time. Catching sight of our waitress coming through the kitchen's swinging doors, I stopped her and whispered, "Please bring my friend over there a piece of cake with a candle, and sing 'Happy Birthday.'"

"Flourless chocolate hazelnut or strawberry short-cake?"

"Strawberry."

She smiled conspiratorially and walked away.

For a moment I ached to backtrack to our table as I slipped past the ladies' room, through the kitchen, out the back door onto the shade-dappled side street, and around the corner to the costume shop.

Half an hour later I was getting out of a taxi in front of the entrance to the Javits Center with an orange plastic bag from Halloween Adventure containing my new identity.

I crossed the plaza and entered through one of the giant building's many glass doors. The convention had officially started that morning and people zigzagged along a roped line leading to the registration desk. Most wore street clothes but some had arrived in costume, which reinforced my confidence that I would be able to blend anonymously into this crowd. When my turn came I paid, was given my name tag (which I wouldn't wear), and then headed straight to the nearest bathroom.

When I pushed open the door I was surprised, and relieved, to find three other women openly changing into costumes. One, a young woman with short dyed-red hair who was hitching a Batman cape under her chin, greeted me by saying, "People are leaving bits and pieces they can't use, take whatever you want—it's mostly the girlie stuff that came with the ladies' superheroes . . . *some* of us don't want to be girls today; we want to be boys so we can run around acting like assholes for a few hours." Laughter bubbled through the room.

"Thanks. I think I've got everything I need in here." I lifted my orange bag.

"Anything you don't need, just toss on the chair."

A stall door swung open and out stepped a woman in a red coat dress and a fedora, holding a stuffed backpack in one hand, presumably containing her street clothes, and slipping on black sunglasses with the other.

"Excuse me," I said to the woman—Carmen Sandiego, at least for the next few hours. "Do you know where we can stash our stuff?"

"There's a storage place up the street that rents out lockers, or you can just try your luck and leave it here. That's what I'm gonna do."

"Me too," Batman said.

I slipped into the stall, took off my clothes, ripped open the package, stepped into the red and black fabric of my costume, pulled it up—and was transformed into Spider-Man. It hadn't even occurred to me to buy the ladies' version, if there was one. The spandex hugged every inch of me. Energized me. With the hood and gloves pulled on, I was covered from head to toe. I put my purse in the orange bag, stuffed my regular clothing over it, left the stall to the next person waiting, and added my bag to a heap of bags that had collected in the corner of the bathroom next to the chair covered in cast-off miscellany.

And then I headed out to roam the acreage of the convention center.

I went straight into the heart of it. Into the busiest, the loudest, the most manic cluster of activity I could find, right in the middle of the main area. Everywhere I went I met with copies of my new self; there must have been twenty other Spider-Men at the convention, along with Supermen, Batmen, Catwomen, Green Goblins,

Incredible Hulks, Yodas, Princess Leias. Other disguised pretenders whose very enthusiasm seemed to give license to my decision to come join the party.

Giant banners hung from the ceiling of the huge main area, announcing what you would find if you wandered in this or that direction: Hollywood Highlights, Anime, Autographs, Podcasts, Tabletop Gaming, Graphic Novels, Toys & Props, and something called Variant Stages.

I moved Spider-Man-like past booths stocked with comic books, comic book spinoffs, comic book accessories. People continued to pour into the convention. It was hard to imagine that anyone interested in games, toys, or comic books wouldn't be here. Wishful thinking, maybe. But as far as I was concerned, having made it out of the apartment and slipped my shackles to wander free in the real world—maybe not the *real* world but *this* world—I couldn't let myself think JPP wasn't here. Or couldn't be here. Anything was possible, and so through the eye slits in my hood I searched every face. Every single one. Seeing him. Blinking away the mirage. Not seeing him. Seeing him again.

I left the comics area and entered Tabletop Gaming. Whole subsections in this area were devoted to Chaotic—a card game I'd never heard of—Magic, and Dungeons of Dread. The first tournaments were beginning and were scheduled to continue over the next three days. As I moved through the area I heard the *slap-slap-slap* of shuffling cards, intermingled with conversations, laughter, sales pitches . . . and then blending with the *clack-clack-clack* of falling dominoes.

I followed the snake of sound into a white tent in

which five men in matching orange flower-print shirts sat at small tables awaiting opponents. Of the five, two had partners: an old Hispanic man in a suit and tie, and a young boy with his mother standing nearby . . . the way she hovered, aware of her child as well as their surroundings, made me ache anew for Cece, for the vigilance that had been at the core of every moment we were together. My eyes roamed every face—every face that was not Martin Price.

Disappointment washed through me in an over-whelming sensation of sinking. Sinking, and then shame. To think it might have been that easy . . . that JPP would hand-deliver to my home an invitation, date conveniently circled, to the next place we'd find him. I could hear the sharp tone of Mac's admonishment that I was sure would greet me later today, just as clearly as I could hear his hurt that I had ditched him on his birthday.

"Have a seat," one of the hired players invited me to his table.

I shook my head and left the tent.

Wandered through Anime, where Japanese meta-animation abounded. Autographs, where luminaries and rising stars of the comics, games, and toy indus-tries sat in rows upon rows awaiting their adoring fans. Podcasts, where teams of Internet broadcasters gath-ered information and opinion from anyone willing to offer any for instant publication into the universal ether. Wandered, feeling newly, supremely stupid for being here at all, for abandoning Mac for *this*.

I found myself in Variant Stages, an area at the back of the exhibition hall devoted to special events and contests put on by performers and comedians. Four separate mini-shows were in progress at the moment I walked in. Suddenly exhausted, I chose one randomly and sat down in the nearest empty chair.

The act was billed Vampire Cowboys. Two men dressed as, well, vampire cowboys sat on chairs meant to be barstools, in front of a tall bench meant to be a bar in an old-time saloon. Behind the bar, a poster board meant to be a mirror reflected back what I guessed was supposed to be the image of the same two cowboys but as full-fledged vampires. I didn't really get it. My brain was shutting down. My eyelids grew suddenly heavy and I felt them begin to droop. The ubiquitous loud music pumping through the entire convention center began to fade. And then someone's hands gripped my shoulders and hoisted me up.

"You're falling," he said.

I opened my eyes. The horrid face of the Green Goblin—mossy skin, long yellow teeth, bulbous eyes—crouched in front of me and startled me alert. *That voice.* And the overpowering smell of body odor. Dead fish. *Death.* An urge to vomit rolled through my stomach, up my throat. I swallowed it back down. Stood up, forcing him back two steps. He was shorter than me. Unafraid. Wearing his scaly-green costume with perverse entitlement.

On impulse, I reached out to touch him—to diminish him by acknowledging that his skin was only rubber.

He jumped away.

And then, as unexpectedly as he had appeared to do a good deed, to stop a fellow superhero—a rival, I now remembered, as the Green Goblin was the nemesis of

Spider-Man—from falling to the floor, he darted out of
Variant Stages into the main exhibition hall.

I ran after him. Watching his back so I wouldn't lose
him. So if he crossed paths with another Green Goblin
he wouldn't become someone else—making me think I
had never found him. Heard him. Smelled him.

If he wasn't JPP, he wouldn't run. That was clear: *He
wouldn't run.*

"Help!" I shouted. And then screamed, "Stop that
man!"

It was as if my plea went totally unheard in the ca-
cophony of the convention. Or maybe people thought
we were putting on a show, an escaped team from Variant Stages, good and evil performing an epic chase.

He slowed, just a little. Paused enough to turn and
look at me coming for him. He had heard me. He, too,
knew my voice. He knew it was me. I could practically
hear the ratchets of his sick brain weighing the pros
and cons of making another try for me.

If he still wanted me, now was his chance.

Then he turned and ran faster through the crowd.
Away from me.

I ran harder, faster, after him.

"Stop him!"

Again, no one flinched.

We ran. Past tables. Booths. Fans lined up for give-
aways. Ran. To the pounding beat of the unrelenting
music piped into every molecule of the air. Faster
than the beat of the music. Ran. Double-time. Triple-
time. *Flew.* People stood by and watched. There was
applause. We raced past the final sectioned-off area,
beneath the last banner, into a long deserted hallway.

When he vanished around a bend in the hall, cheers exploded behind us. As if it was over. As if he had evaded me. Won.

I ran and ran. Took the same bend. Followed him as he receded down a long ramp into a dimmer and darker, grimier and grittier area. The delivery bays—their wide throats open onto Thirty-fifth Street. The convention music receded, replaced by an ensemble of street noises: traffic, horns, voices.

Two hundred feet ahead, a slice of city street gaped through an open bay door.

I ran. Faster. Heart pounding. Eyes pinned to him as he jumped into the back of an empty truck aligned with the mouth of an open bay.

I ran. Pulled by gravity as the ramp angled downward. *Ran and ran*.

Because it was him. I had done it. Found him. Again.

Finally I reached the open truck.

The empty truck.

He was gone.

Like a magician, he had evaporated himself before my very eyes.

I stood in the truck, screaming his name: "Martin! You freak! Come and get me!"

Stood there. And stood there. Alone. Listening to my own voice echo back at me.

How could he have just vanished?

I blinked my eyes. Looked again.

He was still, once more, eternally, again—nowhere.

I buckled over, propped my hands on my knees, and labored to breathe as the dusty air entered my lungs in raspy intakes. Coughed. Simultaneously resisted and succumbed as filaments of helplessness began to weave their way into me. That familiar despair.

And then I heard something: up the ramp. The soft *thump* of movement. He must have jumped out of the truck and reentered the ramp off to the side.

I ran fast, faster, racing up the ramp. Filled with the same bright energy of hours ago: hope, faith in my instincts and abilities. Gained on him. Grew closer. So close. Almost close enough to touch him.

"Stop!" I shouted. "Stop right now!"

And he did. To my amazement, he stopped, turned, and faced me as the distance between us quickly shrank to nothing.

He put his hands out to soften the blow of our collision.

My force threw him to the ground and without hesitation I straddled him. Leveled him with every ounce of my weight so he couldn't leverage himself up. Pinched him with my knees so he lost most of his lateral movement. Put both hands on his neck. Leaned forward. Pressed down. Squeezed. And squeezed. And squeezed.

Strangling him, killing him, with my very own hands was a pleasure I had never fully imagined. Never thoroughly appreciated. I began to see how easy it was when you wanted it this badly. Began, in that sense, to understand him as I vanquished him. Felt—as I pressed and squeezed his life away—how lucky I was, how unbelievably lucky I was for the opportunity. Not a chance opportunity, but one I had deliberately sought. The satisfaction was immeasurable . . . and as I thought of Jackson and Cece, I squeezed harder . . . and harder still, as I thought of the Alderman family, one and then another and another and another and another. All those faces. Now ghosts. Crowding out, blotting away the significance of the monstrous face inside the mask.

His hands might have been gripping my arms for whole seconds, a full minute for all I knew, before I realized it. His fingers clenched so hard that my arm muscles suddenly spasmed. All at once my fingers hinged away from his neck. Stiffened. Fanned out, powerless.

And then I became aware that his smell was gone. The putrid odor that had overwhelmed me in my Brooklyn apartment that night: gone. And washed over me just a little while ago, slumping in the chair: *gone*. His identifying smell.

In its place was the smell of pine.

He pushed me off him, gasping for air as he sat up. Suffocating in my hood, I pulled it off in one quick tug. At the same moment, he yanked off his horrid green mask.

We stared at each other in disbelief.

Without thinking, propelled by raw feeling—a chaos of guilt and affection that swept through me without warning—I leaned down and kissed him. His lips were tender, strawberry-sweet. The taste of the shortcake he must have eaten in bereft loneliness, or anger, or both, broke my heart.

"I am so, so sorry," I said.

"You almost killed me."

"You came."

"Of course I did."

"Why didn't you tell me?"

"I didn't want to upset you, in case—"

I put a finger to his lips, and said, "*He's here.*"

A voice over the loudspeaker announced: "All exits have been sealed. We ask everyone to stay where you are. Please sit down. Thank you for your patience and cooperation."

Cooperation, maybe, as thousands of people suddenly fell silent and, one by one, sat down where they were. But patience, maybe not: The central exhibition hall buzzed with panic. People wanted to know what was wrong. What happened? What, who, where, how, when was the danger coming?

Somewhere in this vast place, with its coliseum-sized rooms and snaking halls and rooms upon rooms upon rooms . . . somewhere, hiding, among tens of thousands of terrified people, lurked Martin Price. I was sure of it. The smell. The voice. I was positive it had been him.

A dark blue ocean of police troops seeped into the huge space. Armed forces, keyed for action.

The hunt for JPP was on.

Batman, cape flying, ran toward us in long, muscular strides. A black Batman I didn't recognize until he was closer and he became Billy Staples in cape and mask. Eyes bright, candy-coated, intense. He seemed transported, as if he had actually flown on his own wings to our aid.

"He's cornered. In the men's bathroom." Billy's masked eyes flicked from me to Mac then back to me, reading us.

In my mind I saw a fireball rolling through a room, exploding through a revolving door, igniting everything. Pure, malevolent destruction. Heat spread suddenly throughout my body; flesh-melting heat.

I felt Mac's cool hand rest on my back, trying to calm me. I stepped away.

"We haven't arrested him yet," Billy said. "Karin—thought you'd like to do the honors."

I did. But the *honors* I had in mind for him had nothing to do with reading him his Miranda rights.

We followed Billy through the bright buzzing center of the exhibition hall. Cries of agitation, fear, confusion filled the gigantic space. Everyone—conventiongoers, exhibitors, superheroes—was sitting cross-legged or bent-kneed or straight-legged on the floor. Looking terrified as police roamed among them. Some of the cops held their guns ready in their hands. Others had rifles strapped over their shoulders.

I turned and saw that Billy had removed his Batman mask. Sweat drenched his face, making it glow in the overhead fluorescents. We trailed him through the seated crowd. People watched us, their eyes gummy with questions. I looked above their heads, past them, focused on the undulating black nylon cape flowing off the back of Billy's costume.

He led us out of the main hall and through the Anime section. Everywhere people huddled, officers roamed. Then we entered a short hallway. Turned right into another hallway that was barricaded by a human rope of police that parted to let us through.

"Four minutes!" Billy said in a loud voice, flashing his smile. "That's how long it took us to nail him. That's how bad he is at hiding." I realized that he wasn't just speaking to me; he was making an effort to

insult Martin Price—because he was within earshot.
We were getting close.

We passed through a swinging door adorned with a
stick figure of a man.

Stepped into the bathroom.

And there he was.

Martin Price.

JPP.

The worst kind of human scum. Crumpled on the
dirty floor like a piece of garbage. Stinking up the
bathroom with his outsized odor.

He was on his knees, handcuffed to the base of a sink
in a row of ten sinks in the enormous white-tiled bathroom. Across from a bank of urinals. Surrounded by
six heavily armed police officers.

He looked like a little boy.

Blond and pale.

Helpless.

Pathetic.

Feeble.

None of which he was.

You almost wanted to help him.

But that was the last thing you would ever do.

All six officers hung back, as did Billy, who stood
against the door. Watching. Giving me space—physical,
mental, emotional space. Giving me my moment. Only
Mac stayed right beside me, hovering.

I walked slowly toward Martin Price. In the urine-
stinking room. Tiles sticky under my feet, each step
cracking.

Walked. Slowly. Toward him.

As he cowered. Pretending he was fearless. Dripping

with arrogance. His pale eyes darting between my face and the floor.

Walked.

Slowly.

Toward him.

In the total silence of everyone watching. My breath heaving. Sweat dripping off my face. Fists hanging like stones at my sides.

It was up to me. Whatever I wanted.

I stood above him. My knees inches from his face. Staring down at the crown of his balding head. Thinking, for a split second, that some woman had given birth to him. Repulsed by the fact of his existence.

"Everyone," I heard Billy say, addressing the six officers. "Out."

A few mumbled dissent. But they shuffled out of the bathroom, and Billy joined them. Leaving me and Mac alone with the man, the freak, we had sought so long and so hard, and at a terrible price.

If I had been alone with him, all alone . . . My mind pinwheeled through the possibilities. Saw my foot crushing his pathetic face. Saw my hands squeezing the last breath out of his measly neck. Saw him grow lifeless under the force of my rage. If I had a gun I would have . . .

I turned to Mac, remembering why he was here in the first place: He was working undercover.

"Where is it?"

"No, Karin."

I ran both my hands along the sides of Mac's scaly green costume, an exact replica of the rubbery skin Martin Price was wearing. Felt for his gun. Knowing that when he didn't carry on his hip he carried on his right ankle, I dug my hand into his boot. Grabbed the handle, slid it out.

It was my game now.

"Leave," I told Mac. Wanting to be alone with the man who had murdered my daughter. Murdered my husband. Destroyed my life. Threatened more brutality against the others I loved. Promised to keep coming back until every domino in his sick game had tipped and no one was left standing. Until my entire family was obliterated.

Alone with him. With not a single witness in sight.

"No."

"Fine, then."

I pointed Mac's gun at the top of Martin Price's head. The coward couldn't even look at me. Couldn't face his own death, as he had forced so many others to do—slowly, without pity. At least I would be merciful. I was a trained marksman, and he was so close; a single shot to his head was all it would take.

I unlatched the safety.

Hand, shaking.

Took aim.

"Karin, *no*." Mac's hand tried to leverage down my arm.

"Yes."

"That's murder."

"It's justice."

"It isn't the way. He'll be locked up for life, and that's worse than death. Think a minute. Stop feeling and *think*."

But was it necessary to contemplate moral logic *now*?

When I was milliseconds away from the most critical choice of my life.

No.

But . . .

Martin lifted his face and looked at me.

And then he spoke: "Please. Don't."

And my mind leap-frogged past the moment and my imagination conjured *me killing him.* And when *I saw* the bullet rip through the brain of Martin Price, exploding into him, delivering such a huge and sudden shock to his body and soul that he wouldn't have had a moment to relish the violence of his own death—when I looked into his eyes and recognized a human being . . .

Revenge—what was so wrong with that? Why would I even hesitate when given my one unfettered chance?

Why should right and wrong even matter in a case like this?

Who wouldn't want to destroy such a monster?

Who would not be forgiven for pulling the trigger on this one particular man?

I knew all that. Even in that moment. Understood it perfectly.

And yet I couldn't.

I couldn't.

I learned that I could kill myself more easily than I could kill Martin Price.

Why?

As my arm lowered, Mac's fingers slid to my hand and took the gun from me before it dropped to the floor. I heard him latch the safety as he put an arm around me and moved me across the bathroom, as far away from Martin Price as we could get without leaving the room.

With his free hand he knocked on the inside of the door and shouted, "Staples!"

Billy came back in, looking worried. Mac reholstered his gun and said, "I want a witness to this." And then, to me, "You still want the honors, Karin?"

I felt numb. Frozen and empty. Disempowered, standing there across the room from *him*. A man who would sit in prison and possibly live a long life, learn crafts, read books, throw basketballs through hoops, think thoughts, relive and savor all the people he had brutalized, the lives he took. At the end of all this, he still had the gift of his own life. I couldn't look at him.

"You do it," I told Mac.

The rest of the cops shuffled back into the bathroom and I stared at the floor, studying the grime between the little white tiles, as Mac read Martin Price his rights. Then they unlocked his shackles, lifted him off the floor, cuffed his wrists behind his back, and took him away. Out of the corner of my eye I saw him look at me as he passed, sensed his desire for me to turn around. But why did he want me to see him? Did he need me to recognize his humanity? Did he need to see capitulation in my eyes—again? Or did he need one more chance to relish my fear of him? Because I was his most precious witness. My pain anointed him as special. And as long as I was alive, eternally bloodied by the raw losses he had caused me, his *accomplishments* also lived on.

My gaze stayed down, counting seventeen, eighteen, nineteen tiles before I lost track.

And then the door swung shut behind them. Their cascade of footsteps receded down the hall, leaving Mac and me alone in a bubble of silence.

I was so ashamed—of my passion to kill JPP, and my failure to. For being such a coward, any way you looked at it. I dropped my face in my hands and wept. Mac's arms came around me, enveloping me in his warmth. He whispered into my ear, a murmur of something kind, probably, but I was too dazed to make out his words.

CHAPTER 11

The GPS unit Jon had borrowed from our mother for this trip ran out of battery power, so he pulled over and consulted a paper map.

"Tell me where we're going," I insisted. Again.

"Not until you pull yourself together." Jon's face in profile looked almost flat. Pale. Nearly translucent skin revealing a lattice of fear, tension, and determination that had replaced the bones, muscles and cartilage out of which the average face was built. His was no average face, not anymore, not since every iota of his being had geared itself to the survival of his family. I was proud of my brother for his valor that had emerged in these times of our family's need. Proud as I was pissed that he had colluded with Joyce in what I felt was a kind of abduction.

Not three days after being yanked off Prozac—Joyce having noted its "deleterious effect" on my particular brain chemistry and my "resulting reckless behavior" in chasing down a serial killer unarmed and alone—darkness had wrapped its arms around me again. Now all I wanted was to be home. Alone. In my dim apartment. Mulling over one single moment in my recent past. Contemplating the moral logic upon which I had based the most critical choice of my life. Dissecting and eviscerating my essential failure. Reflecting upon it over and over endlessly. Hating myself for my cowardice. Regretting it. But still, even so, regardless of the clarity of that moment in the convention center men's room when I failed to pull the trigger, when I looked into Martin Price's eyes and recognized a human being, I failed myself in every possible way.

Why couldn't I kill him?

This was the question I wanted to sink into, alone, in my dark basement apartment. Where I wanted to remain. Forever.

It was all I really wanted now. If you could call that *wanting*.

I wanted. Lacked. Everything that mattered: Jackson, Cece, courage; an inner core of *self* that made you a person worthy of occupying time and space on this earth.

If I tucked myself away, out of the world, and didn't bother anyone, or ask anything of life. Didn't beg attention by attempting suicide again. Just existed alone in my darkness. If I just did that, allowed time to verticalize around me as I reflected on that single moment—freed myself from the pain of what had come before it and from any expectations for a life after—then I could live. Exist. Without the raw, jarring reminders brought on by wave after wave of memory in conflict with internal dissent.

"Look at you," Jon said to me, heaped in the passenger seat beside him as he drove. He looked forward at the road, not at me, and yet I felt the spotlight of his complete attention. "Look at you." It was exactly what he had said when he arrived at my apartment two days ago, after JPP was tossed back into jail and Jon had moved his family back home: *Look at you, you are the embodiment of wretched misery. You are so horrible to see that I can't even look at you. Look at you.*

Everything about me had become intolerable. The darkness I had brought into everyone's lives. My family, dead. His family, terrorized. Mac, deceived. My failure to annihilate the person who had done this to us. And yet these people continued to love me. Love me to the point that Jon had left his family to drive me to some Joyce-appointed destination he refused to name.

"You're having me committed." I turned away from his face and watched green flashes of upstate New York pass us by. "Yup. That's it."

A snort of bitter laughter from my brother. "Maybe that'll be next."

"They have psych wards right in the city."

He ignored me and kept driving.

After more than three hours we crossed into Massachusetts and exited onto the Mass Pike, then exited again into the town of Lee. It was a picturesque hamlet with stores and restaurants and, as we drove out of the small village center, houses whose sidewalks were seamed with large old trees. I had never been in this area before and had no concept of where he could be taking me. We then came into to another village, Lenox, a somewhat larger and wealthier-looking town;

but no sooner had we entered it than we were out of it again, driving along a woodsy road marked by signs to Tanglewood.

"*Tanglewood?*" I said. "Where they give *concerts*?" Jackson had once told me about this place—where every summer for a hundred years some of the world's best mostly-classical musicians gathered and performed, drawing thousands of cultural tourists to this area of western Massachusetts. I remembered now: He had wanted to come here to see James Taylor perform live. We had said we would do it, rent a room at a country inn, bring Cece, have ourselves a weekend. I had forgotten all about it until now.

I started to cry again.

"I'm not taking you to a concert," Jon said, not bothering to keep the exasperation out of his tone.

We drove past Tanglewood's many parking lots, then past the main entrance to Tanglewood itself. And then we came to a small sign that read *Kripalu* and turned into a long, curved drive that led up the side of a mountain.

"What is this place?" I demanded, wiping my eyes with the palms of my hands. "Jon, honestly, I'm not some little kid you can just take places with no explanation."

He glanced at me, and I saw that his eyes were bloodshot, that he was exhausted and didn't have the energy to try explaining what he probably didn't understand himself.

"Joyce told me to bring you here," he said. "And I brought you here. As soon as you're checked in, I have to head back."

"You're not staying with me?"

"I can't."

He pulled into a parking lot in front of a large brick building with two extensions angled off a center, like the spread wings of a bird in flight. Atop this mountain we were surrounded by views of other mountains, and the dips and valleys that lay between them, all bursting with early summer foliage. Green, everywhere. Air so sharp and sweet it was almost hard to breathe.

Jon had packed me a small suitcase that he removed from the trunk of the car. I followed him up some steps, through a double set of glass doors and into a crowded lobby. We joined a line that had formed in front of a registration desk. While we waited I got the gist of the place from the words stenciled on the wall behind the main desk: *Kripalu Center for Yoga and Health*.

"You've got to be fucking kidding me," I hissed into the back of Jon's neck. Goose bumps formed on his skin but he didn't respond. "Answer me."

"That wasn't a question," he said without turning around.

"What, do you *hate* me?"

His whole body swiveled at once and he faced me with the fiercest expression I had ever seen on my until-lately easygoing brother. "I love you, Karin, so cut the crap."

As the line diminished, my fury did not. *Yoga?* Joyce was out of her mind. So was Jon. They all were, to think something so silly could begin to touch me where I hurt. I had been a cop. I was a widow. The mother of a murdered child. A worthless coward.

Jon pulled a piece of paper out of his pocket, unfolded it, and handed it to the young woman behind the desk, who read it and smiled. "I heard that's a good one." She typed something into her computer then gave Jon a printout, which he handed to me: *Healing Anxiety and Depression, a five-day workshop with Joyce Goldman-Kerns.*

So! Joyce was on another one of her missions to save everyone and had instructed Jon to bring me to her. Here: to this place where I absolutely did not belong and didn't want to be. I crunched the paper into a ball and tried to toss it into the nearest garbage can, but it missed and landed on the floor instead. A smiling barefoot older man in sweatpants and a T-shirt who happened to be passing seemed to note my agitation without expression, and kept walking. A young boy ran past, laughing, trailed calmly by a woman with blond dreadlocks, wearing stretchy black pants and a bright orange camisole. She wore a ring on one toe, and every toenail was painted a different color. When she passed us she smiled but didn't miss a step as she followed the boy.

"I can't do this," I told Jon. "This place—it's *Joyce*'s thing, not mine. How am I going to sit in a room with people in spandex and dreadlocks? I cannot do this."

"Why not? Why not just give it a try? You're here."

"I want my Prozac back."

"Joyce said no."

"I felt better with it. It worked. This won't work."

"Joyce said you didn't respond well, and she said you weren't honest with her about how it was affecting you."

Ah, but the pure energy of it . . . how could I explain?
It had been good. My daily forty milligrams had introduced me to the power of flight. I was convinced that,
without it, I never would have had the audacity to trick
Mac into letting me take him out to lunch—and then
ditching him for the hot pursuit of my burning intu-
ition. I would have talked myself out of the gut feeling
that I *had* to go to the convention, and maybe we never
would have caught JPP; maybe he would still be out
there.

"Jon, don't you get the feeling that this is more for *her*
convenience? Her *guilt*? Because she was scheduled to
be out of town *again* when I crashed and needed her?"

He shook his head, sighed, and said, "Yes. I think
you're right. I also think she's trying to find a way to
help you, whatever that turns out to be." He kissed
my forehead. "I'll be back in five days. Everything
you need to know is on that piece of paper." He bent
down, picked it up, flattened it out, and handed it
back to me.

And then he left.

I couldn't believe it.

As soon as he was gone, I went to the front desk,
asked for a bus schedule, and soon learned that the last
bus to New York had left an hour ago. It was Sunday,
and here in the deep country things shut down early;
I would have to wait until morning to leave. I perused
a bulletin board full of activities and meal schedules,
then found the room number listed on my crinkled registration form.

It was a shared room with four bunk beds—an option
chosen instead of a private room, I assumed, not so

much to save money as to stop me from being alone. I parked my suitcase next to the nearest lower bunk and looked around for the bathroom, which I soon discovered was a communal bathroom off the public hall. Joyce's workshop classroom, called the Sunset Room, was off the same hall.

I lay on my bunk, stewing. Failing to rest. Ignoring my roommates as they filtered in. Skipping dinner and then skipping the first workshop that night. Expecting Joyce to come and chastise me; feeling a little disappointed when she didn't. I realized I was being as stubborn as a disgruntled child but just couldn't get over the fact that Joyce and Jon—and Mac, too, I guessed . . . and possibly my parents—had colluded in this. I had felt their proverbial eyes all over me as I had sunk back into despair after stopping the antidepressants. Sensed their communal pondering as to how to levitate me back out of myself without a chemical pulley. I couldn't blame them for their concern; in fact, when I really thought about it, I told myself I ought to be grateful for it. By morning, most of my anger had baked off. I woke hungry.

At breakfast in the communal cafeteria—a cavernous room full of sunshine, whole grains, fresh fruits, and groggy friendly faces—I spotted Joyce. She was standing in line wearing black yoga pants, green flip-flips, and an embroidered long-sleeved sheer purple tunic over a white camisole, balancing her tray while selecting a muffin from a serving dish.

"The apple-walnut one's good." I came up behind her.

She glanced backward at me. Smiled. "Okay."

"An apology would be nice."

"For what? You look more relaxed than I've seen you."

I had slept well, yes, and chalked it up to the country air. She had a lot of nerve to take credit for that.

"I'm leaving after breakfast."

"May I join you before you go?"

I returned to my table and waited. I watched her as she put a few slices of not-bacon on a small plate, chose a dish of plain yogurt, and poured a mug of mint tea. She carried her tray through the dining room, smiling at the many people who greeted her.

"Seems like you know everyone here," I said, as she put down her tray and sat across from me. We were alone at the far end of a long table.

"I've been coming here for years, since my twins were killed."

That silenced me.

"A car accident," she explained. "Eleven years ago, when they were in college."

I stared at her, stunned. She had never indicated anything about having children or about having herself experienced the kind of terrible loss I resuffered on her couch every week.

"I probably shouldn't have told you that." She looked at me with such directness I couldn't look away. "But to tell you the truth, the way you greeted me just now—well, I thought maybe it would help if you knew that someone *does* understand the essence of what you've been going through."

"I'm sorry."

"Don't be sorry, Karin, please. Just *be here now.*

It's all we can do." She leaned across the table and gripped my hand. Stared me directly in the eyes. "*It's over.*"

"It will never be over."

"It's over in that he's in prison now."

"He escaped before."

"Do you really think they'll let him escape again?" She shook her head so emphatically, her bobbed hair swayed at her chin. "No way."

"It's just—"

"No." She squeezed my hand harder. "You have to find a way back. It's time."

Paralyzed at the thought of *letting go* and *moving on* in a way I had long felt was impossible, I looked into her pale brown eyes, realizing I had never before noticed the chips of green and yellow suspended in her irises.

"You *can* do this. You *have* to do this. We'll do it *together.* You don't have to come to my workshop or take any of the yoga classes. There's plenty to do here. Or you can do *nothing* here—there are miles of walking trails, there's a lake, there's a nice little town nearby. Just hang around for a few days and see what happens, okay?"

"Maybe."

"Think about it."

"I will." But the truth was, she had already hooked me. Joyce was good, and she had excellent timing. She knew when and how to brandish the tools in her arsenal.

"With or without meds, it was going to come back to the same thing. You need to find a place inside yourself where you can remember your lost loved ones from a distance that's been forced on you. And you need to forgive yourself for surviving."

"But if we find I need to try meds again?"

"We'll see. You didn't need them before the tragedy, so I don't see this as a clinical depression, and we may have discovered that medication isn't a suitable temporary treatment for you."

"That's a big *we'll see*."

She smiled. "It is."

And so I stayed, telling myself it was just for a day or two. I took her suggestion to avoid both her workshop and the yoga classes. For the first two days I basically hung around the grounds, taking walks, reading alone on a bench in the shade, cautiously avoiding all the yogis who floated around the place seeking their own versions of healing. Now and then, Joyce and I took a walk together and talked. Just as in her office in New York, she let me vent and offered guiding wisdom.

On my third full day, I grew bored. It was a strange sensation: an emptying of mind I hadn't experienced for a very long time. I had tried every unorganized activity available and nothing else was tempting. Succumbing to curiosity, I ducked into the Sunset Room to listen in on one of Joyce's workshops. About forty people sat in a loose circle on the floor, facing her as she talked. Yoga props were scattered around the room, giving the impression that the workshop was part practice, *doing*, in addition to listening to Joyce's trained insight. I had missed so much I could hardly follow the special vocabulary she had built over many hours and days.

She kept talking about "bodies," as if we had many.

And she mentioned our "story," as if we had only one. I listened, letting her words wash over me. She seemed to allude to a system of emotional and physical bodies stuck in a self-perpetuating cycle, a repetitive dance. I got that: being trapped inside yourself. But she also seemed to say that you could break that cycle by re-defining yourself—changing the life story you told yourself and others over and over—thereby slipping out of the skin of who you thought you were, slough-ing off the single-minded story that had become your identity.

I remembered how empowering it had been to slip into Spider-Man's skin at the convention. But it had never occurred to me that you could slip *out of* a skin, and transform yourself, as readily as you could slip into one.

The next morning, I returned for the final workshop and watched as Joyce guided the group in a yoga prac-tice, confident that I wasn't limber enough to join in. After a while a woman near me burst into tears and collapsed on her mat. Joyce went over to comfort her.

"You okay?" I heard Joyce ask.

The woman nodded, and then shook her head.

"It happens," Joyce whispered. "The stuff that's buried sometimes bursts out." She stroked the woman's back a few times before drifting away.

Gradually the woman began to quiet. Meanwhile I couldn't stop thinking about the irony of "stuff that's buried" bursting out. In that moment, the phrase became a metaphor and glued itself to my *story*, which was rife with buried "stuff."

Graves.

Inside the graves: bodies. *Actual bodies.*

Seven, to be exact: the five Aldermans, Jackson, Cece.

And then there was the eighth body: the empty grave of eluded death. Mine. Susanna's. JPP's. The eighth body required for the rest of the dominoes to fall. For the nightmare to really, truly, irrevocably end.

The eighth body was where I was trapped. It was the essence of my story: my own death, for which I had yearned. Martin Price's death, which I had failed. And all the undone deaths—the fears and terrors—that lay between. It had become my skipping record, the single note that had continuously replayed in my mind . . . even now that the threat was over . . . even now that a full year had passed since the loss of my beloved husband and child.

On Friday, as I waited on a bench outside Kripalu's main entrance for Jon to pick me up, my phone rang.

"How're you doing?" Mac asked me. It had been only a week since we had captured Martin Price at the convention center, and less than a week since Mac and I had seen each other. Why did I feel as if we hadn't spoken in half a year?

"How are you?"

"I asked first."

"Fine, actually."

"It's good to hear your voice, Karin."

The bright green lawn in front of my bench dipped perilously down, flattened briefly to accommodate a narrow asphalt parking lot, then plunged into a valley of gardens, fields, and forest, rising on the other side in the magnificent specter of a distant mountain. It was beautiful.

"I'll call you when I'm back in New York."

"Sounds good. Bye—"

"Wait! Mac?"

"Still here."

"It's good to hear your voice, too."

CHAPTER 12

Everything was damp with an early morning mist that the July heat was sure to burn off in an hour. Jon had mowed his vast lawn yesterday, and the smell of fresh-cut grass was still poignant. I stood on the kitchen deck and watched Susanna dart barefoot down the four steps onto the lawn and run circles before throwing herself on her back. Laughing. Her nightie now thoroughly wet.

Today she was three. The age of memory. A true beginning.

"Susanna—come inside, let's get you ready."

She ignored me. I didn't want to raise my voice because Jon, Andrea, and David were still asleep in the house. So I joined her on the wet grass. Stood above her and said, "Come on, sweetie, we should get started."

She rolled away from me, swiftly, like a marble.

And so I did the only thing I could think of at the moment: lay down in my nightgown on the damp grass and rolled in her direction. Grass prickly on my skin. A film of dew enveloping every inch of me. Surprised by a sensation of happiness that radiated throughout my body. Susanna rolled back in my direction until we were lying face-to-face.

"We're so wet, we won't need a bath now," I said.

She threw her little leg over me and climbed on, giggling as she fell forward and blew raspberries into my neck. I tickled her off.

A truck rumbled to a stop in front of the house.

"Come on," I said.

We ran inside and upstairs. In the guest room, where I had stayed last night, I stripped off my wet nightgown, left it puddled on the floor, pulled on yesterday's shirt and pants, and ran outside to accept the first delivery. The white truck read *Bouncy House* along the side. I greeted the driver halfway along the front walk.

"You Mrs. Castle?"

"I'm her sister-in-law."

"Good enough," the man said. "Sign here. What time you want pickup?"

"Any time after five."

He noted it on his yellow carbon of the delivery sheet and handed me the top copy. Meanwhile two other men had already started unloading a long roll of multicolored plastic and hauling it to the backyard along with a big battery-operated air pump.

"Over there." I pointed to the spot Andrea, my mother, and I had already designated as the best place. The men unrolled the plastic until it lay on the grass in a red square. Set up the pump. And slowly an immense red, blue, yellow, and green cube arose on the lawn.

By the time it was fully inflated, Jon had appeared with Susanna, now ready for her big day in her new green-and-purple flowered party dress, with her hair gathered into a high ponytail and tied with a purple ribbon. She squealed when she saw the bouncy house and ran directly across the lawn to be the first to try it out. While she bounced and bounced inside the inflated net-sided room, Jon and I sat together on the deck, drinking coffee and reviewing the schedule for the day.

Susanna's birthday.

The fourth of July.

Independence Day, on so many levels.

Even though JPP was no longer a threat to Susanna, he still loomed in our minds. It was as if we would not be fully finished with him and the dread he had inserted into our lives until July fourth came and went and we could see and feel his warning pass unfulfilled. And so today's celebration would mark not just Susanna's birthday but also the end of our nightmare. A denial of the inevitability of the eighth body that had haunted my family for too long. Today was our chance to reinvent our story. It was an important day for all of us, for all these reasons. It had been a magnificent thrill to wake up this particular morning, alive.

Because the table had been moved to the lawn for the party, Jon balanced his empty mug on his bent knee. He looked tired; more than tired, *older* after the past few harrowing months. The crow's feet by his eyes had deepened and a vertical furrow had developed in his brow. And if I was not mistaken, in the clear morning light, wisps of gray were visible in his short blond curls.

"Got good weather today," he said.

"We're lucky. Rain would have—"

"—put a damper on things."

He smiled. I smiled. We both turned to watch Susanna tumble, laughing, in the bouncy house. The sun rose another inch and the morning perceptibly brightened.

"We really *are* lucky." He lowered his head and rubbed the tops of his eye sockets with his thumbs the way a glasses-wearer does, though Jon's eyesight was fine. "I got a call yesterday about a project. First meeting's next week."

"Did you take it?"

He nodded. "But I haven't told Andrea yet."

"She'll be okay. Mom and I are here—we'll help her out."

"The bank account's getting a little slender. I have to get back to work."

"I know." I reached across the space between us and squeezed his hand. Like me, Jon loved working almost as much as he loved his family. I knew it was not only the income from the next project that was drawing him back, but his restiveness. "You have to go back to work sometime. She'll understand."

"I hope so. Luckily the first few meetings are in New York. I won't have to go to L.A. for about three weeks, I think."

Nearly August. Deep, sultry summer. The perfect time to escape my city apartment. "I'll come and stay with them."

"You're sure?"

"I'll take Susanna to the public pool and give Andrea some quiet time with David."

He looked at me, trying to read me.

"I'm *sure*," I said.

Out front, a car door slammed. Jon went around to greet the next delivery. I went upstairs to shower and get dressed.

By noon the party was in full swing. All twelve children from Susanna's regular Tuesday playgroup had been invited, and with them their siblings and parents. With family and assorted other friends and neighbors, there were over fifty guests.

Four tables with pink paper tablecloths were set with Cinderella-themed paper plates and cups. White helium balloons were tied to trees, the deck railing, the backs of chairs. On a serving table were platters of sandwiches, crackers, cheese, cookies, vegetables, and various snacks. A large sheet cake decorated with pink and purple flowers magnetized the attention of half a dozen small children at any given moment: standing on their tiptoes, fingers gripping the edge of the table, as if staring at the cake hard enough would transport it into their impatient mouths. But they would have to wait for lunch *and* the entertainment before they got dessert. When we had interviewed Elizabeth Stoppard, a.k.a. Loopy Lizzie the Clown, she had made it clear that the serving of the cake was her act's big finale.

Amid the happy chaos, my mind drifted in and out of memories of Cece, when we celebrated *her* third birthday, when I was the mother of a little daughter who loved princesses and fairy tales. And then my mind would drift away. Just as Joyce had tried to teach me: not digging into the memories, just letting them come and letting them go. Allowing them without effort. It was hard, but I was practicing, and today it was going well. Cece existed in my mind, at this moment, at this party, in Susanna's movements, in every molecule of the humid July air. She existed in all these things. And yet she didn't. The goal was to be here and there, present and past, simultaneously, without trying to fight off either. And now that my chemistry had fully realigned itself after the shock of stopping the meds, I found I could sustain myself on a middle ground between misery and hypervigilance. I no longer missed the keen sensation of my mind racing into the heart of every single thought that settled there. Now, I could sit still. Observe. Think. Feel. Take a walk, tend my garden, watch a cloud take shape in the sky, listen to rain patter against a window—and not incessantly re-experience the catastrophic ending of my universe.

Across the lawn, Mom was serving plates of food to a growing line of guests. On my way to help, Andrea intercepted me and handed over David.

"Do you mind?" she asked.

"My pleasure."

She went off to help serve the food in what amounted, for a young mother, to a moment of freedom—doing something, anything, without a child attached to you—while I very happily cradled David in my arms.

I kissed the soft crown of his fuzzy head, and whispered, "Hello, Maestro." He was wearing a onesie designed to look like a tuxedo. Ten days past his official due date, he had developed the weight and girth expected of a smallish baby his age. He had sparkling blue eyes and had mastered his beautiful smile. He was doing it now—his little face brightening, his mouth opening, the corners of his lips lifting—so I carried him over to my father, who was parked on a chair off to the side. I sat beside him and angled David so Dad could get a good view.

Finally, when everyone had had their lunch, more and more children began to agitate around the cake. The clown was late.

"What should we do?" Andrea asked, having just returned from putting David down for a nap in a cradle in the kitchen where she could hear him if he cried.

"Serve the cake," my mother said. "Everyone said she was punctual—she must have gotten caught in traffic on her way over. Who knows how long she'll be?"

Just as Andrea was about to cut the cake, the clown came around the side of house into the backyard, saying, "Sorry I'm late! Battery died in my van, had to wait for a jump." She hurried to the center of the lawn, started pulling things out of her bag of tricks—rubber chicken, can of ribbons, bottomless milk bottle—and within minutes had all the children and most of the adults gathered around her on the lawn, laughing and clapping.

Loopy Lizzie was less stout than I remembered her from our one meeting, and she must have had a cold because her voice seemed slightly different than I recalled. But dressed in her baggy, hyperpatterned costume and her floppy orange wig and covered in globs of face paint and a big red ball of a clown nose, you wouldn't have been able to identify her gender or age. She had told us that, having started as an actress before being waylaid by motherhood, she had made her living as a clown for the past decade, earning herself the reputation of the most sought-after children's party clown in the area. Watching her perform, I thought she was a pretty good clown, but I couldn't really understand what all the fuss was about. Maybe clowns just weren't my thing; at the circus, I had always preferred the high-wire acts.

After about forty-five minutes of entertainment, she pulled out balloons and wowed the children by transforming simple tubes into cats, dogs, hearts, hats, swords, and wands. Then, as promised, she served cake, doling out a joke with every piece. She had spent exactly ninety minutes with us, as contracted, and eager to move on to her next appointment, she told us not to bother seeing her out; she only needed to use the bathroom and would then find the front door herself. Jon paid her and showed her into the house. When he came out he told Andrea that David was still asleep.

Minutes later, we heard Loopy Lizzie's van start up and pull away, and another car arrive and shut its engine.

After a moment, Mac appeared around the corner of the house—late, but no matter. He said hello and stood at my side. Since our kiss at the convention center, a vague tenderness had hovered between us but neither of us had been willing to breach our long-established comfort zone. I, for one, felt safer un-coupled, keeping myself free to remember Jackson. It scared me that sometimes now I couldn't vividly recall my husband's face or his smell or his laugh; it was as if my sensory memory had started to release him, and I hated that. With Cece, though, every atom in my body still possessed her. But that was different; she was my child.

"Where'd they get those?" Mac asked when he noticed all the children running around with their special balloons.

"The clown just left."

"The *clown*?"

"Loopy Lizzie . . . I told you all about her."

He looked at me, his eyes probing my face. "Lizzie Stoppard's dead."

"No she isn't; she was just here. She left a minute ago."

"A runner in Memorial Park nearly tripped over her body this morning."

And then, from the house, an electrifying scream silenced our debate.

We found Andrea in the kitchen, on her knees, in front of a large basin on the floor. A dozen red apples bobbed on the surface of the water into which her arms were plunged, reaching for something.

Details came into quick, sharp focus.

The long hand of the wall clock ticking forward to three thirty-six.

A squeezed juice box with a protruding straw on the counter by the sink.

The blue velour bear that Susanna believed David liked best, the one she insisted he keep near him at all times, on the floor next to the cradle.

The cradle itself—empty.

The water streaming down Andrea's arms as she lifted a small penguin out of the water.

Not a penguin; no. A tuxedoed . . . *baby*. Limp. Still. Dripping. In the moment I recognized the tuxedo onesie David had worn all day, in my mind I also saw David. Andrea must have seen the same thing—or, like me, thought she saw it and suffered the same jolt before realizing that the baby was in fact a doll dressed in David's clothes.

"*Where is he?*" she demanded of anyone, everyone, who had heard her scream and run into the kitchen: me, Mac, Jon, and some of the guests from the party. "*Where's David?*"

"I've got him!" My mother's voice preceded her entrance. Wrapped in a pale green blanket, David fussed in her arms. "His diaper leaked and he needed a change. Who put his outfit on that doll?"

Andrea took David and gently rocked him with an expression of embarrassed relief. "I'm sorry," she said, "I didn't mean to upset everyone. It's just that I thought—" She stopped talking when she saw Mac's expression, the emotions that jiggered across his face before he could stop them: surprise, as he noticed something in the tub of water; curiosity, as he walked over for a closer look; apprehension, as he crouched down and dipped in an arm; dismay, when he pulled out two black, white-spotted, sickeningly familiar rectangular tiles.

Dominoes. Two of them. Three numbers: four, two, one.

They glistened, wet, in the palm of his hand.

"Is this some kind of a joke?" Jon came up beside Mac and looked at the dominoes. "I mean, *what the hell?*"

Family and guests released a communal murmur of denial. If dressing up a doll in David's onesie and dropping dominoes into the tub of water had been someone's idea of fun, no one was willing to admit to it. In my gut, I didn't believe it was a joke; I couldn't believe that anyone among us, here at this party, was capable of being so cruel.

Mac looked at me; without speaking, I knew his thoughts. "He's in prison," I said. "It isn't possible." But a feeling was crackling through me, a terrible sensation of dread.

Drying his hand on the front of his jeans, Mac pulled his cell phone out of his pocket and speed-dialed Alan, his partner, with the tip of his thumb. A minute later we had confirmation that Martin Price was where he was supposed to be: locked up tight in New Jersey State Prison in Trenton.

And then the numbers started dialing through my brain: *four, two, one, two, four, one, two, four, two, four, one . . .*

"Two four one," I said, staring at Mac, whose eyes sharpened with the same recognition. "*Two-for-one. Two for the price of one.*" And then my eyes snapped around the room, scanning the crowd of faces that had gone suddenly quiet.

Where was she?

Through the kitchen window I saw a small group of children jumping around in the bouncy house: three boys and a little girl who was not my niece.

"*Where's Susanna?*" I asked.

Mac stuffed the wet dominoes into his pocket. "Everyone, *start looking.*"

For a moment I felt faint as images came at me piecemeal: the hand of the wall clock ticking another minute forward; the chaos of people suddenly moving throughout the house and grounds; the sharp tone of a father's voice chastising a child who wanted attention *now*, at just the wrong moment, when there was none to spare. Closing my eyes, I breathed, steadied myself, and then crossed the wet floor to comfort Andrea, who appeared frozen in shock. I touched the back of David's fuzzy head, so warm, as he nuzzled into her neck and she held him tightly. Her expression of terrified disbelief: I'd seen it before, at the hospital, when she learned that JPP had either targeted Susanna or planned something for her birthday—or both.

"I don't understand," Andrea whispered in a quavering voice.

"Neither do I," I said, but it wasn't fully true. If Susanna wasn't located soon, there were two strong possibilities, neither one good.

Either Martin Price had spawned a copycat, or he had a partner.

I wanted to console Andrea, tell her this was all some kind of freakish coincidence, a terrible mistake. But how could I? I had been a cop. A victim. And I knew, everyone did, that we had just turned a corner no one had seen. The moment felt surreal, when you don't understand what's happening; as in a dream when you can't move forward because some overwhelming force is pulling you back.

PART III

CHAPTER 13

"Susanna's still missing," I told Alan Tavarese, who had driven up in his white Prius behind a contingent of police cars that brought reinforcements for the search. "We've looked everywhere for her." Though *everywhere* did not begin to encompass the possibilities.

The house sat on the edge of woods separating Walton Avenue from the fields of Waterlands Park, a situation that had seemed an asset when Jon and Andrea were house hunting and now felt like a set of terrible liabilities, made worse by the train track that lay just beyond the park. There were so many places a child could get lost or hide, too many ways someone might flee with her. Because Susanna was so young, we had started by searching inside the house. I myself had checked every nook and cranny in the attic, a last-resort place I hadn't expected to find her and didn't. Jon, Andrea, and some friends had searched every room, every closet, every corner. Mac, who had just returned with a group of neighbors from a search of the surrounding yards, came around the side of the house when he saw Alan.

"Better put out an AMBER Alert," Mac said.

"Already did," Alan said. "Statewide, NFA and LIM—"

My stomach clamped when I heard the official acronyms for Nonfamily Abduction and Lost, Injured, or Otherwise Missing applied to Susanna. I felt suddenly hot and then realized that it wasn't just me: We were all sweating. Since he'd stepped from the cool of his car, perspiration was gathering on Alan's forehead. Rivulets dripped down Mac's temples. The hot day was getting hotter; a heat wave had landed.

"—and the task force is getting put back together stat, already happening when I left. Better late than never . . ." Alan stopped himself from finishing the sentence because it wasn't true. Sooner would have been better than late, late was possibly no better than never. "Already started running the numbers on the dominoes—everything we've got on your family, Karin—but no hits as of yet. But listen to this. Martin Price: Someone over at Trenton tried talking to him, to find out if he knows what the hell's going on here, and he wouldn't say much except it isn't a copycat we're dealing with. He wants us to know he's got a partner. But beyond saying that, he won't talk."

"You believe him, about a partner?" Mac asked.

"The thing is, I do," Alan said. "The less this guy says, the more I believe him, you know what I mean?"

Behind us, from the house, we heard Andrea weeping, and Jon's agitated voice: "You don't know that!"

I stepped in close to Mac and Alan. "We shouldn't assume anything he tells us is true."

"I agree," Mac said.

"We'll go with it both ways," Alan said, "see what takes us where."

"Listen," Mac said, "Susanna's been missing as long as the phony clown's been gone. They start the secondary distribution?"

"Yup. Already got a text on my phone, so it's definitely out there."

Text message networks, content alerts by Internet providers, in-store announcements by major retailers—along with a broadcast to law enforcement, the news of Susanna's disappearance had already been transmitted into the consciousness of tens of thousands of ordinary people, possibly before Susanna herself fully realized what was happening (if . . . I couldn't complete the thought: *if she was still . . .*). It was her birthday, a clown had come to entertain, and then the clown had invited her along on an adventure . . . I wondered what was going through Susanna's mind right now.

One two four two one four two . . . the numbers kept running through my head . . . but other than the implicit announcement—two for one—I couldn't think of what they meant. Martin Price had always left dominoes that were an indication of who his next victim would be, so wouldn't his partner or imitator do the same thing?

The sensation of Mac's hand on my back returned me to the moment, and also told me that my shirt was wet. I was sweating more than I had realized. Uniformed police were spreading out to conduct a more thorough canvass of neighbors' homes, while other searchers who had started earlier were gathering on the lawn behind us, waiting for further instructions—as if someone had a clue.

Jon's voice sailed again over the din: "Keep looking! *Please.*"

I turned to see my brother standing in front of his house, dripping sweat, ropes of tension lengthening his neck as he pleaded with friends and neighbors not to give up. One by one, searchers who had come to a standstill put themselves back in motion, setting out to look and relook anywhere and everywhere, knowing the only thing we all knew for sure: Keeping still was not an option. Even my father was wandering the yard, near my mother, who was on her hands and knees dragging the beam of a flashlight back and forth across the crawl space beneath the house.

"Karin," Mac said, "Alan and I ought to get over to the task force, ride the search, start figuring out the rest."

I felt surprised that he was going to leave—surprised by the raw sensation of a safety net being yanked from beneath me—but reminded myself that he was at work, I was not, and my place was with my family.

I nodded, and without another word, Mac and Alan drove away.

Kelly, another detective from my old unit—a stout, fortyish African-American woman with a booming voice—had taken charge of the search operation. Speaking into a bullhorn she didn't need, she was organizing people into small groups and directing them not to overlap. As I approached for my assignment, she lowered the bullhorn and flung her arm around my shoulders, pulling me close. She was powerfully strong and wore a sweet perfume.

"Go check out your people inside. I don't think they're doing so good."

I looked at the house: its white stucco and brick, its curved path from the driveway to the door. A lone helium balloon, attached by a long ribbon to the outside doorknob, angled upward toward the sky and swayed almost imperceptibly.

"If you hear anything—"

"Don't you worry," she interrupted, "I'll find you in a nanosecond."

The air in the house was cold in contrast to the heat outside. I heard murmuring voices from the direction of the kitchen, and footsteps upstairs. But the first person I saw was Andrea, in the living room, cradling angelic David as he slept, blissfully innocent of what was going on. She looked at me and pursed her lips to form a *shush* without actually making any sound. Silent grief was etched into her face as if she already knew the outcome of all this, as if Susanna's disappearance had already lodged itself inside her and registered as a permanent loss. I padded as quietly as possible across the room and leaned down to kiss her cheek, to reassure her that we still didn't know, but she turned away before I even touched her.

"Andrea—" I whispered.

David's eyes popped open, his face scrunched up, and he started to cry.

"Now look what you've done!"

"I'm *sorry*. I'm sorry I woke him. I'm sorry I—"

"Go away, please!" Tears spilled down her cheeks. "I can't look at you right now."

"We'll find her," I said, but it was a promise we both knew I couldn't honestly make.

She stared at the wall, crying along with David, until I gave up and left the room.

I found Jon in the kitchen, speaking with a detective I didn't know. The man was taking notes, jotting particulars beyond her appearance: her favorite things, how she tended to react under stress. When there was a lull in the conversation I introduced myself and learned that the detective was new to the unit. When he heard my name he stared at me a moment before his eyes pulsed away. He was smart enough not to verbalize the obvious fact that he had realized who I was. Instead he introduced himself as "Detective Third Class Gerry Mober," and then continued interviewing Jon.

I walked away, feeling stupid and useless. They didn't need me; I was only getting in the way, reminding them of exactly what they *didn't* need to think about right now: the dark possibilities of how this could turn out. I went back outside—grateful for the punishing heat— crossed the lawn, and walked past Kelly, feeling her eyes on me all the way. I kept my gaze down because suddenly I couldn't bear her or anyone else's attention, couldn't tolerate the stares of everyone who knew my story; knew that I, by dint of my former work and my own losses, had brought this on my brother's family. His *innocent* family. I had made the monster hungry for more, and now the monster had multiplied. Did it matter that I loved Jon and his family more than I valued my own life? It did not. It only mattered that Susanna was missing and I was to blame. If only there was some way to strike a bargain: to trade my life for hers. If only it was possible. If only I *could*, I would do *anything* to have her back. But how? I had never felt more aware of my essential helplessness or culpability. I felt everyone's accusatory looks all the way across the lawn and to the street . . . until finally, turning to glance back, sure I would turn to salt in punishment for my greedy attempts to hang on to life, I saw that in fact no one was paying me any attention at all. That I was alone in my thoughts and my feelings came as a relief. Shaking off the distraction of my own guilt, I summoned focus, cleared my mind, and headed into the broader neighborhood to look for Susanna.

Houses. Lawns. Streets. Cars drifting past. And everywhere people roaming, muttering *Susanna, Susanna.* Looking in and over and under and behind. No possible hiding place went unexplored. As the minutes grew to hours, and the hours transformed day to night, we looked: Hundreds, now, had converged on the area. Kelly's bullhorn could be heard from such a great distance that it was possible to know, without returning to home base, that despite the steady accumulation of goodwill and effort, the search had yielded—nothing.

It was dark when I found my way back to the house. Media were now camped out on the lawn in force: five television vans with their tall satellite antennae, reporters holding microphones to anyone willing to talk, floodlights bathing the front of the house in an overbright greenish glow. All the attention had summoned a new wave of searchers who arrived with undaunted energy. The last time I had witnessed this circusy scene I been on the inside of the house—a different house; *my* house—mourning my husband and child. I took a breath and started across the lawn as cameras and microphones chased me and I repeated, "No comment," until I was at the front door waiting for someone to let me in.

Finally a sliver of my mother's face appeared in the cracked-open doorway and she pulled me inside. Detective Mober had turned the dining room table into a desk where he sat hunched over a pad of paper and took notes as he talked on the phone. Beside the pad, an empty mug and a napkin with crumbs. My father sat across from him, gripping his own empty mug. When he saw me, his confused eyes lit up with relief, but he said nothing.

My mother steered me to the kitchen where a half-eaten tray of party leftovers sat on the counter. There was no pretense of plates or utensils. She handed me a napkin and said, "Eat."

I wasn't hungry, but with no energy to argue I took half a sandwich. She handed me a glass of ice water, the drinking of which informed me of a terrible thirst. I drank another full glass before we even spoke.

"Nothing?" I asked her, knowing that if there had been any news I would have heard it by now.

"All those cameras," she said, shaking her head.

"How are Jon and Andrea?"

She sighed, and fixed me with her warm, loving eyes. "They're afraid. They expect the worst—*but I don't.* I can still feel her. I just don't feel she's gone."

My mother's optimism was infectious and for a moment I also felt hopeful. But one look at Jon's ashen face, when he walked into the kitchen, banished any glimmer of confidence. His agitation silenced us. We stood there watching him pace the room, breathing heavy intakes and outrushes of air as if he was struggling not to suffocate. When he abruptly stopped walking and looked at me, all my guilty apprehension came rushing back.

"How did this happen?" he said. "You people had *how much time* to investigate this guy? Two years? And you never even had an inkling that he might not be working alone?"

I felt my head vibrate, as if it was trying to shake *no*, to deny that we hadn't done everything possible to see this coming. Martin Price was captured. Put away. It was supposed to be over.

"I . . ." Faltering. "I . . ."

"You can't blame Karin," my mother said softly, touching Jon's arm no sooner than he fiercely pulled away. "Of all people, you can't blame *her*."

Jon glared at her with red-blue volcanic eyes, a conflagration of fury and sadness. And then he looked at me. "I don't know how to deal with this. It should never have happened. It didn't *need* to happen. She was only three!"

"Don't say *was*." I was crying now and so was he. "Don't *say* that yet."

My mother came between us, rubbing my back with her right hand, Jon's back with her left. "I think—" she was just starting to say when Jon ran out of the kitchen. "Well," her voice now empty of intention, "it doesn't really matter what I think, does it."

She was right. It didn't matter what any of us thought. Only the facts mattered and so far we had only these: A woman had been murdered, Susanna was missing, and there was a new set of dominoes—the cipher of yet another unknown.

It was midnight and I hadn't heard from Mac since he and Alan left in the middle of the afternoon. My resolve to leave them alone to do their work with what

I knew was a hyperactivated task force finally melted. When I called Mac, to my surprise, I received some actual news.

"They found the clown's van. I'm on my way right now."

"Susanna?"

"Just the van, they said. How are the folks there hanging in?"

"Every time I walk into the room Andrea bursts into tears. Just looking at me reminds them of how bad this could turn out to be. Let's just say that my being here isn't exactly helpful."

A pause, the horn-honking sound of traffic that told me Mac hadn't yet reached the highway, and then: "I could swing by and get you."

Seven minutes later he pulled up in front of Jon's house and I hurried through a hungry mass of reporters to his car. He started driving practically before I had shut the front passenger door.

"Where's Alan?"

"Task force. They're crunching the numbers but so far no dice."

"The game is dominoes."

He flashed me a halfhearted smile. "If you can joke now, you're either too optimistic or too pessimistic."

"Just numb." He merged us onto the Garden State Parkway, and I stared at the diminishing red taillights of a car speeding past. Looked at Mac: his forehead a worried grate.

"We can't jump to any conclusions about Susanna," he said. "Partner or copycat, either way we're dealing with a different person, so it could be anything."

"But the dominoes have always been about *who* would be next, and the task force has all the numbers on everyone in my family, and it isn't clear."

"Okay, but think about it—it's gotten less clear over time. Last time he left us a pointer, more a where to find the who. And that who was also possibly a when. We just haven't figured out yet what they gave us this time: a who, a what, a where, a how, or a why."

"A why? Who cares why? They're insane."

"A why might signal their intentions for Susanna. My point is that the numbers this time could mean anything, couldn't they?" The rhetorical question lingered between us as he revved the engine to pass a car that had slowed us down.

We pulled into the massive parking lot at the Willowbrook Mall in Wayne, gloomy with the ambient light of a backlit *Macy's* sign on one concrete side of the building and the portable police lighting that turned the area into the set of a horror movie—except that what was so disturbing about the scene was how real it was. A couple of cars were parked near the main door and the lights were on inside the mall. The lot was otherwise empty except for a single white van around which crime scene investigators worked, their cars askew, doors gaping, headlights slashing the mealy darkness. A radio had been left on in one the cars, leaking Bob Dylan's "Tambourine Man" to which a photographer cop sang along while methodically snapping his pictures, each of which came with a single blinding flash of light. Shading our eyes, Mac and I approached the van. The side door, slid open toward the rear, was painted with a large smiling clown face that under the circumstances appeared cruelly taunting.

An older man in white shirtsleeves and blue slacks came forward to greet us. His thinning hair had been neatly combed to one side and he repeatedly squeezed a worn-out blue stress ball. He slipped it into his pocket and extended his right hand.

"Detective Harry Ramirez. You must be Detective MacLeary from Maplewood."

"Mac." They shook his hands. Mac introduced me and asked, "How's it going?"

"So far what you see is what you get. No sign of the girl but we got people in the mall and back in that field there, looking." He pointed to the distance at the right. It was too dark to see the field he meant.

A gloved technician hopped out of the van and said to the photographer, "Yo, Roman—wanna get this before we start bagging?"

"Yeah."

We stood back and watched as Roman, a grizzled man with black hair puffing out beneath a red bandana, photographed the van's interior. Each flash brought another clear view of what was inside: a dirty brown shag rug; three plastic crates of clowning props; a large plastic bag spilling colorful snakes of balloons; a half-used case of water bottles. When I saw a plungered-in hypodermic needle lying on the brown rug my heart drummed frantically. In the next flash I saw the vivid orange wig atop the puddled fabric of the costume the clown had worn to entertain at Susanna's party.

"Did he leave anything else behind?" Mac asked Harry Ramirez. "Anything of the girl's?"

"Haven't found anything yet. Maybe they'll get some trace hits at the lab."

Mac and I looked at each other: We both knew that meant more waiting, and more waiting meant maintaining the assumption that the clown impostor had kidnapped Susanna, and an investigation based on assumptions had vast potential to implode. It wasn't good news.

By three A.M., the interior and exterior of the mall had been searched. By four, a canvass of the surrounding neighborhoods was under way. By four-twenty, the mall's security director had been located and summoned. At a quarter to five, she pulled into the parking lot and got out of her car wearing a purple bathrobe and sneakers. Her identification card and a key ring hung around her neck.

"Who's in charge here?" she shouted. "I got like two minutes to get you into the security station so *come on.*"

Mac and I were standing with Ramirez next to a squad car, the top of which we had turned into a coffee table for our Styrofoam cups.

"Whoa, slow down Miss . . ." Ramirez squinted, trying to read her ID card in the dark. ". . . Diana Spencer . . . like the princess?"

"I am a single mother and I left my kids alone in the middle of the night so come on and hurry this up. I gotta get outta here *now!*"

She got back in her car, sped to the main entrance, jumped out, and left her engine running. Ramirez, Mac, and I followed on foot and met up with her just inside the building. The air-conditioning hadn't switched on for the day, and the trapped air was dank. We passed a string of unlit storefronts to a door that led us downstairs to a basement and into a drab hallway with beige-painted cinder-block walls and a series of plain doors. I knew we had come to her office when we reached a door with a picture of a sparkly pink crown taped in the middle. She opened the door with a key from her collection, flipped on her overhead fluorescents, booted up her computer, typed in her password, and then led us into another room three doors down along the same hall. The lights were already on in the security monitoring room where a bank of eight screens cycled through a variety of interior and exterior mall views.

"There you got everything from yesterday this time on. You got my password. You need anything else from me, you got my number. I'll be back at nine. You need to copy something, I'll do it then, no problem." And she left.

Mac sat in one of two chairs facing the monitors. "Where to begin?"

"I should get back out there." Ramirez pulled the stress ball out of his pocket and tossed it back and forth between both hands. "You mind?"

"Go," Mac said.

We quickly learned that there were seventy-two cameras posted in and around the mall. That times twenty-four hours made one thousand, seven hundred, and twenty-eight hours of footage to review. Split between us, it was eight hundred and sixty-four hours each . . . which would take us thirty-six days total if we didn't sleep. An impossible task. But we had to start somewhere.

Mac pushed the play arrow above a sticker reading *One: East Entrance*. I took on *Two: North Entrance*. We fast-forwarded through the hours until three-thirty yesterday afternoon, about the time both the clown and Susanna were last seen at the house, and reviewed the footage carefully after that.

Outside, the sun rose, but we missed it. The mall stayed closed for business and we missed seeing streams of customers turned away from their errands. Seconds upon seconds, minutes upon minutes, and hours upon hours passed in a blur of grainy images until finally, just before noon, I spotted the van—igniting the hope that hard on the heels of its smooth pull into the parking lot would be a view of the clown and, more importantly, Susanna.

CHAPTER 14

Lizzie Stoppard's white van, with the smiling clown face painted on the side, curved into the parking lot and then drove out of view. Again. And again. Mac and I replayed the nine-second digital clip over and over and over, staring hard at the HD screen in the new tech division of the Maplewood Police Headquarters, where we had come, just past noon, with a DVD copy of the relevant footage we'd gleaned so far from the mall's security system. But all the high-tech equipment in the world would not reveal more than a distant image of a van driving in and out of the camera's range. The rest of the footage was being reviewed, but right now this was all we had. Only nine seconds, time-stamped 4:03 P.M., and no Susanna.

"Man or woman?" Mac leaned in to peer at the fuzzy image of the clown driving the van.

"Can't tell."

"Come on, Karin. *Man or woman.*" His fingertip punched replay harder than necessary and the clip spun through its nine meager seconds. As soon as it finished, he punched the button again and leaned closer to the screen. It was impossible to see exactly who was at the wheel of the van other than a person of undetermined age and gender wearing a floppy orange wig. And when the person removed the wig and the costume, emerged from the van, and went *somewhere*, no camera we currently knew of had followed the transition. The man, or woman, lost himself or herself in the crowd—along with Susanna, presumably—and was gone.

An autopsy of Lizzie Stoppard's body was under way but for now the cause of death was still unknown. A preliminary report revealed no blood, no signs of assault, strangulation, blunt force trauma . . . or anything that indicated a violent attack, other than some fresh bruises and scratches that made it appear she had tried to fend off her attacker. Possibly the empty syringe found on the van's floor had something to do with the murder, but we wouldn't know until the autopsy was finished exactly how and when she had died, or if in fact the needle had been used on her.

Mac sat back and looked at me. His eyes were soupy, bloodshot. Mine couldn't have looked much better.

"The way she was killed," he said, "organized, quick, clean, and careful. Nothing overtly violent. No interest in seeing any blood. No interest in torture. Unlike Price, who needs all that."

I pushed the images out of my mind: the violent snapshots that had lodged themselves in my brain. Planted my attention in this moment, this conversation.

"I say the clown's a woman," he said.

"Maybe. But the costume was left behind in the van. A woman wouldn't do that."

"So then we're looking for that rare bird—a *messy*

woman." Mac crooked a half smile. "I have to tell you, Karin, I'm a little surprised. I didn't think you trafficked in stereotypes. Especially you—you're not exactly a neat freak yourself."

"Leaving behind the costume wasn't messy," I argued, "so much as careless, impulsive, *thoughtless*. I don't know a single woman who doesn't strategize out every aspect of her life. A woman who accomplishes anything, even this, would think through every element."

"Multitasking."

"It's deeper than that. *Strategizing*. Every woman I know, including myself, really thinks things through. I know that *I* wouldn't have left that costume behind. It's kind of a no-brainer. He—she—went out of his way to leave the dominoes, and also left the costume. It was a decision made in advance."

"Granted. Then it shows ambivalence, because obviously we're going to find her—his—DNA traces. Skin, hair, something."

"Martin Price was never ambivalent about anything he did."

"Then she's either ambivalent," Mac said, "or she wants us to find her, because she doesn't want to go through with it—or she's a novice at this. Maybe, after killing Lizzie, she discovered she didn't like it . . . maybe that's why we haven't found Susanna."

What I liked about Mac's theory was the built-in wishful thinking that this killer wasn't as bloodthirsty as JPP had been. *Maybe Susanna was still alive.*

"So let's say, *maybe*, this person is a woman," I said. "If she *is* a partner, she would be connected with the prison system, don't you think? It could explain how JPP managed to escape—twice. And narrowing it down further, she'd be connected with the New Jersey State Prison system."

"Or a woman connected to someone connected to the prison system. Or someone connected to someone connected to someone connected . . ."

"Mac. Stop."

"Sorry—this is just so frustrating. The task force already went through this; they've been calling down the list, and so far every female employee of the state prison has a solid alibi for July fourth. Barbecues. Fireworks. Everyone busy having good old-fashioned fun."

The way he said that: cloaking each word in cynicism. As if plain-old fun had ceased to be a possibility. I couldn't say I disagreed with him, but still, it was painful to hear.

"Mac—"

He shook his head as if to shudder off the pessimism that crept into the skin of every cop sooner or later. "You want to get some coffee? I could use some." He stood up and went for the door. I stood up, too, but before he turned the knob I put a hand on his arm, stopping him.

"I've been thinking about what we discussed earlier and I think we have no choice." The idea of going back to Martin Price with a second request for an interview had been floated between us and put aside. Every theory we tested took precious time, and we had none to waste with a notorious game player. But the scant digital footage and total lack of any sign of Susanna felt like running full-speed into a solid wall. We were nowhere—and it *hurt*. If we could take the temperature of his claim that he had a partner, maybe we could hone in faster on whoever we were looking for.

Mac nodded. "Let's see if he'll budge."

As soon as we stepped out of the tech division into the hall, we were met with the sounds of phones ringing with callers responding to the AMBER Alert. In a situation like this, all hands were on deck to log tips. We passed the conference room where a reinvigorated task force was hard at work. Through the glass wall we could see but not hear them: Alan, rumpled and tired, gesticulating to the FBI liaison in front of a dry erase board where numbers had been charted, while a dozen other men and women worked their computers and phones. Still dozens of others were out working the field.

In the kitchenette down the hall, a new pot of coffee was dripping. We stood there and waited.

"If you talk to JPP," I said, "remember he's playing with you. Don't take his bait. Don't think about me or Jackson or Cece or the Aldermans of any of that. Just ask your questions."

"You really think you have to tell me that? If I let any of that enter my mind, I wouldn't talk—I'd kill the guy bare-handed."

The coffee was so hot it burned my tongue. But it was good: It woke us up. Mac got right to work, putting an urgent request for an interview with Martin Price through the channels. In an hour, we had our answer: The prisoner had reassessed, though he still wouldn't talk with Mac or anyone else on the police force.

He would only talk with me.

* * *

Mac handed me a piece of gum as soon as I came out of the ladies' room. Peppermint. I unwrapped it and put the flat rectangle into my foul-tasting mouth. I had just thrown up for the second time since we left the station house. A prison guard posted outside the bathroom—a skinny woman in a blue uniform and red button earrings—smiled and shook her head when she saw me, indicating that I wasn't the first person she'd seen react this way before stepping into a room with a notorious prisoner. What she didn't know was that I wasn't just any investigator or psychologist or writer looking for information. I was the aunt of the missing girl, and I myself had nearly been one of the Domino Killer's victims; I had come *that close* to being the eighth body in his sequence of murders. The guard couldn't possibly have known that, for me, this was not business as usual, that every minute now was a painful resurrection, or that I came with a heart full of hatred for the man I was about to visit.

"Take it easy in there." Mac placed a hand on my back as he walked me along the shiny linoleum floor toward the first interior guard station separating the public hall from the prisoners. "Here's another in case you throw up again." He slipped a wrapped piece of gum into my jeans' back pocket. "Make the next one a projectile, and aim right for him."

That made me smile. Or at least I thought I smiled. By the look on Mac's face, it might have come off as more of a grimace.

He left me at the guard station, where I removed my shoes, emptied my pockets, handed over my purse, spit out my gum, and walked the rest of the long hall-way alone. Mac would be watching and listening from behind a one-way glass. I had thought that that knowl-edge would be a comfort, but as I approached the in-terview room I found myself trembling uncontrollably.

A large male guard put his hand on the doorknob, hesitated. "You want me in or out?"

"Out. But keep your ears open."

"Will do. You got four guys watching on monitors, so don't worry. We never lost a visitor yet." He smiled broadly with crowded, ghoulish teeth and pushed open the door to let me in.

And there he was: man of my nightmares. Not creep-ing up on me. Not pushing a knife into my ribs or a tongue into my mouth. Not taunting me through a digital distance. Not running from me in scaly Green Goblin skin. But here: right here, in front of me, sitting on a normal chair like a regular person . . . almost. He wore an orange jumpsuit with a number stenciled below his left shoulder. His handcuffed wrists rested in his lap, and from there a chain fell to the floor where his ankles were bound to the base of the chair, which was bolted into the floor.

I stood ten feet in front of him. Just stood there, look-ing at him, with his attention glued to me. I could sense his twisted brain writhing, frustrated by the cold fact that if he tried to get up he would fall flat on his face. I wanted to see that: wanted to watch him come for me and get yanked back by his chains. His skin looked pasty. His thin blond hair was greasy and lay in chunks atop his shiny scalp. He sat very still, appearing to read my mind, and then a grin spread across his face.

He was about to speak when I turned my back to him and walked across the room to the chair that had been set up to face him at a distance. I didn't want him to take control of the conversation; that would be a mistake.

I sat down. Crossed my legs. Crossed my arms. Would have curled into a ball and rolled myself into the corner of the room if I hadn't felt so determined to pry some information out of him. He was stuck here, facing a long, cruel, lifeless life; he wouldn't escape this time because no one was giving him an inch. But that wasn't good enough. I wanted more.

I looked into the milky blue mirrors of his eyes, took a deep breath in, exhaled, and issued my first question.

"Who is your partner?" I asked, without a glimmer that I might not believe he had one.

He looked at me but didn't answer.

"Who killed the clown?"

His frozen face: nothing.

"What do the numbers mean this time?"

His grin curled into a smile.

"*Where is my niece? Who took her?*"

The smile abruptly faded. "Took?" A shudder passed through his face, turning his cheeks briefly gelatinous. Convincing me I had hit a nerve: that his claim of a partnership might well be true.

"That's right. *Took*, not killed—we have evidence she's still alive. Does it disappoint you that your partner doesn't work as fast as you do?"

It was a gamble, peppering him with information I didn't have, trying to provoke answers out of him; a gamble that fell flat in the response of his icy gaze and his silence.

"Of course it disappoints you to hear she's alive," I pressed. "Why would I even ask?"

"Why would you? It's a disappointment you know well."

Rage burned through me and I felt my body inflate with an urge to fly across the room and wrap my hands around his throat as I once had, or thought I had, but failed at, in the convention center . . . when I had almost strangled Mac instead.

"Don't you wish you had that gun back in your hand right now?"

I tamped down the rage, gathered myself, ignored the echoes of my personal history.

"No. I made a conscious choice not to kill you, Martin. I'd rather see you rot in prison the rest of your life. All I want is my niece. *Where is she?*"

He cocked his head and stared at me.

I shifted slightly forward and tried again: "Where is my niece?"

"You wish you did it. I can see it all over you—regret. You reek of it."

I stilled my twitching face. Reminded myself not to let him get to me.

"You lie in bed at night telling yourself you're a coward. Why didn't you have the guts to kill the guy who *did that* to your little girl?"

Cece—oh, Cece, my baby—I saw her now, singing at breakfast, cradled half asleep in my arms—I saw her and smelled her and heard her and wanted her and needed her. Saw her . . . lifeless body on her blood-soaked bed . . . then saw Susanna . . . *saw her.* And fireworks shot through my body. Uncontrollable pinwheels of fury and pain.

A spasm rose from my stomach, sending vomit into my mouth. I swallowed it back down. Closed my eyes. Took a single breath that lasted minutes, hours, years. And then let it out.

The moment my eyes opened, he spoke.

"Come here."

I stared at him. Was he kidding me? Stared and waited for an explanation.

"I have something to tell you."

It was why I was here. So I stood. Shaking. Walked, slowly, until I was in front of him.

"Closer."

I leaned down until I could smell his rancid odor mixed with industrial-strength prison soap.

"You can do it right now. Put your hands around my neck. *Do it. Kill me.* And I'll tell you what you want to know while I'm dying."

Oh—it would be the perfect moment! I would get everything I wanted: his death, my revenge, the name of his partner—and Susanna. And he would also get what he wanted: a final, delectable thrill of violence that would put an end to his helpless boredom.

"*Do it,*" he whispered so close to my ear that I felt the heat of his breath.

Pulling myself in from the center, I gathered all the loose, flaming threads of the past year and braided them together into one tight rope and held on for dear life.

Straightened up.

Stood back.

Turned around.

Crossed the room.

Sat down on my chair.

Faced him.

"Where is she?"

Silence.

"Who is your partner?"

Martin Price's upper lip curled into a sneer. His confident plea of a moment ago turned to syrupy resentment, oozing through his tone, as he said, "*That* is the wrong question."

"The wrong question."

"Don't repeat. It makes you sound stupid."

"What is the right question?"

"'Who am I?' Or better yet, 'Who was I?' Answer that question first." And then he shifted his attention toward the door and shouted, "Guard!"

We arrived in twilight at Mac's place—the furnished bachelor apartment he'd rented after his split with Val—where he put me in the bathtub to clean off the third and final sickness that had overcome me as we drove away from the prison. While I soaked in the tub, he went to his building's basement and put my clothes in the washing machine, then he spent a few minutes in his car with a bottle of spray cleaner and a roll of paper towels. I couldn't stop remembering a poem I'd read in a high school English class by Edith Wharton, with the line, *Every night she comes and puts her thin white lips to my heart and sucks till morning.* It was how I felt: my soul sucked right out of my heart by the lifeless lips of an inhuman creature. Sucked and sucked, all night long; only my night had lasted a year.

I felt empty, spent beyond emptiness, and I hadn't

even gotten anything concrete from the interview. He had managed to taunt me, to touch every raw nerve he could find. He had come close to making me believe he *did* have a partner. But he hadn't answered my questions about Susanna. Twenty-nine hours had passed since her disappearance, and despite everyone's frantic efforts to find her, statistically her chances of survival were quickly dwindling.

When Mac returned, he sat on the toilet seat and we went through it all one more time.

"He gave you something," he said, "when he said we were asking the wrong question."

"He gave me another question."

" 'Who was I?' " Mac mulled aloud. "Meaning . . . before he started the domino murders."

"Or before that. How long before?" I found the lost bar of pine-scented soap with my feet, took it into my hands, and returned it to the soap dish protruding from the white-tiled wall. "Do you have a towel? I'm getting cold."

Mac handed me a towel and averted his eyes as I stepped, dripping, out of the bath. At first I didn't even think about that: being naked in front of my former colleague, my good friend. It was his eyes twitching away that sexualized the moment in a way that hadn't occurred to me before. It made me realize how comfortable I felt around him, how natural, but it also reminded me that he was a man and I was a woman. Then, as quickly as the awkwardness materialized, it slipped away. Mac followed me out of the bathroom and I heard him puttering in the kitchen while I put on his robe.

He met me on the couch—a blue plaid pullout that took up half his living/dining area—with two glasses of red wine. I curled my feet under me to keep them warm and leaned in close so I could see the case file he held open on his lap. All those old papers that had been handled and read and copied countless times, along with some new ones. The problem was that, when the information became too familiar, you stopped reading between the lines. Now, with Susanna missing, the lab and autopsy results not yet in and the only other clues—three numbers and a vague question—feeling like dead ends, we had to relook at everything.

"He's twenty-nine years old," Mac said. "He's been at this for two years that we know of. So we start digging backward from there, from the beginning, looking with new eyes."

I brought the glass to my lips. The wine was a little bitter but I liked it; my brain wasted no time warming to its influences.

"Dropped at the orphanage when he was two," Mac read through a cursory bio the first task force had drawn up for Martin Price, "too young to remember his birth parents, mediocre kid, orphanage fire destroyed early records, yada yada yada."

On the face of it, it looked as if Martin Price had been a lonely, pathetic child just as he was a lonely, pathetic man. After the fire at the orphanage, some cursory notes had been made in his new record when he was eight. He was a middling student and an obedient-enough child. Ten years passed, and on his eighteenth birthday he was released into the world with three outfits and fifty dollars and told to make his own way. Which he did, mostly without event, until he decided to turn other people's lives and deaths into a game he played for . . . what?

Mac set aside the bio and picked up a new printout—Martin Price's rap sheet from before the domino murders began. It was short, listing only one item: an arrest for shoplifting about three months after his release from the orphanage. He had stolen a pair of handcuffs from a porn shop in Trenton, an inauspicious beginning showing that bad things had already been brewing in his mind. No big surprise there.

And then, a few documents down, we came upon an old problem.

"This doesn't sit right," Mac rattled a copy of a driver's license application from the East Orange Motor Vehicle Agency. "How do you apply for a license when you're sitting in jail for shoplifting?"

I could hardly read my old scribble on the page, but I remembered the discrepancy. "Bureaucratic incompetence, basically. Someone typed in the wrong date."

"You still buy that?"

"Motor Vehicles? Totally. And we visited the address listed on the application and the guy—"

"—Paul Maher—" Mac read from another sheet of notes.

"—told us he never heard of any Martin Price living there, and he'd been there ten years."

"Yeah, I remember him. Shifty eyes, remember?" Mac parodied Mr. Maher's metronome eyes, how they refused to make eye contact with us back then. It was strange. But people could be strange. We didn't make much of it at the time.

"I remember."

"And he couldn't recall the name of the people he bought the house from." Mac consulted his old notes again: *"Bought house seven years ago. Lived there three years prior to purchase, as a renter. Does not recall name of seller. Recalls only that seller was around fifty years of age.* A seller who was his landlord for three years, then sold him the house, and he doesn't remember his name? Weird."

"Ann and Arnold Selby," I said. "That's who sold me and Jackson our house. We only met them twice, at the inspection and at the closing."

"Terry Silverman sold me and Val our house sixteen years ago."

"It *is* strange." I remembered Paul Maher, his reluctance to talk to us, but the rationale for his poor memory eluded me now. "How did he explain it away?"

"Something lame. But that neighborhood ten years ago? It was junkie city; another house on that street was busted wide open. Dealers. Got shut down, and slowly the street came back to life. If Maher was living in his house ten years ago, which he was, then he was either stupid or broke or he was using."

"Maher bought the house he was living in," I said. "Maybe he cleaned up with the neighborhood."

"That's what I'm thinking." Mac leaned forward, picked up his wine, sipped. "He acted spooked when we talked to him two years ago. Remember that?"

"I do."

"Let's go back."

"And if he tells us it *was* Martin Price who sold him the house? And we find out that's the person who applied at Motor Vehicles? It must be a common name."

Mac set his glass down on the coffee table, leaned forward, and looked at me. "I know. But a fifty-year-old homeowner living in the suburbs who doesn't drive? It says right here"—he pointed to the license application—"*first-time applicant*. When you think about it, Karin, it doesn't make any sense."

"You're right; it doesn't."

"Get dressed. I'll meet you out front in the car."

CHAPTER 15

Paul Maher opened the door and stood there, staring at us. He looked much the same as two years ago when we first appeared, unwelcomed, in his life: short and stocky, with pale skin, thick jet-black hair, and close-set green eyes. A dusting of gray at his temples now. He stood under the porch light of his freshly painted white clapboard house, wearing expensive-looking jeans and a bright-white polo shirt, and didn't greet us. Instead he called behind him: "Honey! I'm taking out the garbage!" He shut the door and ushered us down the steps.

He led us off the front walk—neatly laid slate edged with a brushcut of thick grass—and around the side of the house. Past three garbage cans—a black one, a blue one, and a green one, each labeled for recycling or not—and into a backyard with a swing set that in the dark shimmered a silvery purple. A pink tricycle sat beside a small tassel-handled bike with training wheels. It looked like he had a couple of young daughters. I swallowed back an emotional burp of envy, resentment, joy, grief . . . suspicion. This was a man who knew something about little girls—and was nervous.

We followed him into a backyard gazebo that was so new it was still off-gassing a Christmassy smell of fresh wood. He gestured for me to sit on one of the five built-in benches. Mac sat beside me. Paul Maher remained standing and furtively glanced behind himself at the house, where a light in one window snapped off—child number one had just been put to bed, child number two still to go, with limited time before his wife came looking for him. It was late to be putting kids to bed, an indication that they were *very* young, still taking long afternoon naps.

"Okay, I'm gonna make this fast. That girl who's missing? I have no idea where she is, but I can tell you *this* for whatever it's worth in finding her: My real name isn't Paul Maher, it's Marty Prizinsky."

My heart leaped when he said all that, and we hadn't even asked. I glanced at Mac. He'd held on to his poker face; I pulled mine back down.

"I've read the papers all along, and I'm *sorry*. I had no idea. It freaked me out when you showed up last time, I admit it. I'll talk to you now, but *please*, we have to make this fast."

"Okay," Mac said, "maybe you should just tell us everything you don't want your wife to know."

Paul Maher nodded quickly, as if that was the plan, sat down across from us, and spoke in a tense whisper. "Two years ago you wanted the name of my landlord—Fernando Garza. He owned a few houses on this street and sold them off after the dealer was gone."

"Your dealer?" Mac asked.

"Everyone's. Most freaked and left after the bust. Some hung on awhile. I'm the only one still here. I kicked, cleaned up, got a job, bought the house. Now I've got my own business—I'm a Web site developer, I just opened my first out-of-the-house office and grew my staff"—he paused to read our reactions to his success; I smiled, Mac nodded, and Paul restarted what seemed half rant, half confession—"and now I'm married to Carly and we have two beautiful children."

"Girls." I smiled again.

"Yes." He looked at me with a flash of warmth and inched closer.

"I can't let *anything* ruin this."

"Okay," Mac said. "Anything . . . like what?"

The second bedroom window darkened. Paul Maher's eyes flicked to the house, then back to us.

"Look. Ten years ago I was a total loser, I mean in every way. That's out on the table, okay? So when a lady found me and offered me ten grand for my identity, offered me a new one, I thought, *What the hell*, you know?"

"A lady *found* you?" I asked.

"What lady?" Mac.

"Found you *how*?"

"The county needle giveaway. They used to knock on our doors, hand out new hypodermics. We thought they were nuts, but hey—some of us didn't actually want to die, not consciously, anyway."

Yesterday: the spent syringe lying on the floor of the clown's van. My pulse was hammering now. He knew something.

"Who was she?" Mac leaned forward now, the whites of his eyes shimmering in a shaft of light from the back of the house, where a downstairs lamp had flicked on.

"Don't know. White lady. We didn't ask each other any questions, just made the transaction. Cash. At the time I didn't much care why she wanted the name—it wasn't my real name, anyway, like I said before. I was Marty Prizinsky at birth, then when my birth parents stuck me in the orphanage when I was two, I guess the director didn't like my name. Too *ethnic*, probably." His eyes shifted back and forth; his avoidance strategy, apparently, when something upset him. "Changed it to Martin Price, legally. I only found that out when I was eighteen, when I *graduated* . . . that's what they told me: I was *graduating* into adulthood, bam, just like that. So. When I heard that name, Marty Prizinsky, fall off the lips of the head matron for the first time, it hit me why Martin Price never really felt like *me*. I went looking for my birth parents and found out my mother died in childbirth and my father died a drunk a few years after I was dumped. You know what? When the offer came up to sell that orphanage name, I jumped on it. I was happy to cut away from my so-called childhood, and I needed the cash. Slipped right into Paul Maher—some old guy who died; she handed me his ID when I sold her mine. Only screwed up that one time, at Motor Vehicles. Last time you came, you told me that was how you found me. I got scared. I knew you wanted to find out who Martin Price was, if he used to own this house, if I could help you locate him." Paul Maher shook his head, looking down into cupped hands as if gazing into a mirrored pool. Trying to find himself, still, after all those transformations.

"You knew that." Mac held his unruffled tone.

"When I read about those murders—" He stopped

talking, shook his head. "I was shocked. I realized that lady was up to some bad business when she bought my name and social . . . but believe me, you wouldn't have guessed that, meeting her."

Two years ago. *Two years ago* he realized the connection between the sale of his identity and the Domino Killer. *Two years* and he sat on it. Had he come forward then, we would have had a full year to find *the lady*— we would have known to look for a lady, it would have introduced the idea that JPP had a partner, an idea that now seemed more plausible than ever—and maybe we would have stopped them before he, or they, murdered Jackson and Cece. Before Susanna vanished.

I stood abruptly, seeking darkness, any shadow, where I could hide the tears that had sprung to my eyes. I left the two men in the gazebo, stood by myself off to the side on the plush grass, buckled over, and silently wept.

Their voices floated across the yard:

"I told myself, if you guys ever came back, I'd talk to you this time," Paul Maher said. "When I heard the news yesterday about the murder and the kidnapping, I figured you'd come back. And here you are. I'm ready. How can I help?"

Any remaining self-control abandoned me. A moan of despair issued from my throat with the stubborn rage of an unexorcisable demon, a disturbing sound that stilled their conversation a moment.

Then, "She's the one whose family . . . ?" I heard Paul Maher say. "Wow. I'm really sorry."

Mac said something, I couldn't hear what, and there was a shuffling of feet in the gazebo just as the back door of the house swung open: a slanted rectangle of light in which stood the silhouette of a woman. Behind her, a six-burner red-enamel stove.

"Paul? Are you out there with someone?"

"No." He darted out of the gazebo, across the lawn, toward his wife. I watched him kiss her cheek and pull the door shut behind him.

Mac waited in the gazebo until the kitchen light turned off, darkening the back of the house. I met him at the foot of the gazebo steps.

"Sorry," I whispered.

"You're not the one who should be sorry."

He held me against his side as we walked across the lawn, past the color-coded garbage cans, straight down the driveway and back to the car. Only after he started the engine and drove us off the gentrified street—where Paul Maher had remade himself, at any cost—did Mac fill me in on the rest of their conversation.

"Guy's a jerk," he said. "Junkies always are, clean or dirty."

I nodded. Couldn't speak—not yet. Watched the passing houses' new affluence drain away the farther from them we got.

"He promised to come into the station in an hour, look at some photo arrays of women who fit the general description of *the lady*." Mac smirked. "As long as . . ." He shook his head without finishing.

"As long as *what*? Did he *bargain* with you?"

Mac nodded. Waited for a green light, then turned onto Bloomfield Avenue and began the journey past the series of car dealerships that led out of East Orange. Finally he spoke: "He'll help us as long as we don't narc him out to his wife. He likes being Paul Maher. Wants to keep it that way."

I fixed my attention back on the outside world—a vast world in which Susanna, somewhere, in unknown condition, was waiting to be found. We turned onto Valley Road and drove past a succession of restaurants and strip malls. Massive, mostly empty, late night parking lots. Shopping carts stacked in gleaming rows, ready for tomorrow's shoppers. The odd cart abandoned haplessly on an endless asphalt checkerboard. A patch of trees, then another strip mall and more of the same.

"If only . . ." I started, but didn't finish. Looked at Mac, whose profile was arrowlike in its steady gaze forward.

"That's right, Karin. Don't go there."

Silently we exited and drove through the tranquil residential streets of Montclair until we reached my parents' house. My mother's car was parked at the curb, which surprised me, as I had assumed they would still be over at Jon's.

"I'm heading back to the station," Mac said, "but I think you should get some sleep if you can." He glanced at the stately yellow house, then back at me. "I'm assuming this is where you want to be."

For a moment, I was flustered. There was nowhere I wanted to be, exactly. The encounters with Martin Price and Paul Maher had finished ripping off an emotional scabbing, a healing, that lately had steadied me but yesterday had been torn loose. Now, again, I was back to craving something I couldn't have: my family back. I yearned to reverse time, to travel to the other side and find them. Where my body parked for the night didn't matter.

"I could go in and give Jon a call," I said, "tell him we might have a lead."

"Not a good idea."

"If they have some hope, it'll help them."

"Not if it's false hope."

At that, my face spontaneously twisted into a knot, another failed effort at stopping tears.

Mac reached tentatively, as if to touch my face, but pulled his hand back and gripped the steering wheel. "It's been a tough couple of days for everyone—but for *you*, Karin . . . Listen, I think you should give yourself some space. It's not good for you to be right in the soup while it's cooking, you know? Let us find her."

"What am I supposed to do right now? Sit back and twiddle my thumbs while she's out there? I *have* to help look for her. What exactly are my choices?"

A car passed, illuminating an intensity in his eyes, something that went beyond Susanna's disappearance, before dragging a shadow across his face.

"Karin . . ." He was about to say something, stopped himself, started again. "I don't know what your choices are right now. But I shouldn't have picked you up last night and taken you with me—it was a mistake. A *personal* mistake." His hand loosened around the steering wheel and slid down to his lap. As his fingers balled into a fist, I felt his loneliness—for me. Felt him hold on to it, own it, so I wouldn't feel its pressure. And saw, at that moment, that he would never attempt to breach my solitude for fear of going too far and losing me completely. Mac's desire to help me in every possible way, to stop the relentless crimes against my family, had never been a secret; now I understood that he also yearned to calm my inner turmoil . . . perhaps, even, to love me. But he couldn't bring himself to try. As for me, the thought of love was like the blur of a spinning top: something that dazzled until you tried to grasp it and then it was gone.

"Mac . . ." I began, but couldn't parse anything of what was running through me into simple words.

He looked through the driver's window, away from me, onto the dark street. "Go inside. Get some sleep. *Please*."

I muttered good night and got out of the car, aware of him watching me walk up the path to the house, making sure I got in safely, despite the police van posted outside. I heard his car drive off only after I'd closed the door.

The house was eerily quiet. Upstairs, I listened at my parents' bedroom door and heard my father's familiar gruff breathing. It was comforting to think of them there, safe and sound in their bed, sleeping; though chances were my mother was wide awake. I stood there for a minute, listening to the silence of her wakefulness, before I heard movement in their room and the door opened.

"Did I wake you?" I whispered.

She shook her head and stepped into the hall, closing the door behind her. "I had to bring your father home; the stress over there . . . he was very confused."

"What's happening at Jon's?"

Her eyes teared, but she refused to cry. "Everyone's searching—hundreds of people, Karin. It's incredible the love that's pouring out of all those strangers. Andrea's keeping to the house, she's in bad shape, but Jon's turning all that rage into action because . . ." Her words trailed off as she pulled me into an unyielding embrace.

How could I tell them? My parents? Jon and Andrea? How could I tell them how blind we had been? That JPP had a partner—*all along, there had been two of them.*

CHAPTER 16

"We have an update now on the search for Susanna Castle, the little girl who went missing from her birthday party two days ago," said the host of *Good Morning America.*

A police sketch of a woman's face filled the small television screen on the kitchen counter—and the sizzling of the eggs, the fact that they were ready to be served, that the coffee smelled good, that my mother was halfway to the table balancing three bowls of cubed cantaloupe, all that evaporated. I stared at the face on the screen and knew I was looking at *the lady.* Straight, shoulder-length brown-and-gray hair, wide eyes, prominent cheekbones, narrow jaw, thin unsmiling lips. I recognized the work of Narciso Jones, the Maplewood Police Department's staff artist, and the crooked flourish he always added to the outside of eyes to indicate middle-age. My stomach cramped. Lungs froze. Time whooshed out of the kitchen, out of my parents' house, out of the past two years, and suddenly I was standing in front of a woman who could be the other half of JPP.

My mother abruptly turned to see the TV and one of the bowls slid out of her hand, sending pieces of cantaloupe and shattered porcelain across the floor.

"This woman is being sought for questioning by New Jersey detectives," the host said. "Now, they stress that she's a person of interest, not a suspect. They'd just like to speak with her."

"So folks out there," a cohost chimed in, "take a close look, and if you know this woman or can help the police locate her, call the number at the bottom of the screen. Or call us here and we'll give you the number. ABC will be broadcasting this sketch throughout the day along with the other networks, I believe."

The sketch was replaced by two phone numbers—one for the Maplewood Police and the other for the television studio—that hovered in place for what seemed an eternity as the cohost kept talking.

"You know, it's been really incredible the way people have shown up for this family."

Jon's front lawn appeared: people gathered around a white tent under which a table was organized with piles of photocopied information. Two women stood near the table with clipboards, doling out assignments. A third woman in a pink visor handed out water bottles. The shot then switched to the parking lot at the Willowbrook Mall in Wayne, where a similar scene played out.

"There are now *two* search stations where all kinds of people are coming of their own free will to spend daylight hours searching for little Susanna."

A close-up of Susanna's smiling pigtailed face filled the screen, followed closely by a photo of Cece . . . and my heart did a somersault.

"No one wants a repeat of what this family has already gone through."

"Which is *more* than understandable."

A new angle of the two hosts facing each other instantly changed the mood, as one turned and smiled and the other introduced a new subject.

I got down on my knees and began picking up white shards of the broken bowl and dirt-flecked pieces of cantaloupe, placing them together in the palm of one hand.

"The eggs," my mother said.

Only then did I become aware of the burning smell. I looked up at the stove and saw dark smoke billowing out of the pan as my mother hurried over and turned off the gas. I jumped up and used my free hand to wave smoke toward an open window by the sink. While I was there, I emptied my hand of glass and fruit into the under-sink garbage.

"*Karin*," my mother said, "*you're bleeding.*"

I was barefoot, and smears of blood traced my steps from the stove to the sink. The sole of my right foot was cut; I saw that now. I sat down at the table beside my father—whose eyes darted between us, trying to understand what was going on—and reached for a napkin to stanch the bleeding.

Once the smoke was mostly dissipated, and my mother had swept the floor, she brought some first-aid supplies to the table and attended to my foot. She pulled a half-inch sliver of porcelain out of my flesh and cleaned the wound. We both agreed it wasn't deep enough for stitches, so she disinfected it and bandaged it up. Then she looked at me and asked, "What was that picture on the TV? Did you know?"

"Not about the police sketch." I had not yet had a chance to tell my mother about the events of yesterday.

"They might have warned us." Mom sat at the table looking mystified.

"I'm hungry," Dad said.

"It isn't right to turn on the TV and have to be surprised like that."

"Where are the eggs?"

"I'll make some more." Mom got up and set to work reinventing our ruined breakfast.

I sat there with my father, thinking that she was right. They should have warned us. Mac, specifically, should have. I went to the kitchen phone and called his cell, got his voice mail, and left a message. I stewed through breakfast and a shower, growing more upset. What, exactly, was going on? Had they made real headway, or was the sketch a shot in the dark? Obviously Paul Maher's visit to the task force had not yielded *the lady*'s identity . . . but had anything else come of it? Mac's determination to give me "space" began to feel like a punishment. I tried him again, left another message . . . and then it occurred to me that my cell phone had been turned off, charging, since the night before. I powered it up and immediately saw that there was a message from him, left early that morning.

"I didn't want to wake your parents so I'm calling your cell. I got your messages but it's been crazy around here . . . you know how it is, Karin. Maher couldn't ID anyone so we're going to run a sketch in the media this morning. Just a heads-up. Talk to you later. Sit tight."

All my anger drained away. I *did* know how it was. But Mac always had his phone with him and he had

never ignored my calls before. That, in itself, made me
uneasy; I couldn't lose him, especially now.

I dialed him, left another message, and slipped my
cell phone into my jeans pocket, on vibrate, so I would
feel it ring. Then I gathered my parents into the car
and drove over to Jon's house to join the search. Did
I believe we would find Susanna somewhere near her
home, when the clown's van had been discovered in
Wayne? Only if she was still alive. Practical sense told
me that, if she wasn't, she would be found closer to the
mall . . . and therefore I didn't want to be anywhere
near there.

Half a mile away, we began to see wandering people
with photocopies of Susanna's picture and to hear the
urgent chanting of her name. They had come prepared
with broad-brimmed hats, their skin gleamed with
sunblock, and many carried water bottles as if they
expected to be out a long time. When we pulled up to
the house we saw coolers dotting the lawn like licks
of salt in primary colors. Beginning its third day, the
search had taken on an air of workaday preparedness
and lost the edge of hysteria that had charged us all
on day one.

My mother led my father into the house, where he
could sit with Andrea, and then met me under the tent.
She greeted the pink-visored woman, then joined the
other two at the table. Immediately she launched into
grandmotherly conversations about Susanna, doling
out equal measures of information to help searchers identify our little girl and loving reminiscences to
help her feel close and hopeful. I understood that this
was how she was coping with the vast unknown of her

granddaughter's fate and avoiding dark memories of Cece's. The tent ladies seemed unsure how to handle me, the nexus of yet another tragedy, and vacillated between treating me with the reverence of a celebrity and as the harbinger of plague. I had to get out of there. And so, despite my injured foot, I took a photocopied map with a local route highlighted in blue and struck out on my own.

My path through the wooded area that edged Jon's backyard led to a tennis court and eventually a soccer field. From there I walked beside the train track about a quarter mile to the narrow end of Waterlands Park, stopping frequently to carefully scan the surroundings. Plenty of other searchers had also taken the blue route and so I wasn't alone, yet the sense that somehow we were all missing the telling detail gnawed at me. The sound of strangers calling Susanna's name began to blend like birdcall. All along the way, *Missing* signs with her picture and personal details had been posted on trees.

After tracing the edge of the park, where a Little League game enlivened one of the three diamonds with heartrending normality, I reentered the woods, calling, "SusieQ!" again and again and again.

"Karin!"

I turned and there was Jon: map-less and water-less and pale as a ghost, with eyes set deep in volcanoes of dark sleeplessness.

"You look *terrible*," I blurted.

In less than a moment, he flew into my arms and dropped what felt like all his weight against me. I staggered backward, steadied myself, and held him.

"*I miss her,*" he whispered. "*I can't take this.*"

Silently I rubbed his back, and listened.

"Not knowing where she is, it's unbearable. But *knowing* . . . if the worst happens. . . . that would be worse, wouldn't it?" He pulled a few inches away and looked right into my eyes, his burning with dread and a new, unspeakable comprehension. Tears spilled down his face. I lifted my flattened palms, uselessly, to try and wipe them away.

"You'll never find that out," I said, "because everyone is looking for her right now *and we are going to find her and she is going to be okay.*"

He sucked in a breath and nodded like a child determined to accept the implausible.

"Mom told us what you've been doing, Karin . . . that you went to the prison and talked to him. It must have been so hard for you."

"It doesn't matter if it's hard for me. If I hadn't become a cop in the first place then none of this would have happened and now you wouldn't be—"

"*No.* You became a cop to do something worthwhile, so you could help people—it's more than I can say for myself—and the price you've had to pay for that . . ."

His words dissolved in tears, and I held him again.

"I'm so sorry for the things I said to you the other day," he said. "So is Andrea. We know this isn't your fault."

"Thank you. But it is."

After a few minutes, arm in arm, we found our way back to the house.

By evening, there was still no sign of Susanna—anywhere.

As darkness fell, the searchers packed up their things and headed home, vowing to return tomorrow.

Jon retreated into his house to continue the vigil with Andrea and David.

My parents and I drove back to Montclair, where we ate a small meal in the kitchen and withdrew to our rooms.

I collapsed on my bed in a stupor of exhaustion and tried calling Mac one more time. In all the hours of another long day, despite three more messages from me pleading for a response, he still hadn't called back. It was intensely frustrating not knowing what was happening with the investigation aside from what was reported by the media, which experience told me would be just the tip of the iceberg. Mac's number rang five times before routing me to his voice mail. This time, I didn't leave a message. I knew that broadcasting a police sketch always incited a reaction from the public and sometimes even an identification. I knew he would be busy. There would be the inevitable hundreds of calls from a spectrum of people who thought they knew *the lady*, did know her, or just craved attention. But by now I had convinced myself that his silence was about more than the case; our parting conversation in the car last night had been fraught with so much else. As the day had moved forward into night, and my mind had spiraled through excesses of blank-minded doing-ness into oceans of wishful thinking into valleys of memory into tunnels of blind rage, every now and then my thoughts would land on Mac and I would feel a muddle of paralysis and yearning.

I put my phone on the bedside table and lay there

in the quiet, my brain buzzing, certain I would never sleep.

It was a feeling at first, a visceral memory: the smooth, dry, dense hills and valleys of muscle and skin. And then the landscape of his body, the parts and pieces that were abstract form, gathered into something, someone, familiar and finally recognizable. The sensation of Jackson's skin beneath my hands, the long muscles that ran the length of his back, and the awareness that I could both touch him and that my touch passed through him as if we had fused. Only a dream could accomplish this: bring someone back to you so completely, without doubt.

I lay asleep-awake in my childhood bed and my husband rolled onto me, into me, and I ran my hands down the length of him. Feeling him. Absorbing him. Loving him. Having him back.

"Shh," I whispered, my lips touching, feeling, tasting, kissing the soft outer curve of his ear. "Don't wake Cece."

Having her back, too.

Jackson didn't speak. Maybe ghosts couldn't. But he was as real as he had ever been. And our lovemaking was as true and familiar, sending waves of pleasure and adoration throughout my body, fireworks ricocheting throughout my brain. And then it got better, deeper, headier, and I could feel the prick of conception as our DNA fused and our second child was created, honoring a promise we had made to each other before, before, before, before . . .

Now I was standing alone in a field of wheat, hot,

sweating, baking in the sun. And there was Jackson, dressed in the jeans and T-shirt he was wearing the last time . . . the last time . . . there he was standing on a hill in the distance, banging a gong over and over again. Releasing waves of echoing sound. Deafening sound. Confusing me.

Ringing. Someone was calling. Jackson was calling me on the phone. That was it.

I opened my eyes. A beam of car light swayed across the ceiling, rearranged my bedroom's shadows, then faded away. And it was dark again. And quiet. And I was so disoriented, dreaming about Jackson when obviously he wasn't home yet.

Something was flashing on my bedside table: the LED of my cell phone, announcing a call. I rolled over, grabbed the phone, flipped it open, pressed it to my ear.

"Where are you?"

"I'm sorry I didn't call sooner. Did I wake you?"

"I was just dreaming about you. Come home, okay?"

"Karin?"

And then I really saw where I was, and who I was, and when this was. A wave of grief was followed quickly by a wave of shame. Nausea. Then— emptiness, surrender.

"Mac? Did you find her?"

"No." Silence. "Karin, listen—"

Before he could say more, I was crying, helplessly burping up more of the same into the ear of the most patient man on earth. I wanted to hang up, to spare him; but at the same time, as my consciousness sharpened, I became aware that it could be a long time before I got him on the phone again.

"What time is it?" I asked.

"Almost eleven. I'm sorry; I didn't think it would be too late to call."

"It's okay. I've wanted to talk to you all day."

After a moment, he said, "If you want, I'll come over."

"Yes."

I got up, stripped off my nightgown, put on jeans and a T-shirt, and sat on my bed, waiting for Mac to arrive. Waiting. Alone. In a house that was as quiet as quiet could be. My parents in their room down the hall. Why did I feel alone in this house when I wasn't alone?

But I knew why. The intensity of the dream, the replay of my longing for Jackson, had informed me of something definite upon waking: He was dead. It was permanent. I could spend the rest of my life longing for him, for Cece, or . . .

Fifteen minutes later, Mac called again. "I'm outside."

I walked to my bedroom window and moved the curtain aside. There he was, on the front path, hands in pockets, waiting for me.

I brought my purse, locked the front door behind me, and met him on the path. Before he could say anything, before I could say anything, we leaned together and put our arms around each other. Our foreheads touched and we stood there, looking into each other's eyes.

"I know this isn't the time," he whispered, "but I love you. Is that okay?"

I nodded. It was more than okay.

His arm was warm around my back as we walked down the path to his car. The cop in the surveillance

van pretended not to see us. We were quiet all the way
to Mac's place, as if talking would violate our fragile decision to ride out the wait together. Quiet, as we
walked through the parking lot of his building. Quiet,
as we rode the elevator to his floor. Quiet, as we entered
his apartment. Quiet, as we turned to each other and
piece by piece by piece removed each other's arma-
ment of clothing, resistance, and doubt.

"What did you do to your foot?"

We lay beside each other, naked, on Mac's bed. The
air conditioner buzzed a chill into the room but we were
still hot, both of us filmed with sweat. I lifted my right
foot and saw that the bandage had shifted from walking on it all day. The cut was now partially exposed and
looked raw. Dirt had somehow found its way into my
sock and edged the disarranged bandage.

"Walked on glass. What else?"

He grinned, waited for a real answer. His eyes were
sleepy, sexy; I rolled over to snuggle against his side
and told him about the breakfast fiasco that morning.

"Let's get that cleaned up." He walked across his
bedroom to the adjoining bathroom and flicked on the
light. And there he was: It was real. *He* was real, alive,
and we had made love and nothing had changed, only
deepened. Mac, naked, was beautiful. I watched the
muscles in his back shift as he opened the mirrored
door to his medicine cabinet and brought out a box
of bandages, a bottle of alcohol, a small jar of cotton
balls, and a tube of antibiotic ointment. Without clothes
he was leaner than I would have guessed, and he moved
with grace. I watched him, feeling a new, visceral con-

nection between our bodies that sent sprays of exhilaration through me. He had washed away the sorrow of my dream; the dream that had provided me with a bridge to *here* I never would have crossed without that jolt of awakening. His call—it had penetrated my semiconsciousness with precision.

He pulled on his boxer shorts, sat cross-legged on the bed beside me, and reached over to turn on the bedside lamp. The darkish bedroom glowed with vague light, but enough for me to see something I hadn't noticed before: a small, purplish tattoo of a flower just below his left collarbone. I touched it.

"What's that?"

"A dahlia. I got it when I was eighteen—youthful folly. I haven't gotten around to having it removed."

"Don't. It's sweet."

"Give me your foot."

I shifted to half sitting against two pillows and raised my injured foot into his lap. "Carefully, please."

"This looks nastier in the light."

"Doesn't everything?"

"You don't."

"Neither do you."

His eyes flashed at me, he returned my smile, and in one quick stroke he ripped off the dirty bandage. It happened too fast to scream or even to feel stunned for very long. I closed my eyes and winced as he dabbed the cut with an alcohol-soaked cotton ball. It stung more than it had that morning. He waited a minute, gently fanning my skin with his hand until it was dry enough for a clean bandage to adhere.

"You okay with this?" he asked.

I nodded.

"No, I mean with *this*." Us. Sex. More than sex.

I nodded again.

"Don't seem so enthusiastic."

"Mac—"

"I'm *kidding*." He slid under the sheet, against me. "My effort at some levity. It's been a helluva day."

"Tell me about it. I mean, really *tell* me." I pulled myself up to sitting, holding the sheet against my breasts.

"You don't give up, do you." Not a question, because he knew me.

"Come on, Mac. It's not like I can just put Susanna out of my mind."

"I know you can't," he said. "Neither can I."

He twisted at the waist, kissed me, hopped out of bed, and returned a moment later with a thick file folder. *The* file folder, battered and stained with use and time. He stretched his legs out long beside me, opened the folder, and took out a page I had never seen before. Handed it to me. It was a printout of a microfiched newspaper article, eighteen years old.

"Take a look."

The piece was called "Whizzards Unite" and described a Montclair woman named Nancy Maxtor, an afterschool tutor who had gathered her most promising math students into a program called Games for Whizzards. Using games as a method for accelerating math skills, Ms. Maxtor was credited with increasing test scores at a local middle school, a development that had won the school a state achievement prize. Parents were happy, teachers were happy, and the kids were all having fun. A grainy photograph with the article showed a woman of about forty—white, with shoulder-length brown hair, wearing oval glasses—posed with a dozen or so smiling children.

"Nancy Maxtor." I tasted the name. "So this is her?"

"We took a lot of calls yesterday, and nine people pointed us in her direction. One of them was her grown daughter, Christa, who said her mother's been in Myanmar doing missionary work for months."

I reread the biographical part of the article. "It says she did all kinds of community work, tutoring, soup kitchen, homeless outreach, the needle handout program." I looked up from the article. "Mac, she doesn't sound like someone who shops for false identities."

"No, she doesn't. But on the other hand, she's who Maher described."

She was, to the T. I looked closer at the picture: She appeared more innocuous than the first time I'd seen her, in that her photograph lacked the menacing associations of a police sketch. Here, she appeared to be the kind of selfless community activist you had to admire. She wore simple clothing, no makeup, a plain gold crucifix on a chain around her neck.

"Widowed young," Mac read from a page of handwritten notes, "religious, traveled sometimes doing missionary work."

"Do you believe the daughter—Christa?"

"That her mother's away and couldn't have dropped in on Susanna's party? Maybe. Maybe not. We've been trying to reach Christa again but so far no luck."

He inched closer to me and touched the newspaper photo with his fingertip. "Karin, look closer at this."

A collection of young faces surrounded Nancy Maxtor: mostly white children, two Asian, one black, all between the ages of nine and twelve. All smiling, looking genuinely pleased . . . except for one boy whose smile, upon closer examination, looked forced . . . and then, upon even closer examination, the boy came into startling, familiar focus.

"It's *him*." My pulse jerked into overdrive as I recognized Martin Price . . . or the boy he was back then.

"Now read the caption."

I scanned the names of the children, skipping over and over the tiny print. Martin Price wasn't listed. But why would he be? We had learned, after all, that that was not his real name. Using the caption as a guide, I counted four faces in to the right, second row.

"Neil Tanner," I read aloud.

"Neil Tanner," Mac echoed.

Neil Tanner. Here was the true name of my nemesis. This young boy who looked so innocent as a child. Neil Tanner. Who grew up to become Martin Price—JPP. Who had a partner, who now had a name, and who now had a face . . . and who might also have Susanna.

"What I'm thinking now—" Mac began, when the phone rang with a call from Alan summoning him . . . *us* . . . to the station house for a briefing that couldn't wait until morning.

CHAPTER 17

It was an astounding image: the mug shot of a child. And not just any child. Neil Tanner a.k.a. Martin Price looked about twelve years old in the color photo in which his head tilted slightly forward and his eyes focused down as if he had just spotted a fun toy waiting for him on the floor. He was almost smiling, but not quite. He did not look upset to be in custody so much as amused. A chill ran up my spine, looking at that picture.

"So he wasn't an average kid, after all." I lifted my cup from the corner of Alan's desk and sipped from the hot coffee he'd had waiting for us when we arrived. He had temporarily abandoned the chaos of the task force conference room for the respite of his own workspace in the detectives unit as he had already talked the others through this, and they had taken what they could and run with it. You could feel in the atmosphere that morale had lifted with new avenues now open in the hunt for Susanna.

"How come I'm not surprised?" Mac said.

I leaned closer. Peered at that face. Even in a mug

shot, he had an uncanny look of innocence. But he wasn't innocent; I knew that. This was JPP. And I was looking at a booking photo he had earned when he was very young.

"Seventeen years ago," Alan said, "when the kid was twelve, he slaughtered both his parents."

I stared at Alan: his pebbled, unshaven face, short dark hair, bluish bags under his eyes. "What do you mean—slaughtered?"

"Stabbed them collectively forty-five times. Dad took thirty-two hits, Mom only took thirteen but he struck her heart."

"*Only*." I imagined a woman I didn't know and couldn't visualize, instantly sensing her through the shared membrane of every mother's unconditional love for their children. Guessing that she had absolved him of his cruelty even as he killed her.

"Set the house on fire and ran," Alan said.

"They lived where?" Mac asked.

"Glen Ridge. Social services records show Neil was a battered child. His abuser? Dear old Dad. But he was never removed from the home. I guess one day he went bazookers."

"So he butchered the folks, lit the house on fire," Mac said, "and then he turned himself in, tormented by guilt?"

But we all knew that wasn't what happened. JPP didn't suffer any guilt, and he didn't give himself up.

"Got caught sleeping in a garage someone left open in Hackettstown. Walked some miles to get there. The booking report notes he was proud of himself for that."

"That's our guy," Mac said.

"And get this: In seventh grade he got suspended for cursing at an English teacher who made him rewrite a lousy paper."

"So?" Mac looked as bemused as I was by what had seemed an irrelevant remark.

"Mr. Alderman. As in Gary Alderman. As in victim number one."

Images of the Alderman family's final moments flashed through my mind. To think that a preadolescent grudge had blossomed into such rage . . . but psychopaths were famous for latching on to any shaky rationalization for the destruction they reaped. The domino murders had nothing to do with a seventh-grade revision.

Alan scrolled down screens until he got to a scan of a bad photocopy. "Neil slipped into the new name, Martin Price, just about when he was released from juvie at eighteen, which checks out with Maher's story. See here?" His fingertip landed on the top half of the screen on the line where Tanner had signed himself out of kid prison. "Signed it Neil Tanner. And"—he minimized the document and opened a new one, also a scan of an old form—"here we have a chit showing one Martin Price, also age eighteen, signing himself out of an orphanage. Kid never even entered the foster care system; lived years in one of the last orphanages in the area before they all got shut down. Hardly anyone likes adopting older kids."

I thought of Paul Maher, who had been sheltered and fed and renamed but not loved. Maybe if he had been loved, by his parents or even by someone at the orphanage, he might have felt connected enough to humanity to care about the common good. He might have come forward sooner and told what he knew. Maybe. *If only.* I felt Mac's eyes on me, and glanced at him. He shook his head almost imperceptibly but I got the message: *Don't go there.* He was pulling me back from that tempting precipice again, and again I resented the emotional discipline he required of me, and again I was grateful.

"Okay," Mac said, "so at the age of eighteen, Neil Tanner ceases to exist and Martin Price shape-shifts from a junkie into a killer. And Paul Maher is reborn a new man."

"Correct. No record of Neil anywhere after that, except for one thing." Alan clicked open another page and skipped down five or six screens, landing on another signature. "See this? *Nancy Maxtor.*"

I leaned in and squeezed my eyes to sharpen the blurry signature. Nancy had dated it and entered her address in Montclair. My heart jumped when I saw that she lived on Harvard Street. "That's not far from my parents'."

"We noticed that," Alan said. "Coupla guys just went out to the Maxtor house but no one was home. Neighbors haven't seen anything suspicious. Apparently the daughter's been living there. We'll go back."

"What are we looking at there?" Mac lifted his chin to indicate the computer screen.

"Tanner's release form. Eleven years ago, Nancy Maxtor got a waiver from the Office of Juvenile Parole and Transitional Services, personally taking on Tanner's supervised rehab, room and board and all that, when he was released from Bordentown."

The juvenile detention facility in Bordentown was for boys, the hardest cases, most of whom were in their late teens. At twelve, Neil Tanner would have been a relative baby in a very tough environment. They said most kids came out of there honed criminals.

Alan continued: "All six years Tanner was locked up, she drove more than an hour every week to teach math to the kids at Bordentown. Obviously she made some friends there because they don't hand out transition waivers to just anyone."

"But *why*?" I couldn't fathom why anyone would feel safe enough to house the kind of people cops called *born killers*.

Alan shrugged. "She was his tutor before the murders. She knew him. Probably believed he was good deep-down, yada yada yada. Maybe she didn't believe he was the one who killed his parents. You see that all the time: self-appointed saints—the one person who decides to uphold the innocence of the falsely accused. She knows it'll be tough making a life for himself with his infamous name, so she gets him a new one—a soft landing spot."

"What about the real Paul Maher?" Mac asked. "The fake one said he was dead when he lost his identity. Strikes me as strange that none of his people would come looking."

"I ran the socials and found him in Iowa: died in 1990 without family or friends in a nursing home, age ninety-nine. Farmhand, owned nothing, never even had a credit card. He was a clean slate. Highly salable identity."

"But she didn't sell it. She gave it to the real Martin

Price and paid good money for his. Why the obfuscation?"

"Good question."

"Any evidence Nancy stole other IDs?"

"Not yet, but I'm still looking. Obviously she knew how. Can't help wondering if she's a pro . . . got in on the identity theft action on the ground floor."

"This is where you lose me," Mac said. "It doesn't match the rest of her profile at all. I believe she's the type who'd take in the worst kind of scum. But buying identities? Murdering people? Kidnapping kids? I don't see it."

"Look, *if* she's JPP's partner, then she's just as psycho as he is, so prepare yourself to believe anything." Alan minimized the page on the screen, clicked and clicked, and up popped a new screen: "Here she is, nine years ago, getting kudos for her involvement with a water-education program run by UNICEF. Doing good works, just like her daughter said. But look at her, really *look*. Size, build, age—she could pass for Lizzie Stoppard, know what I mean?"

As soon as he said that, I saw it: She was average height with a boxy shape, just like the clown. Had her daughter, Christa, lied about her mother being away at the time of Susanna's birthday party? Which would make Christa an accomplice. It was a big bite of speculation, a lot to chew all at once.

"Okay," Mac said. "Point taken. But putting aside what she would and wouldn't do, keeping in mind that this is all circumstantial, let's say she *wasn't* a pro— then where'd she get ten grand to buy Neil his new ID? Ten grand's a lot of money."

"Exactly. I asked myself the same thing while you were busy sleeping."

Alan didn't look up when he said that and I wondered if he suspected something between me and Mac. Wondered if it mattered if he did. As Mac liked pointing out to me, I wasn't a cop anymore, and as a civilian and a single woman I could love whomever I wanted. It was a foreign, jarring thought.

"Check this out." Alan clicked and we were looking at the cover page of a .pdf file of an IRS audit report for Nancy Maxtor, dated fourteen years ago, but he scrolled down pages too fast to make sense of the data. "I read through this thing until I was dizzy. Bottom line: Her grandmother dies and leaves everything to Nancy. Grandma's not just religious, she's evangelical. She knows Nancy's not gonna piss away her money like the rest of the godforsaken family. Died and left everyone else twenty grand apiece. But Nancy? She got nearly two mill. Next question: Where'd Grandma get that kind of money? Answer: While Grandma was going to church every day, Grandpa was busy selling cars. Built up a very successful dealership, died a rich man, left it all to his wife. And when *she* died she more or less skipped over her own kids and gave most of it to her favorite grandkid, Nancy, the only one of the bunch who saw things her way."

"I can imagine that family feud." Mac lifted his mug and inhaled the steam before sipping.

"You bet. Lawsuit, etc. Nancy won. Will was iron-clad."

"So she had real money," Mac said.

"And she spent it wisely. No fancy clothes. No fancy house. She spent it on God's work."

"You realize her inheritance blows a hole in your professional-identity-thief theory," I said. "She didn't need to work for money."

Alan cocked an ironic eyebrow, reminding me of something every cop learned to take for granted: The criminal who didn't love the so-called thrill of breaking the law was the exception to the rule.

"I don't care *how* Nancy Maxtor got her money," he said. "The way she spent it makes the old lady who left her fortune to a dog seem like a genius. Buying a new identity for a killer? What the hell was she thinking, if she wasn't in on it on some level?" He sat back and released a momentous yawn.

"Go home," Mac told him.

"Are you kidding me?"

"It's your turn to grab a few hours of sleep. Trust me, it'll do wonders." Mac didn't so much as glance at me when he said that; I knew *he* hadn't slept a wink.

"I want to head over to Harvard Street first." Alan looked up at the wall clock. It was four A.M.

"If Christa's home and she didn't answer the door before," Mac said, "she won't answer it now. For all we know she sleeps with earplugs. It'll have to wait until morning, and I don't think you can keep yourself upright that much longer."

"I'm fine." But Alan's eyes were bloodshot. He was pale. And he couldn't stop yawning for more than five minutes.

"I'll head over to the house around seven," Mac said. "Go say hello to Sandy."

Sandy, I assumed, was Alan's wife; but the truth was I didn't know him well, and for all I knew Sandy was his cat.

Alan stared at his partner a moment before relenting. "Right. Okay. But promise you'll wake me up if you find Christa Maxtor in. I'm a little interested in talking to the woman."

"Will do," Mac said. "But it's going to be a while so *go home*. Give Sandy a kiss for me."

"No way."

His wife.

Alan stood up and yawned again.

"Before you head out," Mac said, "any word yet from the lab? I'd like confirmation that Susanna was definitely in the van."

"Nada. But my gut tells me they'll pick up something from her. And since they only found one hypodermic, and Stoppard's the one who turned up dead, it doesn't take a psychic to predict she was the one who took the needle. Poison, something fast and nasty, considering how clean she looked when they found her, just the surface bruises and scratches."

"A good possibility," Mac said. And then, to me: "Which statistically fits the m.o. of a female partner, you have to admit."

I couldn't deny his point. Female criminals were famous for avoiding overt violence when killing their victims; quiet methods like poison or suffocation were more typical than bloody mayhem, making them harder to track. And I was aware of a sordid history of male/female serial killer teams. They were rare, and notoriously lethal.

"You got that right," Alan said. "Remember that mother/son duo that killed people for their real estate? And the husband/wife team who buried kids alive and picnicked on the grave? And how about the woman who supplied her boyfriend with her younger sister to rape and murder—and watched."

"Hey, Alan." Mac glanced at me; my expression must have shown my distress. "Can it."

"Sorry, Karin, I wasn't thinking. Guess I *am* pretty fried." Alan yawned, bent down to open a file drawer, took out a backpack, and slung it over one shoulder. "See you two later."

He left his computer on with various pages loaded and minimized across the bottom task bar. We drank another cup of coffee each as we reviewed the research. After a while, Mac turned his exhausted, tender eyes on me. "Breakfast?"

"Are you really hungry?"

"Yes and no. But we should eat."

"Okay."

"Just let me touch base with the group." He stood. "Back in a flash."

He disappeared to visit with the task force and was back ten minutes later, without any news. "They're cranking it."

"The dominoes—?"

"Nothing yet. But there's a lot of new ground to cover now, which is good."

The six A.M. shifts were starting to filter in as we walked through the first-floor lobby. Sunrise glowed through the windows in shades of pink, amber, and full-out orange. I was so revved up by the onslaught of revelations about Nancy Maxtor that I felt light-headed—by the possibility that we might find her, that she could be JPP's partner as well as his aider and abettor, that she could have Susanna, that her charitable side might have kicked in to spare my niece's life.

We passed through the glass doors into the crisp early morning air and were immediately confronted by a flock of reporters who had arrived to start a new workday.

"What's the news about Susanna Castle?" a young woman asked before lifting her camera and snapping our picture.

Mac smiled and tried to maneuver us past, but the woman blocked our way.

"We understand the police sketch is of Nancy Maxtor," she said, "but no one's seen her. Can you confirm that?"

"It's being investigated. When we have more, we'll call a news conference. Our priority is finding Susanna. Excuse me, we need to get through."

They moved aside so we could squeeze by and we made our way to Mac's car.

After a quick breakfast at a local diner, we drove to the Maxtor house on Harvard Street in Montclair, and pulled up in front of a modest two-story brick house with a row of tall hedges obscuring the downstairs windows. The front lawn looked newly mowed. A newspaper, folded into a clear plastic sheath, sat on the front walk. There were a few steps up to a crooked walk that led you to a short stoop. I followed Mac to the front door and stood behind him as he rang the bell. I checked my watch: It was seven-o-five A.M.

We waited. No one answered.

"Maybe she already went out," I said.

Mac shook his head. "The newspaper's lying there."

"Maybe she's still asleep. Maybe she doesn't live here. Maybe she's got a boyfriend and she mostly stays at his place."

"Maybe, maybe, maybe." Mac smiled at me, brought me back. Lifted his hand to ring again when the front door suddenly opened.

CHAPTER 18

"Yes?" Irritation in the woman's voice was offset by a magnificent smile: cherry-lipsticked lips stretched across white teeth. She was a teacher; I knew it in my gut. The long black hair, the dangling strawberry earrings, the scoop-necked pink T-shirt over the comfortable brown skirt, the practical sandals, the droopy canvas purse hanging from her shoulder. And that smile: forced patience, her mind one step ahead, the determination to bring everyone along with her. She appeared to be in her late twenties, possibly thirty—too young to be Nancy Maxtor, but just the right age to be her daughter—and looked fit and strong, as if she spent her off hours at the gym. She was average height but exuded a confidence that made her seem tall and imposing, though in fact both Mac and I were taller than her by half a foot.

Mac brought out his police identification and went through the standard introduction. When her eyes landed on me, I had another gut feeling, skipped my name and simply introduced myself as his "friend."

"That's not too professional, is it?" she said to Mac in a tone that was half criticism, half charm.

"Got me there."

"I assume you're here about my mother."

"That's right."

"I wish you people would correct all the misapprehension that sketch has created about her."

"That's why we're here, to talk to you so we can clear that up."

"I told that detective on the phone—"

"Detective Tavarese."

"Yes, that's it. I told him my mother's in Myanmar, helping rebuild schools in the Irwadaddy Delta. There's just no way she could be involved in that girl's disappearance—or that murder."

"How long's she been gone?"

"Almost seven months now. I miss her, but she's doing good work. I'm proud of her." Christa glanced at her watch. "I'm running late; camp starts in twenty minutes. Can we please talk later?"

"How I can reach her so we won't have to take up any more of·your time? We'd like to ask her a few questions about one of her former students from a while back, from her afterschool math club—Neil Tanner."

"My mother's had so many students over the years."

"She might remember this one. I'd like to talk to her."

"Well, she's really very hard to reach, but you can try calling the World Mission headquarters in D.C. Usually I just wait to hear from her when they travel into Yangon, which isn't often. They *might* be able to get a message through in the weekly mail run."

"How long exactly did you say she's been gone?"

"I'm sorry—but I'm the teacher and I can't be late."

"I thought you said camp."

"I teach drama at a summer camp for underprivileged children." She opened her purse, pulled out a scrap of paper, jotted something down, and handed it to Mac. "Here's my cell number. Can we talk later this afternoon? I really have to go." Her smile faded and all her prettiness went with it, transforming her face into one of the plainest I'd ever seen.

"Sure," Mac said. "Don't want to hold you up."

She pulled the door shut behind her, and bent to pick up the newspaper and put it under her arm before walking quickly to her car without so much as a glance back at us. We walked to Mac's car as she got into hers: an old model Nissan, blue, with two bumper stickers we read as she drove away: *I Brake for Unicorns* and *Christian Democrat and Proud of It.*

"She didn't flinch when I mentioned the name." Mac opened the passenger door for me, I got in, and he came around the other side.

"You'd think if her mother was involved with him," I said, "she would know."

"Right." Mac started the car. "And this whole thing about Myanmar . . . well, we shouldn't assume Nancy Maxtor is the partner, because maybe she isn't."

"Still, I have a funny feeling about this."

"Me too. But I'm so wiped out from last night I'm not sure I trust my thought process right now, you know? It's been a long night. A good night"—he turned to smile warmly at me, and I felt the kind of release you get from a slow, deep intake of air—"but a *long* one."

I put a hand on his shoulder as he drove. When he turned the wheel I felt the taut shifting of muscle beneath his cotton shirt; felt him, with my fingertips, as if he was part of my own body. In that moment I was startled by the realization that I not only liked him, enjoyed him, trusted him, cared for him, desired him—I also loved him. As simple as that. I knew that being with Mac would never be the same as being with Jackson—but Jackson was gone. Mac was a new journey, a different person, whose love would offer its own garden of surprises.

"I'm heading back to work," he said. "I'll drop you at your parents."

"Mac, please—"

"Sorry, but she was right when she said it wasn't professional to bring you along." He slid me a half smile. "Get some sleep for both of us."

"As if I *could* sleep."

"I'll call you as soon as I know something."

"Promise?"

"Promise."

"I want to know what's going on."

"Got it. But Karin, remember—"

"Don't say it again." I was not a cop anymore. How many times had I heard that by now?

"You'll be in on whatever it's safe and legal for you to be in on, as a bystander."

Which I wasn't, not exactly. "What is the opposite of *innocent bystander*?" I asked, wondering how to define yourself when you didn't fit in neatly anywhere.

"Guilty party," he tried. "Victim."

"Maybe I don't mean *opposite*. Maybe I mean . . ." But what *did* I mean? And why was it so hard to redefine the classifications that typically guided our thinking and expectations? To think outside the so-called box?

"Injured participant," Mac kept trying. "Suffering casualty."

"Getting closer."

He pulled up in front of my parents' house, put the car into park, and looked at me. "You know, we don't really have to come up with the exact answer to this. How about we chalk it up to D, none of the above, and move on with our lives? Stop hitting our heads against that one particular wall."

I couldn't argue with that. Our goal was to find Susanna, and to identify and stop JPP's partner, not realign our positions in the universal karma. I knew by now that my own personal ghosts were not banishable, that they would haunt me always; that I would have to learn to live with them while I relearned how to live.

I smiled at Mac and he smiled at me, and there we sat like teenagers in the front seat, awkwardly silent a moment before edging closer.

"They'll see us," I said of the perpetual security van. "And my parents are probably up by now."

"I'm forty-one years old, Karin. Legally separated, getting divorced. And you're, what?"

"Thirty-three. Widowed." The bald facts.

"So what are we afraid of?"

He was right. There was nothing, really, to be afraid of anymore when it came to each other. We pulled ourselves together and kissed tenderly, slowly, deeply. Already his mouth was becoming familiar, already I was learning the feel of his lips and his tongue, already my raw desire for him was transforming into a steady yearning. I drank in the soft flexibility of his skin, his smell: the pine soap, the sex neither one of us had had an opportunity yet to shower off.

"I'll talk to you later," he whispered in my ear.

"Make sure your phone's on."

He laughed. "Karin, it will be on, right here in my pocket, as always. In fact . . ." He leaned back to maneuver his phone out of his pants pocket, flipped it open, and assigned me a ring tone all my own: old-fashioned ring, a steady set of bells with regular interruptions. We kissed again and I got out. Not until I was inside my parents' house did I hear the *thrum* of Mac's car driving away.

I knew my parents were home because my mother's car was parked out front; it was early, and assumedly they were still in bed. I went to my room and lay down, feeling energized by all the developments of last night, yet exhausted to the bone. Despite my protestations to Mac that sleep would be impossible, I had spent very few hours in my bed over the past three days and my body didn't waste a moment succumbing to unconsciousness.

I woke up lying facedown on my bed, fully clothed, and was immediately gripped by a sense of disorientation so strong that I couldn't remember what day it was or even, for a moment, where I was. Then the images of my childhood room coalesced around me. I looked at the clock: four fifty-three. It had to be afternoon because strong light edged the shades, which I now remembered pulling down when I got back that morning and came upstairs for a rest that evidently had turned into a deep sleep.

My cell phone was on the bedside table where I had left it. There were no messages. After a shower I went downstairs to the kitchen, where two things immediately caught my eye: a packet of chicken cutlets defrosting on the counter, and a personalized envelope from my mother's stationery with my name written on the front in Mac's handwriting. He must have come by while I was sleeping and accepted an envelope from my mother, refusing to wake me—so it couldn't have been all that important. I took out a folded white page and opened it. A second paper fluttered out, landing on the floor. I bent down to retrieve it and saw that it was the copy of the old newspaper article about Games for Whizzards, Nancy Maxtor's afterschool group of math students, with the photo Mac and I had studied together last night after making love.

Look at the photo again—carefully, he had scrawled on the page. *See what I see? Call me when you're awake.*

I held the article up to the window but the bright sun turned the page translucent, blurring the images together. Flattening it on a counter, out of the sun, I bent over it. There was Nancy Maxtor, smiling, wearing her oval glasses and gold crucifix. And there was young Neil Tanner in the second row. I scanned the other faces, scanned the background of the room where the photo was taken—a classroom, it seemed, with one end of a blackboard in view—rescanned the faces of the other children, one by one.

And then I saw her, first row, far right: Christa Maxtor. That is, I saw her smile. But the broad, effusive smile was sitting on the face of a different person.

I looked closer, *carefully*, as Mac's note had urged. Stared at the chubby, small-eyed face of the girl whose short black hair might have made her look like a boy if not for the frilly dress she wore. It was an ill-fitting, overdecorated dress that created the illusion that she was verging on fat, when on closer look she was merely a bit chubby. It was the kind of dress forced on children by anxious parents desperate to help their child fit in and therefore making all the choices that prevented it. The girl appeared squat and timid . . . except for that smile. It was Christa's smile, without a doubt.

I leaned in and read the tiny print of the photo caption, counting rightward to four: Christa Viera. It was definitely Christa, with a different last name.

My eyes jumped from young Christa to young Neil. There were only eleven children in the group. Certainly they would have known each other. So why hadn't Christa even flinched when Mac mentioned Neil Tanner yesterday? There had been no signal of recognition in her face, none at all. *Could* she have forgotten him?

No. You did not forget the name of the kid in your class who killed his parents. You didn't forget him especially if your mother offered him room and board after his release from juvenile detention. Christa would have known his name and known it well—so why had she acted otherwise?

Questions swirled through my mind as I picked up the kitchen phone and dialed Mac. His voice mail answered and I left a message, then tried Alan's landline at work, which rang and rang. I went upstairs to get my cell phone, found Alan's personal number, and tried that. When I got his voice mail I left him a message, too. I almost didn't care who called me back. I wanted answers.

Had they reached Nancy Maxtor in Myanmar, if she was really there?

Had anyone gone back to talk to Christa again? To ask her why she had pretended not to know Neil? To question her about how much she knew about her mother's relationship with Neil Tanner? Martin Price? JPP?

How had it come about that Christa had been named Viera and was now Maxtor?

"You saw the chicken," my mother said, walking in when my back was turned, making me jump. "Oh dear, I didn't mean to startle you!"

"It's okay." I folded the two pages Mac had left and slipped them back into the envelope, following an instinct to protect my mother from worry, then on second thought took the pages back out and unfolded them. I handed her the printout of the article. "Have you ever seen this woman?"

Mom took her reading glasses out of her skirt pocket, slipped them on, and held the paper half a dozen inches from her face. "It's the woman from TV, the one we saw yesterday morning." She looked at me, surprised. "What is this?"

"An old article about her. Did Mac say anything when he came over before?" I didn't have to ask if she'd seen him; I knew she'd given him the envelope.

"Just that they were doing everything in their power to find Susanna. Karin, you weren't in your bed this morning when I woke up. I almost worried, but then . . ." She paused. "Was that Mac's car I heard driving away early this morning? Dropping you off?"

"Yes. What time was he here this afternoon?"

"About one o'clock, after we got back from Jon's. I had to bring Dad home . . ."

"How are Jon and Andrea doing?"

She sighed, didn't answer. "So you were with Mac last night."

"Yes."

"I realize it's none of my business, but I want you to know that I'm glad. And no, he didn't say anything else. He wasn't here a minute. I like him, Karin. He's a good man. Very *capable*."

She made me tear up, saying that, because it was true: With Mac on the case, or in your life, you didn't have to worry. In that instant, I put all my questions aside. If I had thought of them so quickly, then Mac would have thought of them and more. I felt confident he had all the answers by now.

"I'll make the salad if you do the chicken," I said.

"You've got yourself a deal. And I'll put on some rice, too."

She was definitely the better cook, and it was hard to ruin a salad. In the end we had a simple dinner with my father at the kitchen table. I volunteered to clean up and later joined my parents in the living room where they were watching television. A sitcom about people in a city . . . I could tell my mother couldn't concentrate, and neither could I. With dinner behind us, with my body at rest again, my brain took off in another direction.

Mac still hadn't called me back. This time, I had no

rationalizations for that; I felt sure he wouldn't deliberately avoid my calls now. Alan hadn't called back,
either. But it was Mac's silence that troubled me.

I went upstairs, fired up my laptop, and one by one
sent my questions into cyberspace. *Neil Tanner* brought
up old news coverage of his parents' murder, and after
that, nothing. *Martin Price* brought up a vast number of
stories and blogs and links about the domino murders.
There was a lot of chatter, but no new information,
no answers. It was too late to call the World Mission
in Washington, D.C., so I went to their Web site and
poked around. Nancy Maxtor's name was mentioned
in an undated list of volunteers who had aided refugees in Kosovo, which would have happened a decade
ago, but this at least corroborated Christa's assertion
that her mother was working with the group. When I
searched their activity in Myanmar, I learned that their
most active site was half a day's trek from Yangon, as
Christa had mentioned.

Next I Googled *Christa Viera*, the name in the newspaper clipping. It was a popular name but connected
with Essex County it elicited only one link, an archived
notice from the *New York Times*, dated eighteen years
ago.

In East Orange, New Jersey, a fire raged through a
two-story house, taking the lives of four members of
the Viera family, originally from Galicia, Spain. The fire
is believed to have been ignited by faulty wiring in a
space heater kept in the parents' bedroom. There is
one survivor, ten-year-old Christa. Her older brother
and younger sister perished in the fire along with both

parents. Efforts to find relatives in Galicia have been
unsuccessful.

That explained it: Christa had been orphaned suddenly and Nancy Maxtor must have stepped in to fill
the void by adopting her. Much as she had *adopted*
Neil Tanner. It made perfect sense; Nancy Maxtor was
exactly the kind of person who would have done such
a thing, unasked. On paper, anyway. In reality, taking
in the world's strays would be a risky prospect, if not
an insane one. I could understand adopting the girl.
But assuming responsibility for a young man who had
murdered his parents? I couldn't wrap my head around
that one, which automatically made me question Nancy
Maxtor's motives in everything else she had under-
taken. The more I thought about it, another thing that
seemed patently insane was the idea that Christa and
Neil hadn't known each other, in fact fairly well.

What else did Christa know that she wasn't telling
us?

I tried Mac again, eager to confirm my guess that he
had reached the same conclusions and asked himself
the same questions, but to no avail.

My parents were still watching television when I
went back downstairs and made myself some tea in
the kitchen. I stood at the open window, breathing in
the sweet, cool evening air. It was dark out now. Quiet,
except for the chirping of unseen grasshoppers. Occa-
sionally a car drove past, dragging its sound through
the street and then leaving it quiet again, a lonesome
summer night. The fourth night since Susanna had
vanished: an eternity. After a few minutes I took my

tea onto the front porch, my cell phone in my pocket so I would hear it ring if Mac or Alan called back. Sat there, alone, thinking. I was so used to seeing the surveillance van across the street that I hardly noticed it anymore. There it sat: light blue in the dark blue night, utterly still, the driver cop with his head tilted back against the headrest, dozing. After a moment I heard the van door slide open and closed on the opposite, curb side of the street, and watched as the second cop walked away. There was a thicket of trees fifty yards down where I'd long guessed our guards went upon occasion to relieve themselves—always a challenge on long surveillance jobs.

I finished my tea and thought about going in for a refill, but didn't move. I understood in that moment that there was a possibility that I would get up and go. Because I could, without escort or explanation. I sat, empty mug on my knee, and thought about passive and active opportunities: the ones you let happen to you and the ones you made happen. Thought about Paul Maher, whose turning points, or the ones I knew about, had been entirely passive: meeting Nancy Maxtor when she rang his bell and offered clean needles, then returned offering money for his name; waiting for us to appear at his door a second time before he told us what he knew about an urgent life-and-death police investigation. Waiting. Until someone came along and knocked on his door. Just as I sat here, right now, waiting for my phone to ring.

I looked at my watch: It was now nine forty-seven P.M. Almost five hours had passed since I'd left my first messages for Mac and Alan. I put down my mug.

Dialed Mac, then Alan. Left two more messages. Went into the house and said good night to my parents. On my way out of the house I quietly lifted my mother's car keys off the hook by the door, picked up my purse, and walked to the car, which was parked in its usual spot at the curb. Neither the grind of the engine starting nor the quiet rumble of the car driving away woke the sleeping cop or alerted his AWOL partner. I kept expecting one of them to come alert in my rearview mirror, but they didn't. And then I was alone on the road, driving.

To Mac's. I would start there. He hadn't slept in three days and there was a chance he had gone home in the middle of the day and crashed into a deep sleep, just as I had earlier that morning. If he was there, I would get all my answers, then join him in bed. If he wasn't there . . . I didn't know.

CHAPTER 19

"Thanks," I said to the building's superintendent—Mikhail, according to the embroidery on his shirt pocket—who stood at the front door holding his massive ring of keys. I had met him once before, with Mac, and he had remembered me. I had told Mikhail that today was Mac's birthday and I wanted to be here when he got home, to surprise him. It amazed me how easy it was to fool some people.

"No problem." Mikhail smiled, revealing a gold front tooth. "Tell the boss I said happy birthday."

"I will."

Mikhail shut the door behind him and I stood alone in the small space that passed for an entry hall and led to a living room off of which Mac's kitchen and bedroom sprouted. The apartment was so quiet you could hear the faint buzz of his appliances.

"Mac?"

I walked into the living room: off-white walls, one wide unclean window overlooking the building's parking lot. He had set out to find himself a temporary, furnished landing pad after the split with Val and this was the first place he'd seen. Until now, I hadn't registered how desolate it felt.

The bedroom door sat half open and spilled darkness. I walked in quietly, thinking I would find him sleeping. But his bed was exactly as we had left it in the middle of last night when Alan called: covers bunched and twisted over a wrinkled sheet, two pillows mashed together on one side. There was a musty smell I hadn't noticed before.

I checked the bathroom, which felt similarly abandoned. As did the kitchen, where I looked for signs that Mac had eaten dinner here tonight and found none.

Then, walking back through the living room, I noticed a detail that told me he *had* been here sometime today: The slip of paper with Christa Maxtor's phone number sat atop a copy of *Newsweek* on the coffee table, next to a take-out cup. I picked it up and saw the wet film of coffee at the bottom. It couldn't have been more than half a day old, otherwise the residual coffee would have dried. When I replaced the cup I noticed something else. Mac had jotted another note on the slip of paper: *62 river htwn.* I had no idea what that meant.

He had left his landline phone on the coffee table. I picked it up and pressed redial. Christa Maxtor's cell number appeared on the LED screen with a time stamp of twelve thirty-three P.M.—he had called her just before stopping by my parents' house.

I let it go four, five, six rings before hanging up.

Harvard Street was quiet at this hour. Cars were parked in their driveways, where they belonged. Porch lights glowed. At least half the houses were totally dark and the rest were a checkerboard of lit windows. When I pulled to a stop in front of the Maxtor house, I thought for a moment that I saw a downstairs light flick off, then thought better of it. The neighbor immediately to the right was just then hauling his garbage can to the curb and had stepped in front of my headlights the moment before I'd turned them off, creating, I decided, an optical illusion. The flash of light had been his figure breaking my beam, while everything about the Maxtor house was quiet, still, and dark.

Putting the house to bed, we used to call it when I was growing up. No matter where we lived—one of the many houses along the itinerant route my father's army career took us, or the big house on Upper Mountain Avenue my mother inherited from her parents and where we finally settled after Dad began his second career with the police—it was always Jon's and my job to make sure all the doors and windows were closed and locked and every light was off before we went to bed. We would run through the house counting locks and lights and then compare our totals. The winner accomplished a moment of pride before we crawled under our respective covers in a house that felt safe and peaceful. And then we would wait for sleep. Despite the usual sibling rivalry, Jon and I had always felt especially close; it was the two of us against the world. To think that David could grow up and never know his sister lowered a boom to my heart.

Sitting in the car, I felt an urge to call Jon to see how he was doing, to tell him I loved him and ask him to also give my love to Andrea. I took my cell phone out of my purse, opened it, dialed. Stopped the call. Tamped down the wave of emotion that felt too melodramatic. Dialed Mac, then Alan, one more time each—unreciprocated calls that reminded me why I had come here: for answers.

Slipping my phone into my pocket, I locked my purse inside the car, crossed the front lawn, rang the doorbell, heard the distant chimes, and waited a minute before ringing again. Finally I gave up and walked away.

Christa's car wasn't parked in the driveway or at the curb. I had noticed that some of these houses had detached garages in the back and so went around the side of the house to take a look. If there was a garage with no car inside, then I would be satisfied that she simply wasn't home.

By now the neighbor had put his house mostly to bed, with only one upstairs light still on. It cast a spotlight across the space separating the two houses, about thirty feet of lawn halved lengthwise by a seam of shrubs. Nearly at the rear of the house I could see there was no back garage and so I turned around to leave. I decided to backtrack to Maplewood, go to the police station and look for Mac and Alan. If they weren't there I would drop in on the task force and share my concerns. But then the neighbor's remaining light went off, plunging the passage between the houses into darkness . . . and suddenly I realized something.

62 river htwn was an address, possibly in Hackettstown.

Neil Tanner had been found sleeping in a garage in Hackettstown after killing his parents seventeen years ago. Why had he gone there, of all places?

Back in the car, I got my mother's GPS unit out of the glove compartment, fired it up, typed in *62 river* and selected Hackettstown as the city. After a moment a single address appeared: 62 River Road, Hackettstown, New Jersey. I selected it. A tingling sensation spread through me as I watched a route appear on the screen with a notation along the bottom: *42 miles, 51 minutes.*

Nearly an hour later I was in Hackettstown, driving along River Road, a curving single lane through a densely wooded area. It was late, almost midnight. I was alone on the country road dotted with individual mailboxes announcing houses tucked out of view, my headlights on bright, casting long shadows in front of my slow-moving car.

Viera, painted in faded letters, came into focus on a mailbox that stood at the opening of a turnoff. I pulled over and stared at it. The tingling that had stayed with me now blossomed into a full-out burning sensation.

After failing once again to reach Mac and Alan on their cell phones, I called the main number for the Maplewood Police and was put through to the conference room taken over by the task force.

"Yeah," someone answered. A man.

"This is Karin Schaeffer, former detective Karin Sch—"

"Yup. Hi. Detective Gerry Mober here, we met at your brother's."

"Is Mac there? Or Alan Tavarese?"

"Not since morning. Last I heard they headed out to Hackettstown."

"Sixty-two River Road?"

There was a pause—Mober checking notes. "Yup, that's it."

"I'm there right now. The mailbox has *Viera* painted on it."

Before I could ask him if the task force knew that that was the original last name of Nancy Maxtor's daughter, Christa, Mober muttered, "*Shit*." He must have pulled the phone away from his ear and told the others, because I heard a conundrum of voices behind him. Then, back to me: "You go in the house?"

"Still in my car on River Road—can't see any houses from here."

"Good. Stay there. We're sending a unit from Hackettstown to check this out."

"I won't move," I promised.

But as soon as we'd hung up, an imperative to move forward, to not waste a moment, propelled me into the dark mouth of the turnoff. As I angled past the mailbox, my brights illuminated the ghost of a number that had long ago worn off—62—and without thinking, my mind halved the threat that had multiplied when JPP's partnership announced itself at Susanna's party. *Two-for-one* had been only part of the message, a numeric anagram, which rearranged became 124, which divided became 62.

As soon as we'd realized the threat had doubled, we should have understood that it had also reduced by half.

I drove slowly along the narrow unpaved road beneath a canopy of trees so verdant that any moonlight was totally obscured. It continued for nearly half a mile until opening onto a dead-end clearing and a small, forgotten-looking house. Burgundy paint had mostly chipped off to reveal weathered gray planks. Nailed above the front door was a wooden sign that looked like something a child had made in shop class, with inverted V ends, announcing pride of ownership: *Villa Viera*.

The house was dark and would have appeared abandoned except for Mac's little green car parked out front, the white squares on its top glowing in the reflection of my headlights. I left them on in the otherwise complete darkness and got out. The rush of blood in my ears was so loud that it took a moment to register the sweetness of the air and the rowdy band practice of crickets. I walked to the side of the house to see what lay beyond, and saw Christa's blue Nissan parked near a lopsided toolshed that had also evidently once been painted burgundy.

I returned to the front of the house. A horseshoe door knocker groaned when I lifted it and clanked once, twice, three times. Waited. Clanked three more times. Still no response. The knob wiggled as if it was loose but the door didn't open.

Dry leaves crunched underfoot as I walked around to the back, stepping out of the swath of illumination from my headlights into the bulky shadow of the house that lay like a tarp across what appeared to be an expanse of nothingness. And then, as my eyes adjusted to the moonlight, through a rear screen-obscured window—I saw it.

A silhouette, completely still. Someone sitting in a kitchen, in the house, in the dark. I could see the hulking outline of an old stove, and on the wall above it a three-shelf rack of spice bottles. As my vision strengthened, objects clarified themselves: a sink with an empty dish drainer, a hand towel folded over the curved neck of a tall faucet, an old Frigidaire, a back door leading onto a screened-in porch that seemed to float off the back of the house. A man sitting still-as-stone at a kitchen table.

There were four rickety steps up to the porch door. I tried the handle: locked. But a quick rattle of the door told me it wasn't much of a lock, and a swipe of my credit card proved that guess correct. The door fell open and I walked in.

Rotted floorboards were spongy underfoot, in places threatening to give way. A picnic table was mottled with black mildew. There was an old wooden chair against the wall of the house, and a lantern hanging from a bracket, but nothing else. The porch felt unused, as if Christa—because obviously this was her hideaway, assumedly a summer place she had inherited from her first family after they perished in a fire at their main residence—was waiting for it to fall away from the house, disown itself.

A curtain hung in the back door so I couldn't see inside the kitchen from here. The door was locked. I tried the credit card but it didn't work. Growing cold, trembling, I pried away the rotted frame near the back door handle. The soft wood splintered in my hands, its pieces falling like feathers to the floor. I pressed a corner of my credit card into the lock mechanism at a newly liberated opening until I heard a pop. Took a deep breath in, let a long breath out, tried to slow my pulse. Pushed the door open into a dark kitchen that seemed too quiet.

The person sitting at the table didn't move, or speak, or breathe.

"Mac?"

No answer, just heavy stillness. A strong nutty scent hung in the air.

I noticed a light switch beside the door and reached back to flip it on. A dim glow bathed the shabby room in sepia unreality.

And I saw him.

His expression was as surprised as mine must have been, but his appeared frozen while I could feel my facial muscles cascading with the quickly shifting thoughts and feelings of disbelief. His face looked claylike, as if someone had thumbed idioms of emotion onto his features. I wasn't sure if what I was seeing was really there: Alan, still as a mannequin, with a game of solitaire laid out before him on the kitchen table. King of spades. Queen of spades. Two of clubs. Set out in the same formation as the game I had played in the moments before JPP attacked me at my own kitchen table in Brooklyn last spring. The cards and the dominoes that fell over them that night were burned into my memory, indelible snapshots.

I felt myself move toward him in extreme slow motion; at least I thought I was moving. It was possible I wasn't moving at all.

"Alan," I whispered, "what are you doing here?"

Light shone off his eyes, white spots reflected off his pupils, the position of which didn't alter as I moved toward him. Slowly. I was too terrified to move any faster. A prickly awareness told me that anything could happen. I had to be ready.

"Alan?"

I was close to him now. The floor creaked under my

next step. He shifted incrementally, as if finally he planned to rise and greet me. Relief crackled through me, but just for the briefest moment.

Something dark now appeared in the right corner of his mouth, moving in the direction his body had shifted. Gathered and fell in a rivulet down his chin.

I pulled my foot away from the gimpy spot in the floor but his body didn't sway back into place and the blood didn't furl itself back into his body.

To be that stiff, he had to have been dead for at least three hours, no more than three days. I had last seen him sixteen hours ago, just that morning, around dawn, on his way home to get some sleep. Mac had stopped at my parents' at about one o'clock. Had he gone by Alan's house after that? Found him awake? Invited him along?

Three steps to my left and I saw that he sat in a pool of blood. There were no visible wounds, no rips on his clothing, no place where he appeared to have been injured; it seemed as if he was leaking blood from his orifices.

The ice in my veins trickled into my muscles until, standing there, looking at Alan's propped-up corpse, I felt as rigid as he looked. I recognized the sensation of paralysis we had spent weeks learning to overcome in cop school, training our brains to instruct our bodies to function despite the terror that ripped through our consciousness. This was the fear that froze you in front of a hurtling car. That debilitated you when a stranger appeared in your home in the middle of the night. That stunned you when you saw a child racing into traffic after a ball. I stepped forward, into the gale wind of raw dread. Took another step, despite my brain's instinct to shut down. And another.

I crouched near Alan's feet: black sneakers that looked fairly new. We were trained to holster our guns on our right ankle if right-handed, left ankle if left-handed. I recalled Alan's handling of the computer's mouse last night, clicking open pages, pointing our attention where he needed us to look. Shaking, I lifted his right pant leg: His holster was empty.

I stood up. Forced myself to breathe. Felt air enter my lungs. Felt my blood thaw and move. Stood back and looked at the human shell that was once Alan. Thought of Lizzie Stoppard, killed in a similarly undetectable manner.

Thought of Mac.

And Susanna.

If they were also here, I had to find them. Even if they were already dead. Even if it cost me my life.

Through an open door off the kitchen I could see part of a bathroom. Bracing myself, I pushed the door fully open. A worn white sink. An old toilet. A corroded metal shower stall coated inside with droplets—recently used.

Connecting the kitchen to a common room was a short hallway in which were two doors. The first was cracked ajar onto darkness; I pushed it farther open, releasing a current of cool, sour air: a basement. Behind the second door was a food pantry, shelves stuffed with cans and boxes of nonperishable food, the floor packed with toilet paper, paper towels, tissues. From the hallway I walked into the common room and immediately saw that no one was there: It was barren, with hardly any furniture and no place to hide. Opposite the front door, across a brief landing, was a stairway leading up.

I stood at the foot of the stairs, took out my phone, and speed-dialed Mac's cell number, hoping his ring would tell me which way to go: up to the second floor or down to the basement. After five rings, the call automatically ended. I pressed redial and crossed back through the common room. Stood in front of the basement door in the hallway. And heard it, muffled: old-fashioned ring, a steady set of bells with regular interruptions. Five more rings, and again it stopped.

Stepping onto a small landing atop the basement stairs and looking down into a throat of darkness, I pressed redial a third time and the ringing began anew . . . the old-fashioned ring that now sounded closer, sharper, more insistent . . .

CHAPTER 20

I left the basement door open behind me.

Took the first step down. The second. The third. Paused, listened: Something shifted below.

"Mac!" My voice sounded flat, as if the basement was padded to absorb sound. I breathed. Swallowed. Spoke again: "Mac, are you down there?"

No answer.

Halfway down I became aware of a series of red rubber balls, the kind children used in kickball, skewered individually to the wall beside the basement steps. Five balls, descending in size. Like a family: tallest to smallest all lined up in a row. In the darkness I could just make out that each ball had a cartoonish face drawn on it. Only the second smallest face was unique, with hair drawn in, earrings, a smile. I remembered that Christa had been the middle child in her family—the family that had perished in a fire—and seeing these balls, their faces blank except for the one that represented her, seeing this bizarre exhibit of the family lineup, I *knew* in my gut she had killed them.

I stepped off the final stair onto soft carpeting that

smelled of mildew. The darkness down here was almost total, broken only by a vague glimmer of moonlight from the edges of a high shuttered window across the basement. I stood still, breathing into the icebergs of fear that encroached on what little confidence I had held on to, hoping my eyes would adjust quickly.

Another sound: a scratchy minor adjustment against a hard surface, from somewhere in the middle of the room.

"Hello?" I said. Not knowing whom I addressed. Guessing it wasn't Mac.

And then a light turned on and there was Christa Maxtor, standing against the wall opposite me, her finger on the switch. An overhead fluorescent halo illuminated the basement dimly but with ruthless clarity.

The floor, the walls, the ceiling—all covered in a patchwork of carpet remnants. Lining three walls were bookcases crammed with toys and games: every kind imaginable neatly stacked on labeled shelves. One bookcase held trucks, cars, trains, various other vehicles. Another, board games. Another, dolls. Another, elaborate constructions of interlinked blocks. Another, miniature action figures assembled in battle scenes. A small paint-spattered desk held a laptop computer with a three-dimensional double-helix screensaver floating across the monitor. A flat-screen television was mounted on the only free wall; long low shelves beneath it were stacked with video games. Two old armchairs faced the screen at the kind of harmonious angle a feng shui expert might prescribe. It was a child's paradise down here. But dank. Unrelenting. Creepy.

Then something else caught my attention, to the right

of the TV: a homemade poster of a theatrical production staged at the New Jersey State Correctional Facility, showing a blown-up photo of a smiling Christa surrounded by prisoner actors, one of whom was our Martin, her Neil. By the look of it, she was the leader of the group—teacher, director—bringing drama into the prisoners' lives, as if they weren't dramatic enough. Was this how she had, somehow, aided JPP's escapes? Like her mother, building useful connections in the guise of doing good.

"Welcome," Christa said, without irony. Like a hostess watching her event unfold as planned. But without the smile.

My head felt as if it was about to spin off into the stratosphere. I breathed. Breathed again. Again. And again.

"Please." She gestured to a card table in the middle of the room. Two chairs faced each other across the table on which sat Mac's still-ringing cell phone, a set of dominoes stacked in a neat cube, Alan's .40-caliber Glock pistol on a dinner plate, an unlit candle, a book of matches, a syringe half-filled with a pale blue liquid.

Hydrogen cyanide.

It would explain the nutty, almondy scent I'd smelled when I entered the kitchen; and it would explain Lizzie Stoppard's—and Alan's—quiet-looking deaths. But there was nothing quiet about death by cyanide; it worked quickly, paralyzing the heart. If I remembered correctly, you had up to half an hour to administer an antidote, dicobalt edetate, before the cyanide killed you.

Looking at Christa's place setting, *I knew.* The

family of five. Destroyed by a fire. An orphaned child. A mentor. There were no accidents in this game. Had Nancy Maxtor trained these children to kill? A tremor passed through me, and I knew something else: She, too, was here. Possibly upstairs on the bedroom floor—the only place I hadn't yet checked. A person with this kind of agenda stuck around for the finale.

"Where's Susanna?" I asked, hoping against hope that Christa was crazy enough to tell me.

"Ah, Susanna—what a sweetheart." But it was all she said.

She crossed the room, sat down, and waited for me to join her. Beneath the nimbus of light her skin looked gray and shadows fell over her eyes, throwing dark scallops across her face. Her stillness terrified me with the promise of its reversal: unpredictable action. She had a plan. Something came next.

Every step I took toward her was an epic task of persuasion as my brain overrode my body's signals. *Go for the gun*, my arms instructed. *Grab. Aim. Shoot. Now.* But my mind superseded that impulse with an effort to think like her. Everything laid out on the table was a message. Alan's murder was a message. And now she was inviting me to play along. The two things I was unsure of were how, or if, my compliance would affect the outcome; and if help would arrive fast enough, before I had a chance to find out.

I reached the table. Trying not to shake too uncontrollably, I sat across from her. Mac's phone stopped ringing and I looked at it a little too quickly, as if it could tell me something important. But the fact that it wasn't with him already did.

"Do you love him?"

She held on to my gaze as I constructed an answer. What would fit her warped thinking?

"Yes." *And the truth shall set you free*; but looking into her eyes, I couldn't tell if that aphorism was going to be accurate in this case. And so I calculated a risk: "Do you?"

The corners of her mouth curved up, wings in flight, and there was that brilliant smile. "You don't mean *him*." She glanced at Mac's phone.

I shook my head. "Neil."

"He had a little crush on me when we were kids. I didn't really notice him until . . . Well, let's just say he wanted to prove that he could be like me. Make a good impression, you know, the way they try to." She shrugged her shoulders and let the memory of her eager young suitor slide away.

"Did he?"

"What do you think?" She smiled, as if Neil's brutal crimes made their intent obvious. I felt woozy. Was she telling me that he had emulated her? By killing his parents, as she had hers? By continuing to kill?

A tremor crossed her face and then she said: "Who called love 'the uncharted waters'?"

I shook my head; I had no idea what she was talking about.

"The idea was to finish out the game since he *can't*." Her expression hardened; clearly she was enraged that he was locked away from her now. "But I found I didn't like playing it on my own. Loneliness is . . . well, my mother loved me, I never doubted it."

Trying to weed my way through her digressions, and

wondering which mother she meant, I asked: "Doesn't she now?"

"Nancy? I meant my first mother."

It was hard not to ask the obvious question: *Then why did you incinerate her and the rest of your original family, you freaking lunatic?* But I was trying to survive, so I held my tongue.

"Is your second mother here—Nancy?" I asked. "Is Susanna here? Is Mac?"

"If you want answers, you'll have to win them. You know how to play Draw Dominoes, I assume. It's one of the simplest games."

"I can learn."

Her hand lowered suddenly on the cube of dominoes, disassembling the stalwart shape in a noisy clatter. Both her hands moved through the heap of tiles, shuffling.

"Draw seven tiles," she said.

I did.

She drew seven for herself. "The rest stay in the boneyard."

My eyes flicked at her when she said that. *Boneyard.*

"You've *never* played before," she said.

"Not this version."

She stared at me a moment. She knew what version I meant. But she let it go.

"Now we begin."

I followed her lead, hopscotching same numbers in a line across the table. Listening for any sound from above. I couldn't tell how much time had passed since Gerry Mober had told me he would alert the Hacketts-town police. Five minutes. Ten minutes. Half an hour. An hour. A coil of panic tightened in my stomach, warning of dwindling options. I ordered my racing mind to slow down. Focus. Play.

"The lightest hand wins." She placed a tile horizontally across my last tile, matching her double four to my four. "This is a baby's game, just for warming up. Next we'll play Blind Hughie, another easy game. After that, we'll see if you're ready for Sniff—our favorite."

I hesitated, but it had seemed a deliberate opening. "Whose favorite?"

"Neil's and mine, if you've got to know. But since he isn't here . . ." Her smile avalanched across her face with a kind of vengeance I had never imagined could be real. Pure malevolence. As if she had sprung from a different place than the rest of humanity.

She now had two remaining tiles. I had six, having drawn often from the boneyard. I assumed that by the lightest hand she meant that the winner would have the lowest count after adding up her overall domino values. Which would make Christa the winner if she finished without drawing again. On its surface, an untenable risk.

Upstairs: perpetual silence.

And Mac's phone was now a dead end.

I couldn't let her win. In that moment, it was all I knew for sure. A sudden gut feeling propelled me from there.

I reached for the gun.

Reached for it, not knowing if it was loaded, or if it had been sabotaged to explode in my hand. Not knowing anything. Just reaching. In the process, bumping the hypodermic off the table, seeing it roll to the floor and bleed bluish smoke where it landed.

I lifted Alan's gun, heavy as a rock, defying gravity.

Kicked over my chair as I swung back and righted my footing.

One leg slightly back, bracing. Arms triangled in front of me. Left hand supporting right—my shooting hand. Eyes tight on my target.

"I will kill you," I said. "I will kill you." An intention stuck somewhere in my brain, turning me into a skipping record. "If you move one inch, I will kill you."

"I won't move." She held still. Stared at me. Seemingly unafraid of me or the gun or the prospect of her own death. And me, announcing what I would do, not doing it.

"Explain it to me," I said, giving way to the agony that had driven me this past year. "Explain to me exactly *why*."

"I will." Her voice, unruffled. "I'll explain it to you."

And then the table blasted up against my arm, knocking the gun out of my hand. I heard it hit against something hard.

I kicked the table off me and watched her scramble for the gun. Leaped up. Followed. Jumped on her back as her hand reached toward the side of the tall bookcase arranged with brawling action figures, which shivered but didn't fall when our bodies crashed against it. The gun had landed nose-up against the wall, directly beside the bookcase.

I watched her hand fall on the Glock's black handle. Watched her fingers spider around it. Watched them grip. All in strange, slow motion . . . as if the final moments of my life were being given to me piecemeal so I would experience every iota of my ending. Watched my hand hover, lower, land on hers. Felt my hand press her fingers into the metal. Felt the trigger squeeze. Steeled myself against the loud blast as bits of carpet fell on us from the ceiling.

In the moment she cringed beneath me, I overtook her. Pulled her off the gun with one hand, grabbed it with the other. My fingers dug so deeply into a piece of orange carpet that its edge came up from the floor and folded over itself, revealing two long tracks embedded in the concrete.

Twisting under me, she knocked me off with surprising force and came at me so fast I didn't have time to aim the gun. I drew back my right leg, cocked it, and kicked straight into her face. Felt the bandages Mac had so lovingly applied to my sole dislodge, felt my wound rip open.

She fell back and seemed to register the injury to her cheekbone . . . giving me an opportunity to scoot closer, raise my throbbing foot above her face, and level a tight axe kick with my heel across the bridge of her nose.

I jumped up. Stood above her. Aimed the gun at her heart. "Ready for more? Because I'll do it. *I will do it.*"

"No!" Blood pouring out of her nostrils, nose turning green, voice shivering. "Don't! She needs me."

"I think Nancy can make it without you."

"Susanna."

She glanced at the bookcase with the glued-on figures, and I knew. The tracks. The easy-to-remove bits of carpeting.

Susanna was behind the bookcase.

"I'll open it right now, but don't shoot me," she begged, "*please*. You'll need the combination."

"The combination." Breathing. Willing my mind to slow down enough to think. "What combination?"

"If you kill me, Neil will never tell you the sequence."

"I'll get it from Nancy. I'll find her—"

"Go ahead and ask her." The creepy confident smile oozed back onto her bloodied face: plain menace.

"Where is she? Where's Nancy?"

"Blue. One over. Zero up."

My eyes followed her gaze to a rectangular piece of carpet nearly under my feet. Breathing hard, I stepped aside and crouched down, keeping the gun on her. Peeled off the blue rectangle to reveal a false floor: long planks of wood banded together, a leather loop for a handle. Pulled the loop. The wooden flap was heavy. Pulled harder, and finally it gave way, swaying up and over on stiff hinges. My eyes flicked from left to right, from the floor grave to Christa, while she watched me with the bizarre gratification of a voyeur.

"Go on," she said. "It won't bite."

A longer look and I saw: a boneyard. Nancy's gold crucifix on a chain around the linked vertebrae that were the remnants of her neck. A skein of brown-and-gray hair like scattered hay beneath her skull. Rotted remnants of clothing. The disjointed puzzle of what was visible of her skeleton.

Nausea stormed through me. Nausea and disbelief, as my expectations readjusted. *Here she was*, Nancy Maxtor, the woman Mac and Alan and I had set out to find. Dead and buried for years, by the look for it. How long had they waited after she bought Neil Tanner his new identity, his second chance, before they did away with her and pursued their own plans—and her money?

How had they covered up her disappearance for so long? Questions raced through my mind, hitting dead ends; answers didn't matter right now.

I crouched down and grabbed Christa's arm. Hoisted her up. Tears spilled down her battered face but I was sure they had nothing to do with pain. Frustration, maybe. Humiliation. Rage. But not pain . . . because she wasn't human enough to acknowledge a feeling as helpless as suffering. Her body worked differently. Her mind was another planet.

"No more games." I fixed the gun on her.

She stared at me. To her it *was* a game, with players, winners, losers, statistics. Bodies left in boneyards like credit chits for use against future moves.

"Let me sit down," she said.

"Is Susanna behind that bookcase?"

She nodded.

"Is she alive?"

Her eyes lifted, attempted to draw me in. "Please," she said, "I feel dizzy. I need to sit down."

I stepped closer. Demanded: "*Is she alive?*"

"I don't know."

"Open it." I pressed the nose of the gun against her temple. "Open it. Open it. Open it."

I kept the gun on her head as she peeled back three fragments of carpet beside the bookcase, exposing a yard-long double track embedded in the concrete floor. Kept the gun on her head as she braced both her hands against the inner right side of the bookcase and pushed. It slid along the tracks, revealing a false wall—and a door. Six inches above the knob was a keypad: five rows of five numbers each. The combination lock to which only JPP—Christa and Neil—knew the code.

"Open it," I said. "*Now*. Or I will bury you alive, with her."

"I'll make a deal with you."

"No deals. Put in the code."

"I didn't want to hurt anyone. It was his idea."

The flatness of her tone, the deliberation of her words, told me she didn't mean anything she said. Didn't care if anyone had been hurt. Didn't care that *my own child, my own husband* had died at the brutal hands of her accomplice. For the purposes of some game. And I didn't buy it that Neil had masterminded all this alone.

"Put in the code." I pressed the gun harder against her temple.

Her nails were meticulously manicured, I noticed, as she lifted a hand to the keypad. Short, rounded nails with a perfect sliver of moon atop each finger. Her cuticles trimmed. These were hands that didn't *get dirty*. Looking at them, I *knew* who had been the supervisory inspiration of every merciless death. Starting with her family's. Ending with mine.

Five buttons. Five rows.

Three.

Seven.

Zero.

Six.

Eight.

The magic numbers.

The keypad emitted a triple *beep*. And then a *pop*.

"Okay," she said. "It's open, so—"

Was she actually trying to bargain with me *now*?

Rage detonated from my core with irresistible force. Blind rage that demolished my defenses. Obliterated every emotional building block I had so carefully laid in place these past months. Rage so powerful that I could hear Joyce's words materialize inside my mind, summoned by my wavering consciousness to negotiate my finger off the trigger.

Don't do it, the price is too high.

Vengeance won't bring your family back.

Violence can't solve grief.

Arguing with me to look to the future as I held lightly to the strings of my past.

I could hear Mac beg me, *Karin, no*, when I had my first chance to kill Martin Price, cornered in the convention center's men's room.

I could hear Price begging: *Please. Don't.* Because he valued his life.

I could feel myself in that distant moment recognizing his humanity. Changing my mind. Letting him live. So we could end up here, my brother's family terrorized, Alan dead, and Susanna . . . and Mac . . .

I resisted and resisted and resisted and resisted the urge for revenge. It was not why I had come here. And it was true: It wouldn't help.

I pulled the door open to find a narrow chamber, dark, with a disproportionately lofty ceiling. There was a cot with a disarranged sheet revealing a thin, stained mattress. A toilet emitting a poignant stink. A metal shelf chaotic with an arsenal of sex toys, handcuffs, chains. And a haphazard wallpaper of photographs: crime scene documentation: faces I recognized, people I loved.

My eyes darted frantically across the room, searching for Susanna. Any hint of her. Even in this hideous, nightmarish place . . . *Please, let me find her.*

In the corner of the room, ropes: the double strands of a pulley.

High up near the ceiling, a large hammock drooping with weight. Something glinting in the darkness.

Below the hammock, a wet puddle seemed to gradually spread.

A drop fell into the puddle from above. And another. And again.

I felt for a light switch and found one next to the door. Dreaded illumination.

Prostrate in the hammock—which I now saw was studded with toothlike metal spikes—lay Mac, eyes wide open, spread-eagle, still as stone, bleeding from somewhere or everywhere on his body. His clothes were too soaked to tell from my distance where exactly his wounds were.

There was no time to understand what had happened to him before the darkness began to swallow us both, as the door pressed against my back—as it steadily closed me in.

"No!"

I exploded against the door, forced a bent elbow into the narrowing opening. *Refused.* The diminishing sliver of her face was in turmoil as I matched her furious determination. Somehow I got the gun out in front of me. And somehow . . .

I didn't hear the roar of my own scream. Didn't feel it when I pulled the trigger. Didn't register the sound of the gun discharging. Didn't hear her cry out. Didn't see her go down, or recognize the blood streaming from her head as a symptom of the fact that I had just killed her.

The only things I was truly aware of were Mac—suspended as if in flight, bleeding, still as a shadow, and I was sure of it: dead—and a burning imperative to find Susanna.

CHAPTER 21

I raced up both flights of stairs.

Outside, the crunching sound of cars arriving. Parking. Doors slamming shut. Voices.

The second floor of the house consisted of a half-diamond landing and two doors, both closed. I opened the door on the left, felt for a light switch, and dust danced in the sudden illumination. A double bed covered in a patchwork quilt that had been pulled neatly up to two pillows, one of which looked as if it had recently been slept on. A woman's pale blue bathrobe flung across the foot of the bed. A hairbrush, a cell phone, and a black address book atop a dresser with an attached tarnished mirror. The parents' bedroom.

I backed into the hall, turned and opened the other door into the second bedroom. Except for faded yellow wallpaper, the room looked newly refurbished. A bookcase filled with picture books. Colorful stuffed animals in a corner basket. A toy stroller in which sat a baby doll in a frilly pink gown. A doorless closet with a high bar on which tiny dresses hung—Susanna's green-and-purple party dress among them. On the closet floor, pairs of little sneakers and little shoes. A set of bunk beds against one wall and a twin bed against the opposite wall . . . and huddled in the single bed, beneath a flowery bedspread, a small, motionless form.

Downstairs, men. Their voices urgent with discovery.

Little fingers were hooked over the top edge of the bedspread. Trembling, I peeled it down and saw her.

Susanna. Perfectly still. Eyes frozen wide.

Footsteps everywhere: rushing into the basement, rushing up the stairs.

I tried to touch her face, gently, to gauge her. But my hands were shaking uncontrollably and I couldn't move them with any precision. I was so terrified, so dazed, I couldn't tell if she was alive or . . .

Then one little hand lifted to touch my arm, infusing me with warmth, calming me with the realization that *I had found her, she was alive.*

"Auntie Karin," she whispered, "it's SusieQ."

CHAPTER 22

Two years later

They said I was in shock when they found me standing in the children's bedroom of Villa Viera, shaking, with Susanna tight in my arms. Downstairs, in what the police report called a chamber of horrors, people were dead and a gun was lying on the floor. The scene spoke for itself.

I closed the book that was propped on my swollen belly and set it on the towel curled on the sand beside my chair. Adjusted the engagement ring whose brilliant stone kept slipping toward my palm, creating, alongside my wedding ring, the illusion of a double gold band. Lifted a flattened palm to shield my eyes from the burning sun. I didn't know how long I'd been sitting here on this beach, failing to read the same textbook page, indulging in memories of an event that had taken place a long time ago or yesterday depending on how raw my nerves were when the images visited.

The problem with studying forensic psychology was that, when you read about the criminally insane, you made your own references. Mine were legion. The dual faces of JPP didn't terrify me anymore—Christa Maxtor was dead by my own hand, and Neil Tanner a.k.a. Martin Price had been killed by a fellow inmate over half a slice of French toast—and yet they persisted in my imagination right beside Jackson and Cece. When I had decided to go to college after all, they were my natural mentors, guiding me to a subject I felt compelled to understand but probably never really would.

As for details of the crimes, the task force had collected them and closed the case now fat with documentation elucidating Team JPP's trail, including how and for how long—eight years—they had evaded curiosity about Nancy Maxtor's disappearance. Ultimately they had hidden her murder in a sleight-of-hand built of her well-known history of constant traveling in pursuit of international good works. Christa had even sometimes posed as her adoptive mother, flying overseas, staying awhile, and flying back. Like Nancy, she was an intermittent teacher—though Christa's specialty was drama, not math—with a schedule liberal enough to support other pursuits. She led afterschool classes, worked at camps, volunteered at a prison. Christa's other expertise, it turned out, was murder—and she had one very good protégé in Neil.

But the ultimate question remained unanswered: Why had they done it? There were a thousand reasons, and there was no reason at all. The criminally insane inhabited a different country.

In the four days I'd been on my honeymoon, I had gotten to know many of the beaches here on Sifnos, the Greek island Jon and Andrea had insisted was "bliss"—

and it was. The trip was pricey but we'd decided to do it before the baby came. Just before leaving our apartment in New York we'd learned that it was *he*. I hadn't announced my decision yet, but I was going to call him Seamus Cian Benjamin, after a wonderful man.

I stood up. Stretched my arms wide in the blazing sun. Despite copious sunblock my exposed skin was reddening. The dry air here was nice but we had learned that it could mask extreme temperatures. Typically by noon we had reconvened off the beach and installed ourselves at a shady taverna for lunch before heading back to our room for an afternoon nap.

Where was he? I hankered to get out of this bathing suit and cool my skin in the sea. I hadn't wanted him to arrive to find my chair empty, but I was tired of waiting.

I left my stuff behind and walked to the far end of the beach, where a formation of rocks served as a natural wall. On the other side was a small beach embraced by the shelter of the rocks on one side and a thicket of trees on the other. I was alone here, but even if I hadn't been it wouldn't have mattered: It was one of the island's designated nude beaches. I pulled down the straps of my bathing suit, drew out one arm and then the other, and peeled the black spandex off my overheated skin. Left the limp bathing suit on the sand and hurried to the wet shore, where the soles of my feet instantly cooled. Stood there, staring at the horizon: a brushstroke of land in the distance, blurring together with the cloudless blue sky.

A hand landed on my shoulder and I flinched.

"Shh, it's only me."

Of course it was. I placed my hand atop his, and our brand-new wedding rings clinked. "Isn't it beautiful?"

"Gorgeous."

He kissed my neck and I turned around. His skin had tanned deeply; sparkling eyes in a russet face. I kissed him.

"Take off your clothes," I said.

The flicker of a smile. "I'm not an exhibitionist."

"We're married now. I need to see you."

For over a year he had hidden his wounds from me, afraid I wouldn't find him desirable if I saw the peg-board Christa Maxtor had made of him with her spiked hammock. Since then he had never removed his under-shirt in front of me, even to make love; but my finger-tips had traveled the map of his body. I knew that his scars were numerous, that his once-smooth skin had been left a constellation of unyielding reminders.

"It isn't going to be easy for you," he said.

"It doesn't have to be easy."

He looked into my eyes, saw that I meant it. Then he pulled off his shirt and tossed it on the sand beside us. Kicked off his sandals. Unbuttoned his jeans, let them fall, stepped out of them. Removed his underwear.

There he stood, naked to the sun. I watched his pale, ruined skin prickle with goose bumps before relaxing in the brutal heat.

His chest was a canvas of healed-white scars, short and long tears that had been obviously stitched. Some had healed well, others badly. Amazingly, the little dahlia tattoo beneath his collarbone was untouched; a reminder that innocence can never be completely destroyed. He turned around so I could see his back, which was more of the same. Then turned again to face me.

"You're right," I said. "It's hard to look at."

"I told you." He reached down and grabbed as much as he could get of his clothes.

I intercepted his arm. "Put them down."

"Karin—"

"No, Mac, it's okay. I love you." I raised my hand to touch his face.

"I've been thinking," he said. "How am I going to hide this ugly sight from him?" He touched my belly. Our son.

"We'll figure something out. Maybe save the truth for later."

"Or never. It'll scare the hell out of him."

"He'll be his own person. He'll have to know eventually."

"Karin." Mac stepped up to me, put his arms around my back, and drew us skin-to-skin. "Don't you think we can spare him some of it?"

"Maybe," I said. "I guess we can try."

"Let's do that."

Here is a sneak preview of
Katia Lief's next thrilling novel

NEXT TIME YOU SEE ME

Coming November 2010
From Avon Books

I opened my eyes moments before Ben cried. It was the same every morning, as if our bodies were aligned with the sun. I would wake up just in time to see the first trickle of light seep around the edges of the blackout shades on our bedroom windows, banishing the gray from the white walls, revealing the gold bicycle and silver moon in the framed poster across from our bed, and I would hear it: a hum, at first, and then a moan that transformed into my name. Not my name, exactly—not Karin—but *Mommy*. The first time he'd called me that, about six months ago, I burst into tears. Deluded by half sleep, I had thought for a split second that Cece was calling for me; and then I remembered that she had been gone for a very long time. The memory of her small, murdered body, her bloody room, flashed at me. I had to shake my head to disperse the image.

As I moved to get up and go to Ben, Mac's fingertips ran lightly down my back. His touch startled me; I hadn't realized he was awake.

"I'll go," he said.

"I don't mind."

"Let me."

I lay back in bed and closed my eyes, listening as my husband's footsteps crossed our room into the hall, as the toilet flushed, as he walked into Ben's room across from ours, as a mournful "Mommy?" became a gleeful "Daddy!" Silence as the diaper was changed. And then Mac carried Ben to our bed, saying, "I have a present for you." Ben snuggled beside me, and I breathed in his sweet first-morning smell, and ran my fingers through his hair, dark brown like Mac's before it went half gray. We cuddled until Mac returned a few minutes later with two cups of coffee and the morning paper. Before heading into the bathroom to shower and shave, he turned on the TV and Ben crawled to the foot of our bed where he sat bolt upright watching *Sesame Street*.

"It's already hot out," Mac told me, having opened the door to retrieve the newspaper from the front stoop. "Want me to put on the AC?"

"Not yet." I hated the grind of the air conditioners as much as I liked how they dried up the spongy end-of-August heat. Soon it would be autumn and we'd have the respite of cool breezes. I sat up, sipped my coffee, opened the newspaper against bent knees. After fifteen minutes of browsing the front section I picked up the business section and was greeted by Mac's face. He had recently been interviewed by a reporter about his new job.

"Mac!"

"What?"

"They ran the article today."

I got out of bed with the newspaper and tapped on the locked bathroom door. "It's me. Open up." We still weren't ready to let Ben see the constellation of scars covering Mac's body, the vivid reminder of our former lives as detectives. Someday we would have to tell our son the story of what happened to us in our encounters with JPP—Just Plain Psycho, the simplest way to think of the team of serial killers who brutally murdered my first husband and child, and nearly stole Mac's life as well. Someday, but not yet. Right now, Ben was an innocent toddler in what could possibly be the sweetest year of his life; at least that's how I remembered the year between one and two with my daughter, Cece, before the terrible twos struck with a vengeance. She barely made it to three. Eventually, gradually, the world would rob Ben of his innocence. And someday, when the time was right, we would fill in the details.

The bathroom door swung open and there was Mac, naked but for a towel wrapped around his lower half, his chest and back speckled with the tough little whitish scars. Just below his left collarbone was the nickel-sized tattoo of a lavender dahlia he'd gotten in a bout of adolescent rebellion when his father was pressuring him to go to college so he wouldn't end up in the family business, running the hardware store; in the end, he decided his father was right and gave up his resistance, but the tattoo remained. He'd once joked that he didn't need to explain his life to anyone, he could just lift his shirt and his history would be revealed in the ruinous alterations of his skin.

Half his face was slathered in foam (erasing the cleft in his chin) and the other half was cleanly shaven. I held up the newspaper for him to see the photograph of himself sitting behind his desk at the corporate headquarters of Quest Security, above a caption reading:

Seamus "Mac" MacLeary was recently promoted to senior vice president of Forensic Security, and below the headline "MacLeary Replaces Stein in Sudden Shift at Quest."

"He said it would run sometime early this week and that he'd give me a heads-up."

"Which he didn't do."

"Who knows? I haven't checked my e-mail all weekend." He peered at himself in the newspaper. "I'm still not sure it was such a good idea."

"You're in the private sector now," I reminded him. "Fair game. And that kind of promotion always comes with scrutiny, especially since Deidre was well liked."

"True." He shook his head. "Did you read it? What does it say about her?"

I skimmed the article, looking for Deidre's name. "It says ' . . . who was let go abruptly last week in an alleged pay-for-play corruption scandal involving an exchange of money for altered forensic testimony in a high-profile legal case.' That's all it says."

"Alleged," Mac said. "That's good. They'll have to *prove* she cheated. It makes me sick to get her job this way." It had been his mantra the entire week since Deidre had been forced out. His other mantra had been: "I hope she countersues for race discrimination or sex discrimination, take your pick."

I had met Deidre a few times, briefly. She was a light-skinned black woman in her middle thirties, with an impeccable educational pedigree and a reputation as an effective manager and a tough cookie. Mac had worked with her for over a year and had always thought highly of her. Watching her get the axe, seeing himself moved

abruptly into her position, had pained him; but he was
no wilting lily, having served on a New Jersey police
force for two decades, and he dutifully took the job.

"Good news and bad news," he had said upon returning home one night a week ago. "What do you want
first?"

I had stared at him, unwilling to answer. He knew I
didn't want it if it was bad news.

"Okay," he plunged in, "good news first: I got a huge
raise. Bad news is they went through with it. Deidre's
out. I'm the boss now."

I had to remind him to focus on the positive: A promotion of that caliber was an honor, not to mention that
his pay raise would be a boon to us as I was bringing
in nothing at the moment besides my disability income
(those checks were another sad reminder of how my
life and work had fatefully collided). Motherhood
had slowed my progress toward a college degree but
I was still plugging along, taking courses in forensic
psychology at John Jay College of Criminal Justice, in
slow preparation for my second career. After a couple
of margaritas at the local Mexican restaurant over the
weekend, Mac had joked that we should both ditch our
last names and call ourselves Mr. and Mrs. Forensic.
I laughed, but couldn't help wondering if the comment betrayed disappointment that I had stayed Karin
Schaeffer, holding on to my first husband's last name,
especially since Mac's first wife, Val, gave up Mac-
Leary to become Ng when she remarried.

He patted dry his face and kissed me. His skin carried the spicy scent of the aftershave I'd given him for
Father's Day as a kind of joke. Next year maybe he'd

get a tie. The year after, a golf ball paperweight. For Mother's Day, so far, he hadn't risked a silly gift but had taken the challenge to please me seriously: beautiful earrings, a lush silk scarf.

"Have time for breakfast?" I asked him.

"I do."

The phone rang and on his way back into the bedroom to get dressed, he answered it, repeating "Hello?" twice before hanging up.

"Who was that?"

"Unknown caller."

"I hate that guy."

We laughed.

A minute later the phone rang again, caller ID announcing NYPD—New York Police Department. I answered.

"Karin, it's Billy. So Mac's famous now!" Detective Billy Staples, from Brooklyn's Eighty-fourth Precinct—our very own—had become Mac's closest friend since he'd quit the Maplewood Police, moved here, married me, and started a new life. "How's it feel to be hitched to a big shot?"

"You'll have to convince him he's a big shot yourself." I passed the phone to Mac, who took it between shoulder and ear as he finished buckling his belt.

Sesame Street went into a sketch change and I used the opportunity to switch off the TV and transition Ben to breakfast time.

"Can't tonight," I heard Mac say. "Karin's got a class." He listened, then looked at me and asked, "Friday? He's busy every other night."

"Friday we have our dinner at the Union Square

Café!" My tone reminded him how important it was: Our second wedding anniversary was less than a week away. Accustomed to doing things out of sync (I was five months' pregnant when we got married), we had settled for a Friday night reservation when we couldn't get one for our actual anniversary on Saturday. We'd had the reservation for over a month.

Mac cringed, embarrassed he'd forgotten, and whispered to me, "Wants to take me out for a drink to celebrate."

"Go tonight," I said. "I'll ask Mom to babysit."

"You sure?"

"Positive."

They arranged to meet after work at a bar on Smith Street called Boat.

I handed Ben to Mac—handsome in his crisp gray suit, white shirt, and blue paisley tie—and he carried our little boy upstairs while I scrolled open both window shades, flooding the bedroom with light.

I had served in the army. Been a cop and a detective. Had my life, heart, soul, and mind eviscerated by a madman and his muse. And yet here I was, alive and well, on a bright summer morning. If happiness was possible for a person like me, this was it.